shred sisters

Also by Betsy Lerner

The Bridge Ladies
Food and Loathing
The Forest for the Trees

shred sisters

A Novel

betsy lerner

Grove Press
New York

FIRST EDITION

Published simultaneously in Canada
Printed in the United States of America

First Grove Atlantic hardcover edition: October 2024

Library of Congress Cataloging-in-Publication data is available for this title.

ISBN 978-0-8021-6370-7
eISBN 978-0-8021-6371-4

Grove Press
an imprint of Grove Atlantic
154 West 14th Street
New York, NY 10011

Distributed by Publishers Group West

groveatlantic.com

24 25 26 27   10 9 8 7 6 5 4 3 2 1

Here are the ways I could start this story:

Olivia was breathtaking.

For a long time, I was convinced that she was responsible for everything that went wrong.

No one will love you more or hurt you more than a sister.

PART I

Do Not Feed the Fish

1

I was afraid to wake up my dad. He was stretched out on the couch in his den, late afternoon, his brown loafers kicked off on the shag carpet, resting on each other like rabbits. "This better be good, Amy."

He never used my full name. It was Aim or A, or Acorn, Bun, or Bunny.

By the time he reached Ollie, she was soaked in blood.

Ollie had dared me to jump on the couch with her. Using the thick cushions as a trampoline, she made a swishing sound as she jumped, touching the ceiling and dunking an imaginary basketball. Only when she took a jump shot from the side, not realizing the power in her legs, she crashed into the picture window behind the couch. For a second there was silence, then the window splintered into a web of shards that rained down on my sister. She shook her head, and pieces of glass flung like water from a summer sprinkler. She froze in place, afraid to take a step or move. Tiny spots of blood blossomed from beneath her shirt and pants.

My father told me to call 911 for an ambulance, then soothed Ollie with his deep voice. "It's going to be okay, honey. Stay still."

Ollie hadn't moved a millimeter, knowing that doing so would push the shards of glass deeper into her skin. Now in partial shock, she couldn't speak. Later she joked that she looked like a giant tampon, but just then her wit was on hold. Our mother was away on a bridge cruise through the fjords with her friends. The pamphlet for the trip was on the kitchen counter with all her contact numbers, should we need to reach her. In the long minutes before the ambulance arrived, I suggested we call her. My father vetoed the idea.

"Let her have her fun."

The EMS crew arrived, stopping short when they saw her.

"Whoa," the woman EMT said.

"Shit," the guy said, then, "Pardon my French."

The woman slid her hands under Ollie's armpits while the man cut her shirt off from the back. As usual, Ollie wasn't wearing a bra, and my father left the room. While the woman held Ollie up, the man plucked glass from her back. She was silent as they lifted her onto the stretcher. The woman covered Ollie's front with a white sheet. Faintly, then vividly, red slashes soaked through like hash marks. I heard her moan, and they gave her a shot. I started to climb into the ambulance, but the man waved me away and pulled the door closed. Dad started up the car and said I should wait at home, hold down the fort.

I took out the broom and dustpan, the upright kind I used for a game I called Movies. I'd scatter garbage on the floor and sweep it up while complaining with my imaginary ushers about the customers and the sticky floor. The current situation presented more of a challenge. The couch and carpet were covered in shards, shavings, and glass dust. I upgraded to the vacuum. My mother was proud of her new Electrolux cannister; like a dachshund on wheels, the vacuum followed her around as she made her way through the house. It did a good job on the glass dust, but the hose started to buck with the bigger pieces. A puff of black smoke belched from the grid at the back of the vacuum, followed by the smell of burnt plastic.

I called the hospital but couldn't get through. It was getting dark, and I started to panic. Here I was again, on the sideline of another crisis Ollie created, staged, and starred in. My sister was possibly bleeding to death, while my mother dealt another hand of bridge against a backdrop of majestic fjords. The brochure showed a lavish buffet, a room filled with animated card players, a sunset, and a moonrise. I wanted to call her, but I knew my father was right. Except it wasn't about letting her have her fun; he knew she would make matters worse.

Dad returned from the hospital later that evening. There was blood on his sleeve. He hugged me hard and said Ollie was going to be fine; the cuts bled a lot, but they were largely superficial. I started to cry, and he hugged me again and told me not to worry. I wanted to lash out: why hadn't he called? How could he have left me? But I didn't want him to think that I was more worried about myself than about Ollie. He said he needed sustenance, which meant a trip to Chuck's Steakhouse, a martini straight up with olives and a porterhouse, rare.

I loved to police the people in line at Chuck's salad bar, observing how well they adhered to the honor system. When it was my turn, I'd make a show of using the correct tongs to take my fair share from each container, while Ollie would

plunge the same tongs into every container, heaping cole-
slaw on her plate, then olives, and a stockpile of croutons on
top. It wasn't a crime, but it stood for everything I couldn't
stand about her.

The waiter took our order, and my father debriefed me.
He said Ollie would stay in the hospital overnight; they had
given her some strong stuff for the pain. A plastic surgeon had
been called in to assess the damage. Her back was the worst,
he said, but the scarring would be minimal. Not a single shard
of glass had touched her face.

"You're a very pretty girl," the surgeon said. "You're lucky."

When Ollie came home the next day, she let me apply
Neosporin on the deeper cuts on her back. I carefully traced
each one with a worm of ointment.

"Can't you speed it up?"

I was too slow and methodical for Ollie. Even woozy on
pain medication, she couldn't stand waiting for anything.

By the time my mother returned five days later, my father
had had the window reglazed and the carpet and couch professionally cleaned. Dad said it looked as good as new. I
thought Mom would detect the damage right away, but she
was full of bluster and in a generous mood, having won
the tournament. She showed off her first-place trophy and
handed out presents from the ship's gift shop. A baseball cap
that said "Fjords" for my father and a T-shirt for me that
said "I ♥ FJORDS." The bag appeared to be empty, but
then she fished out a polar bear carved from white quartz,
small enough to fit in your hand, and gave it to Ollie for her
collection of souvenir bears.

The tradition had started before I was born. From the moment Ollie saw them, she fell in love with the bears at the Bronx zoo. She was delighted by the creatures swimming, nosing a big red ball into the air, basking in the sun. She refused to leave the exhibit and my parents could not cajole, bribe, or budge her. The story goes that they stayed watching the bears until the zoo closed. At three, Ollie already knew how to exert her power, and my parents, beguiled by their little girl, acquiesced. "Strong-willed," "headstrong," and "stubborn" didn't attach themselves to Olivia until later.

Eventually, my mother put the pieces together from the evidence: the banged-up vacuum, the bloody gauze in Ollie's wastebasket, the bill from the hospital mixed in with the day's mail. My father downplayed the whole thing, said it was nothing. Years later, after Ollie stopped coming home, he said he blamed himself, he shouldn't have tried to hide the accident from our mother. Even then, long before Ollie was in real trouble, she was often out of control, playing too hard, not knowing when to quit. The surgeon had said that Ollie was more than lucky; if a single shard had lodged too deeply in her neck, she could have died.

After the meal, Dad ordered dessert, a piece of Chuck's famous mud cake, with two forks. The waiter set the cake down and winked, "Enjoy, you two lovebirds." My father lifted a bite to his mouth, but then his body started to shudder. I looked away, afraid of what might happen next; I had never seen my father cry. After a few moments, he shook it off, wiped his face with his handkerchief and apologized for breaking down. It had been a long day.

"Is Ollie going to be punished?" I asked.

A mix of disbelief and disgust crossed his face, "Is that what's on your mind?" Suddenly I was to blame; the girl who sailed through glass remained unscathed—Houdini had escaped without a scratch. My father sank his fork into the cake.

Olivia and I fought as if the world existed to fuel our rivalry. We fought over possession of the big chair in front of the television and the remote control. We fought over the window seat on an airplane and the aisle at the movies. There was no taking turns when it came to sitting in the front seat of the car; as long as I was alive, the younger sister would be relegated to the back seat. Even our mother didn't contest it. We fought over the dog we didn't have, what breed it might be, what to name it, which of us it loved most. If Ollie thought that I had a larger portion of food, she'd swap our plates. We fought physically—hair pulling, punching, kicking. Far worse was the name-calling, the insults she leveled at me that still sting today. She called me loser, zero, first living abortion. She said I was a brownnoser, a teacher's pet, and a kiss-ass. I was boring, cloying, a below-average human. She knew I was an A+ student, but she wasn't talking about grades. In Ollie's view I had no charisma, no flair.

My first tormentor, she was ingenious in keeping her tactics beneath my parents' radar. When we fought, they always said the same thing: they didn't care who started it, we should sort it out ourselves. What was there to sort out after Ollie had eaten my dessert, left my beloved markers open to dry, and beheaded my dolls? Every year on my birthday, Ollie would push me aside and blow out the candles. My parents would chide her as they laughed—"Ollie!!!" My father would relight the candles, but I would refuse to blow them out or make a wish as the little wax columns melted into the cake. They would tell me to stop being silly, and I was branded the bad sport while Ollie pushed me aside and stole my wish.

During one of my many scavenging missions through my parents' room, I found an accordion file behind my mother's desk. The "A" slot, labeled with my full name, Amy Claire Shred, was written in my mother's gorgeous handwriting, full of graceful loops. Inside was an archive of information. My Social Security card, with numbers separated by dashes, like Morse code. My birth certificate, with the time I was born, 6 a.m., and my birth weight, 5 pounds, 8 ounces. The doctors had informed my parents that one ounce less and I'd be in an incubator. My father compared me to a hamburger under the warming lights at McDonald's, and somehow that image morphed into the nickname Bun, and then Bunny. Even fully grown, I would remain in the fifth percentile for height and weight, reaching only five feet and weighing under one hundred pounds. Whenever I complained about my size, my mother said good things come in small packages. I was smart enough to know that good things come in tall, willowy packages like Ollie's.

I found my elementary school report cards and fanned them out to admire the solid column of "Exceeds Expectations" on the academic side of the ledger. It was in the personal-development section that I faltered—namely, in social skills. The injustice of it inflamed me. I was desperate to be included, but I was the skinny, clumsy, bespectacled soldier who gets picked off first by enemy fire in every war movie. I was already being shunted away from tables in the cafeteria and had relegated myself to the perimeter of the playground. My teachers reported that I was introverted and socially challenged.

I peeked into the "O" slot and found all of Ollie's report cards bound in a rubber band. I opened one after another showing that her grades were abysmal. She failed Health! I ran to my mother, filled with a younger sibling's indignation; here was proof positive that Ollie was given special treatment. My mother admonished me for snooping; Ollie's grades were not my concern, she said. How could my mother, the Patron Saint of High Expectations, allow Ollie to get away with poor grades?

In high school, it became evident that Ollie couldn't concentrate. Her brain was a pinball machine. She never finished a book or completed a project. She couldn't be bothered with maps or directions. She winged her tests and navigated the world on instinct. When I cried that it wasn't fair, this double standard for our grades, my mother said, with a blend of finality and cruelty, "Who said life would be fair?"

In the spring of sixth grade, a boy in our class was diagnosed with leukemia. He played clarinet, and I remember how small he seemed in the marching-band uniform, his hat like a toy soldier's tilted down on his forehead. In a matter of months, his body grew gaunt, his skin turned greenish gray, and then he disappeared. Our class planted a tree in his memory. At the dedication ceremony, the janitor played guitar and sang in a falsetto voice "Where Have All the Flowers Gone." He wore his janitor pants but had put on a white, collared shirt and a navy blue vest. None of us had any idea that he played guitar or sang, and it was kind of embarrassing.

That night, I went to Ollie's room and knocked.

"Enter."

A few days before, while she was at track practice, I had rummaged around in her dresser and found a packet of pills.

"Are you sick?" I asked.

"What are you talking about?" Her tone was harsh, impatient.

"I found your pills," I confessed.

"What pills?"

"In your bureau."

"What were you doing in my room?" She pinched my neck hard.

I didn't have a quick answer. I couldn't lie the way Ollie did. If anything, I had the opposite problem, telling too much truth, speaking far beyond the required response to any question. This, too, Ollie found irritating. Sometimes my mother would concur. "Sweetheart," she'd say, "can you wrap it up?" or "Amy, please, get to the point." Then I'd try to make myself not talk, or I'd respond in clipped one-word answers, until I could no longer keep it up.

I had no reason to be in Ollie's room, let alone go through her dresser. I knew I risked banishment, punishment. Still, I snooped, spied, and studied her. The smallest details about her life intrigued me: the silver ring on her middle toe, her black nail polish, the way she could talk and floss at the same time. In high school, Ollie was always ahead of the pack trend-wise, fashion-wise, music-wise. She knew about Italian directors and French cigarettes. She wrote in a composition notebook that she called a journal. She wore a bucket hat in the summer and a beret in the winter. She played David Bowie's song "Heroes" over and over as if it were her personal anthem.

"Don't touch my shit," Olivia snapped, still squeezing my neck. "Understand?"

"Are you dying?" I asked, wriggling away, thinking about my dead classmate.

"What are you talking about?"

"The pills," I said.

"Oh my god." Olivia fell backward. "You're such an idiot."

My mother pinned the beginning of Ollie's problems on an ordinary car ride home from the orthodontist. For years to come, she would refer to it as the day Ollie "turned." She was fifteen and I was eleven. It was a year or so after she crashed through the window, and, if you ask me, Ollie had already turned. She flouted the most basic Shred Family rules: not clearing her plate, not making her bed, not taking out the garbage. She no longer watched our favorite lineup of TV shows, instead listening to music alone in her basement room. She and I had previously regarded the downstairs as a terror-filled underworld with spiders, mice, and a disgusting sulfur smell. I couldn't fathom her choosing the partially finished basement with a musty mattress hauled down from the attic. Ollie had made a lair, a psychedelic dungeon, painting the walls black and installing a black light that made the specks of white glow.

"It's my house, and black is not a color you paint walls," our mother railed when she saw what Ollie had done.

"It's my room and I can paint it any color I want," Ollie roared back.

Now she was cranky, her teeth and gums sore from the doctor's prodding and tightening. Her braces would come off at her next visit, but even so she made a display of her suffering. She was one of the few teenagers on the planet whose beauty was not diminished by braces. I would be getting mine soon and was sure to be called Brace Face, Train Tracks, and Metal Mouth. More stoic than Ollie, I had already planned to stop eating at school after Roger Coffin, a boy in our class, had been made the target at Four Square for the world-class offense of being caught with egg salad in his braces. Ricky Testa, class bully, took aim with the intensity of a pro bowler as he scooped the ball underhand, and whipped it at Roger, hitting him in the chest and knocking him back onto the cement. Laughter erupted from the boys in the square and the crescent of girls standing nearby. Long seconds passed, and Roger remained motionless. In what was probably my last act of bravery, I walked over to check if he was okay. His wind back, he sat up and bounced to his feet. Seeing me hovering, he said, loud enough for all to hear, "Eat shit, Shred." Then he jogged off toward the parking lot and disappeared into the woods.

Driving home from the orthodontist's appointment, Ollie brought up the Eric Clapton concert at the Coliseum. She had been hounding our mother for months, ever since the tickets went on sale. My mother held firm; it was out of the question. But now it was the day of the show, and Ollie was relentless.

"All my friends are going," she whined.

"I don't care if the Queen of Sheba is going," my mother said.

"It's the only time he'll be in New Haven."

"It's a school night, Olivia."

"I'm going," Ollie said.

"We don't go to concerts on school nights."

"Do you even know who Eric Clapton is?"

"It's final."

That's when it came out of her mouth: "You can't fucking stop me."

It was the first time anyone in our family had used the forbidden f-word. My mother yanked the car over to the side of the road and instructed Ollie to get out of the car.

"Excuse me?"

"Get out."

"And what? Walk home?"

We were only a mile away from our house, but our mother had never done anything so dramatic; her hands remained gripped on the steering wheel.

"Olivia, now."

"You can't be serious."

Ollie started to massage her aching mouth, which I interpreted as a play for sympathy, but I could see her mentally regrouping. She was used to getting her way, it was only a matter of finding the right combination. She could soften my father with a pouty frown; our mother wasn't as easy to crack. She believed that Ollie had been indulged because of her beauty; she learned that she could take advantage of people and get away with bad behavior. In the supermarket, strangers would coo over the little girl in the grocery cart, with her bright blue eyes and blond ringlets. The bank teller gave her extra lollipops, the man at the shoe store fashioned animals for her out of long skinny balloons. When we went to New York City, to a show or a museum, people would mistake her for a popular actress. One time a man gave my mother his card and said he could get her modeling work. My mother also believed that things came too easily to Ollie. When she started running track in high school, she cleared hurdles and won races; she was the conquering hero carried high on the shoulders of her teammates.

"Olivia, now!"

"Fine," Ollie said.

She took her time getting out of the car and slammed the door. The late-afternoon sun was going down, burnishing Ollie's silhouette. I was well acquainted with the pose, hip cocked, hand on hip. If Ollie didn't get what she wanted, she acted as if she'd never wanted it in the first place. You could never win.

I jumped over and claimed the front seat. I pushed all the buttons, opened and closed the glove compartment, waited for the cigarette lighter to pop out. Now my mother was equally annoyed with me.

"What are you so happy about?"

An insinuation parading as a question. The lighter popped out and I reached for it.

"Don't touch it," she snapped. But I had already pulled it out, the coil glowing red like Mars.

"Put it back before you get burned."

Ollie did not get to attend the concert that night, but it was the last time she took no for an answer. After that she started sneaking out of the house, and when she realized how easy it was, she never stopped.

2

Ollie hated Running Brook Country Club. She rejected the dress code, the food, and the people, who, she proclaimed, were phony and snobbish. Before boycotting the club altogether, she had competed every year in the Labor Day swim meet, where she dominated in freestyle and butterfly, her body porpoising through the water. Winners could eat as much as they wanted at the snack bar, set to close for the season. I can still picture Ollie standing there, a towel slung loosely around her hips, water dripping from her curls, ordering each item on the menu and taking a bite or two before passing the scraps to the younger kids, who worshiped her.

I enjoyed all the rituals associated with the club: pulling into the semicircular driveway, where a high school boy in a crisp white shirt would park our car; my father would slip the kid a buck as smoothly as handing off a baton. The club's interior resembled a cruise ship, with a wire railing and round porthole windows. They offered Shirley Temples to the kids and served sundaes in fluted bowls that reminded me of tulips. Sunday was family night, and our regular table overlooked the golf course, an emerald blanket at twilight, invisible after sunset.

After her braces came off, Ollie deigned to join us for the Sunday night buffet. Mom had urged her to come and show off her new smile, but Ollie didn't care about that. She agreed only to please our dad. He played golf and cards at the club most weekends, and it made him immensely happy to show off his "girls."

That night, in a rare gesture of sisterly affection, Ollie asked me to go to the powder room with her. It smelled of rose and citrus, and the counter was crowded with feminine products, including a basket of tampons and pads that made me shrink, embarrassed to encounter something so private out in the open. Ollie loved to shake the aerosol cans of hair spray and write graffiti on the mirrors. She'd douse herself with perfume, pumping the atomizer like a blood-pressure bulb. One time she sang "I Feel Pretty" from *West Side Story* at the top of her lungs in a crazy frenzy and slammed all the stall doors shut until a lady came in and we collapsed laughing. Those were the times I lived for.

Now, on the way to the powder room, we stopped at a door with a "Do Not Enter" sign. We had probably passed it a hundred times, but now Ollie put her hand on the knob. It clicked.

"Come on," she whispered, as she cracked open the door. I could not move.

"Suit yourself," she said and disappeared behind the door. With Ollie you only had one chance. I retreated to the powder room and watched the women as they lingered by the mirror, reapplying their lipstick and smoothing their hair. I asked myself why I couldn't join Ollie on her adventure. What did I imagine was behind that door?

To my relief, Ollie was at the table when I returned from the powder room. She had not been beamed up to a distant planet or thrown into the trunk of a car. A busboy, filling our water glasses, dropped something in her lap, but she grabbed it too quickly for me to see. I knew I could never enter my sister's world. She was daring and reckless. She slept naked, while I wore pajamas over underpants and undershirts. She scooped out avocados with two fingers and plunged the meat into her mouth. Without hesitation, Ollie would dive off a cliff into a reservoir, jump on a horse and canter into the woods. Ollie was *that* girl. First in, last out. What no one yet understood was that Ollie had no brakes.

In the car coming home, Ollie showed me the busboy's gift, a ring made from an antique fork. The door she had slipped through was a back entryway to the kitchen, and Ollie bragged that she and the busboy had made out in the walk-in refrigerator. He started phoning our home after that, and she'd wave off the call, though she wore the ring on her index finger. Lots of people admired it, astonished to discover that it was fashioned from a fork. We learned later that the boy had dropped out of college because of depression, and some months later, he hanged himself in the club's refrigerator. News of his suicide spread quickly, and when it reached our family, I expected Ollie to be really upset, but it didn't seem to register at all.

By seventh grade, my outcast status was cemented. It seemed as if my classmates had collectively decided over the summer to wear jeans to school on the first day and trade in their lunchboxes for brown bags. That first day I wore a purple dress with white tights and was the proud bearer of a *Lost in Space* lunchbox. Realizing how babyish it all looked, I raced home after school and railed at my mother, tearing the covers off my books.

"I need brown bags! I need jeans! The whole class is wearing them," I cried.

"Bunny," my mother said, "I didn't raise you to be a follower."

Nothing was more abhorrent to her than being a "sheep," going along with the crowd. It's what the Germans did, she'd say, to drive the point home. But I wasn't sending Jews to their graves; I just wanted to fit in. I had also learned too late that my greatest crime in school was raising my hand too frequently, saying the answer with too much certainty, and always getting it right. I could tell that the teachers sometimes grew weary of calling on me when no one else raised their hand. In middle school, a few boys would stick their arms in the air in imitation of an overeager student and make chimp noises, oooh, oooh, oooh, as they passed me in the hall. But I never did that. I raised my hand straight up at the crook of my elbow and demurely waved it, my palm a small cup, to alert the teacher, no sound effects whatsoever. At home if I cried to my mother, she'd say, "No one likes a know-it-all."

The library became my refuge in junior high school. The librarian, Miss Breen, put books aside for me—biographies of Newton and Kepler, theorems, brain teasers. On the last day of eighth grade, I brought her a present. Miss Breen invited me into her office to open it. Teachers' offices had been off limits since one of the coaches molested a star soccer player in the equipment room, but she insisted: "It's our last day!" The couch in her office was covered in burgundy-colored corduroy, and the walls were lined with pictures of her heroes: Johannes Gutenberg, Thomas Edison, the Wright Brothers, Albert Einstein. Like me, she loved science and confided that she had struggled to fit in at school; she saw herself in me. With pride, she mentioned that she owned her own condo; it came with a microwave and a side-by-side refrigerator that dispensed ice right out of the door. Her boyfriend was twenty years older than her; did I think that was bad? I had no idea what to say.

Miss Breen was the opposite of my mother, who opened gifts slowly, her bird-head tilting this way and that, deciding if the worm pleased her. Miss Breen yanked the ribbon off and tore into the package. She clapped her hands and clutched the handkerchiefs to her chest. "I love them. Thank you!" She hugged me so hard, the clasp on her denim overall dress dug into my cheek. Then she told me to wait a minute, she had something for me. She returned with a gift, obviously a book, hastily wrapped with mimeo paper and Scotch tape. "Open it, open it!" she said, plopping down on the couch. The paper unfolded in one piece like an origami fortune-teller.

The book was *How to Win Friends and Influence People*; the man on the cover, Dale Carnegie, reminded me of Dr. Mengele, with his close-shorn hair and tight wire-framed glasses. The concept was absurd. *Influence people?* I couldn't even get someone to sit with me at lunch. The trust between me and Miss Breen was broken; I saw that she was firmly in my mother's camp as someone who believed I needed to be fixed.

⚜

I learned to play bridge the summer before starting high school by watching my mother's Monday game. I had always helped her set up the card table on its spindly legs, pour candy into crystal bowls and carefully set an Entenmann's cake on a pretty platter. Bridge had its own language and logic, and I quickly grasped the rules. When my mother learned of a bridge club at a local college, I started to play on Saturday afternoons. At first the college students were dubious about letting me join, but once they saw how well I played, they fought over being my partner. That was how I imagined it should be with Ollie, but games with my sister always ended badly. If I took the lead or closed in on a win, she would cheat, change the rules, or walk away, often flipping the game board in her wake, leaving me to pick up the pieces.

When our bridge team entered a statewide competition at a convention center in Hartford, I met a wider circle of kids who were into math and science. I hoped we might all be on an equal footing, but a pecking order quickly asserted itself. At the top was a boy named King. While most of the kids were drinking beer, he sipped brandy from a silver flask wedged into the back pocket of his jeans. He had shoulder-length black hair with a widow's peak that made him seem British. He wore a duster and fingerless leather gloves, even at the bridge table. I had a massive crush on him.

On the second day of the tournament, King asked me to take a walk with him. We wound up in a stairwell on the other side of the conference center. We could hear the clanging pots and trays from the kitchen below, the smell of fried fish wafting upward.

"Susan's a rich bitch," he said. It was public knowledge that he and Susan coupled off the year before, only now she was avoiding him. He pulled a bag of Peanut M&M's from his jacket. "She only got into Dartmouth because her parents went there."

"She seems pretty smart." I had no idea why I was defending her.

"She's a tease." He threw an M&M into the air, catching it in his open mouth. "I have a girlfriend at home anyway."

King told me his psychiatrist had put him on Ritalin because he was "hyperactive," but mostly he flushed the pills.

"I prefer my brain, thank you very much," he said. King explained how he could tell the cards in all four players' hands, not via telepathy or X-ray vision, but because his brain could rapidly calculate the odds. The drug messed with that. I kept staring at his knee, sticking out of a tear in his jeans.

He tossed an M&M to me, and I jumped like a seal for a piece of fish. It hit the side of my face and rolled off.

"Like this, Shred," he said and put his huge hands on either side of my head. The feel of his hands was more than I could tolerate, and I jerked away.

"Whoa, steady, girl," he said, as if I were a colt he was trying to break. "Relax."

He tilted my head back the way the lady at the beauty parlor did to wash my hair, my throat painfully exposed.

"The trick is to keep your eye on the candy." He tossed another one at me, and I jerked my head again. This time the M&M hit my ear and bounced down the stairs. Suddenly King's mood changed, and he stuffed the candy back in his pocket. He stood up to leave. I was desperate for another chance, certain I had missed the opportunity of a lifetime, though not exactly sure what it might have been. That night I spied King and Susan making out in the lobby.

Ollie stomped into the family room wearing black combat boots laced up to her knees and a dainty yellow sundress flecked with tiny daisies. It was my mom's forty-first birthday, and we were going to the Golden Door, the Chinese restaurant my family went to for special occasions.

"What are those?" My mother wasn't exactly asking.

"They're Doc Martens."

"They're Nazi boots."

"Jesus, Mom."

"You're not wearing those to the restaurant."

Ollie had started shopping at Goodwill and thrift shops. Her prize possession from the Salvation Army was a suede jacket with fringe that I loved to run my fingers through. My mother said secondhand clothes were for the poor, and Ollie accused her of hating poor people.

"I don't hate poor people; how could you say that?" my mother asked, genuinely baffled. She could not understand why anyone would buy used clothes when they could afford new ones.

She stepped up her interrogation. "Where did you get those?"

"A friend."

"What friend?"

"From track."

I was pretty sure Ollie had shoplifted the boots. A month before she had pulled me into her room, removed her coat, and flashed two albums stuffed into the back of her jeans. She was insanely proud of what she could get away with.

"Aren't you afraid of getting caught?" I asked.

"It's a rush."

"What about the security cameras?"

She said a life of crime wasn't for everyone. She loved all the movie outlaws: Butch Cassidy and the Sundance Kid, Bonnie and Clyde, but most of all, the con artist father-daughter duo in the movie *Paper Moon*. Later, whenever she got caught shoplifting or making a disturbance, she would use the alias Addie Loggins, played by the ten-year-old Tatum O'Neal. I'd read a book about criminal minds and how the FBI could detect when people were lying. The most common behaviors were fidgeting, grooming gestures, and avoiding eye contact. It claimed that people who tell the truth tend to look you in the eye and relay the facts. Ollie knew all this innately and could fool anyone, get away with anything. Clothes, albums, boots, prescription drugs; these were gateway items. Eventually it would be credit cards, cars, other people's friends, boyfriends, spouses.

On the night of our mother's birthday, Ollie refused to change out of the boots, and Mom dropped it "for the time being," though they both remained sullen as we drove to the restaurant. Inside, in front of the koi-filled pool, a sign in lacquered red Chinese-style letters said *Do Not Feed the Fish*. Bright orange fish flicked and darted through the water between the slick stones. Ollie would always jump from one to the next as if she were playing hopscotch. She'd throw the crunchy noodles over her shoulder into the pond as if she were tossing coins into a fountain, delighted by the koi feeding frenzy. I worried that the fish might end up floating on the water's surface; I was convinced the owners would throw us out, but nothing bad had ever happened.

Our mother brought up Ollie's least favorite topic: college applications, looming deadlines.

"Can't we just order," Ollie whined.

Recruiters had been showing up at her track meets, expressing interest. Having been a college athlete, Dad was excited about Ollie getting an athletic scholarship. Our mother floated the question, "What is the future of an athlete?" Then answered it: "a gym teacher?" She hated that her daughter was a jock. She had dreamed of a mother-daughter subscription to the ballet, of shopping trips and lunches at Saks, buying a new duvet with matching accent pillows to decorate Ollie's dorm room. My mother believed that sports were for boys and had worried aloud that "the lesbians might get their hands on her."

"Who says I want to go to college?"

"Don't be ridiculous," Mom spat back.

Ollie hadn't visited a single school or shown any interest in doing so; most weekends she blamed practices and track meets, but this was a first. *Not go to college?*

At the end of the meal, the waiters gathered around, sang Happy Birthday, and presented Mom with a dish of fried ice-cream balls with skinny sparklers, the kind that keep popping back on. For once Ollie wasn't interested in blowing them out. Her leg bounced under the table, something in her lap, while the three of us kept going until the sparklers disintegrated into a pile of ash. Dad gave Mom a blue lacquer pen-and-pencil set; she acted surprised, even though she had picked it out herself. I gave her a box of stationery. Dispatching thank-you notes and condolence cards was a cornerstone of civilization, according to Lorraine Shred, and she praised our gifts as very thoughtful.

Ollie pushed a rectangular jewelry box toward Mom, no wrapping paper, no bow.

"What is this?" my mother asked, somewhat suspicious.

"Open it," Ollie urged.

She shook the box next to her ear.

"Open it!"

Our mother pried open the box. Inside was a gold tennis bracelet.

"My gosh," she said, lifting it out of the box. "Where did you get this?"

"Put it on."

My mother slid the bracelet around her thin wrist and admired the fishbone pattern. The question of its origin hung in the air.

"Do you like it?"

"It's stunning."

Ollie smiled broadly.

The waiter returned with the bill and four fortune cookies wrapped in cellophane.

"You go first, honey," Dad said.

"Eeny, meeny, miny, moe," my mother said, touching each cookie in turn.

"Choose," Ollie blurted. "Come on, Mom."

"Let her take her time," Dad said, as if this were a decision of some consequence.

"It's her birthday," I added.

Mom picked a cookie, cracked it in half, and read the fortune aloud: *"Don't hold on to things that require a tight grip."*

"Hmmm," my mother said. "I'll have to think about that." My father opened his fortune. "You will be hungry in an hour." He always made this stale joke, and we faithfully groaned. Before I could choose a cookie, Ollie smashed one with her fist and pulled the fortune out from the rubble. "*Happiness is attainable, sadness is inevitable.*"

"Screw that," she said, rolling the paper into a tiny scroll between her thumb and index finger and flicking it onto the floor.

"Shall we?" That was how my dad signaled the end of every gathering. I pocketed my fortune cookie to open later. We were silent on the car ride home. Even Dad, always ready with a joke or anecdote to fill an awkward silence, was quiet. We all suspected the bracelet was stolen; that evening marked the beginning of our collective denial.

Toward the end of the school year, Ollie came home with a tattoo on her upper arm. Of all the lines she had crossed, this was the worst. My mother couldn't be consoled. She said Ollie had defiled her beautiful body and couldn't be buried in a Jewish cemetery. My father reminded her that we didn't belong to a temple. We were as assimilated as any family could be; we even had a Christmas tree. My mother said tattoos were for rapists and murderers. Did Ollie want to end up in jail? Throughout Ollie's high school years, my mother's mantra was "This too shall pass." But this transgression was permanent, Ollie's badge of honor for all to see. It was her way of marking herself as separate from us, her first step toward being free. The words etched into her skin came from a New Hampshire license plate: "Live free or die."

3

My parents split slowly, like the subterranean forces that pulled apart the jagged coasts of South America and Africa. You could say Ollie was the force that drove them apart. My mother declared that Ollie, now skipping school on an almost-regular basis, was too much to handle, the skunky smell of marijuana trailing her through the house. Mom would beg our father for help, but he would downplay Ollie's behavior, believing it was a phase that she would grow out of like a pair of shoes.

When Ollie turned sixteen and passed her driving test, Mom said a car of her own was out of the question; soon a yellow VW Bug showed up in our driveway. Dad said she needed it to get to school and sports practices. It would make our mother's life easier. Ollie threw her arms around Dad, jumped into the driver's seat, and took her new car for a spin.

"Why do I always have to be the bad cop?" my mother said, standing in the driveway.

"It's not about being the bad cop," Dad said.

"You're always the hero."

"Lorraine."

"Someone has to reel that girl in."

Ollie had a fender bender within the first months of getting the car; my mother wanted to take away her keys. Dad defended her. "She's a new driver, she'll learn."

Even I knew that she kept a stash of pot, rolling papers, and Visine in the glove box. But then she started missing track practice. At first her coach looked the other way and allowed her to compete; the track team needed her to win. But when she showed up at a tournament reeking of pot, some of the parents complained, and the coach had to expel her. He told Dad he had no choice.

Ben had long hair and drove a van; he worked in a pet shop. His life goal was to open a surf and skateboard shop in Point Judith, Rhode Island, where his family summered. He had graduated from high school two years before Ollie, and his allure was prodigious. He wore work boots and flannel shirts, and when he lifted his arms or jumped to catch a frisbee, a rivulet of dark hair could be glimpsed reaching from his navel into his jeans. Ollie loved going to the pet shop after hours; Ben would let all the puppies out of their cages, and they would climb all over her body. Ollie said it was better than sex, and I solemnly nodded in agreement, though I was still trying to fathom the actual logistics of intercourse. (The word "penetration" terrified me.)

When Ollie said she wanted to surf, Ben filled a cooler with Heinekens and Gatorade, bought beef jerky and Fritos, and made a cassette tape of all their favorite songs for the road trip to Point Judith. Our mother reminded Ollie that it was the weekend of the SATs. Ollie said she didn't care.

"This is your future, young lady!"

"It's *your* future," Ollie shot back.

That night Ollie offered to pay me a hundred dollars to take the test for her. I wanted to help her, and I would have done it for free, but I was terrified of getting caught. She took my refusal as treason.

My mother dropped Ollie off at school the morning of the test. A half hour later, she received a call from the school alerting her to Ollie's absence, her desk empty in a room full of students hunched over their workbooks. She had taken off, leaving the answer sheet with its pale oblong bubbles empty.

My father remained calm. Though Ben wasn't "boyfriend material" according to my mom, we'd all noticed that he had a calming effect on Ollie. She shed her layers of defiance and anger around him; sometimes she was even sweet.

"She's safe with him," my father said.

"You don't know that," my mother snapped.

Dad offered to go to Rhode Island and search for Ollie.

"I guess there's no point." My mother collapsed in a chair in the kitchen, her tennis skirt hiked up, exposing her frilly underwear. She turned her sights on me and said, "How did you get to be so good?" It was a compliment that felt like an accusation.

Ollie didn't return Sunday night, and we realized we didn't even know Ben's last name. Mom started calling around to Ollie's friends, girls on the track team, the coach. My father wanted to post signs with her picture around town, but my mother shot that down. "She's not a lost cat." Early the next morning, my father and I went to the pet store. We discovered it was closed on Mondays, but we could hear the puppies' muffled squeals behind the glass.

Dad dropped me back home to wait with Mom while he searched for Ollie at gas stations and convenience centers, the shopping mall, and strip malls up and down the Boston Post Road. He stopped by the high school track field and walked beneath the bleachers. He saw something white and smooth poking out from under the leaf rot, and for a second believed it might be Ollie's head, his girl broken beneath the bleachers. Getting closer, his knees buckled, and his heart constricted as he fell forward and begged the gods of missing children to spare her. Pushing aside the damp leaves, he saw that it was a bleach bottle.

Finally, my parents broke down and called the police, who said they saw this all the time; teenagers usually turned up in two to three days, but they'd keep an eye out for her. My father wanted us to get some rest, but it wasn't possible. The questions no one could ask aloud hovered: had she hitchhiked and flagged down the wrong car? Was she trapped in the basement with a psychopath? Was Ben a psychopath?

Ollie appeared on our doorstep two days later without any fanfare. My father was relieved and elated, my mother was apoplectic and enraged. She demanded an explanation: Ollie owed us that.

"Do you have any idea what you've put us through?" My mother wanted an account of where she had been and what she had done.

Ollie just stood there. Her clothes and hair were filthy.

My mother's voice rose. "Are you in there? Olivia! Answer!"

Olivia rolled her eyes. "Are you done?"

"Am I done? Sweetheart, I haven't even started." My mother's body was a human bayonet, rigid with anger. Ollie shouldered past her and headed toward the basement. Mom beseeched our father to do something.

"Let's cool down," he said. "Let her be."

"How can you side with her?"

"Honey, I'm not siding with her, but you're not getting anywhere with the interrogation."

After dinner, my father gently knocked on her door, holding a plate of pork chops, corn, and salad.

"Ollie?"

No answer.

"Olly, Olly, Oxen Free?"

No answer.

I never really learned what my father imagined was going on with Ollie, why he defended her that night, as he did throughout his life. What we all knew but couldn't quite admit, was that we were afraid of her, and with reason. If challenged, Ollie had two settings: rage and apathy. By the time Dad returned with Ollie's dinner, my mother was angrily loading the dishwasher. She took the plate from him, and, instead of wrapping it in foil, dumped the contents into the garbage.

"I won't live this way," Mom said.

"What are you saying?"

"It's time we think about boarding school."

"She's a child," Dad said.

"Do you hear yourself?"

I slipped out before Dad answered.

I was afraid to go down to the basement, but I felt bad about not taking the test for her and wanted to know if she was still mad at me.

I knocked gently. "Ollie."

"What?"

"Can I come in?"

She had showered and was wrapped in a towel listening to her new favorite album, Pink Floyd's *Dark Side of the Moon.* The cover had a triangular prism with a refracted ray of light producing a rainbow.

"Are you mad at me?"

There was a box of saltwater taffy on the floor. She pushed it toward me with her toe.

The principal called my parents in for a meeting and informed them that Ollie would have to repeat her senior year, given her grades and absences, and he strongly recommended a psychiatric evaluation. Upon hearing the news that she wouldn't graduate with her class, Ollie exploded.

"No fucking way." She now used the f-word with some frequency.

"It's not up to you," my mother said.

"They can't make me."

"Olivia," Mom said, "you don't have a choice."

"At least Ben loves me."

"Honey, we love you," Dad said.

"Then why are you doing this?" Ollie said, and grabbed her keys. It was classic Ollie; she had a gift for making you feel guilty for something she had done.

I set the table for four that night as if on autopilot, even though most of the time it was just the three of us.

"They're making an example of her," Dad said, pushing his plate away, as if he couldn't swallow what was happening.

"What about getting kicked off the team?" my mother asked, knowing how much Ollie's expulsion from the team hurt him.

"Some good it did them," he said. The team had dropped to the bottom of the division with Ollie no longer there to carry them. "I hope they're happy now," he added.

"That's not the point. What she did was wrong."

"She should have been docked a game is all I'm saying."

"So that's the lesson in all this? What's Amy supposed to think? That taking drugs is okay?" she said, invoking me, the silent and seemingly invisible pawn.

"It's marijuana, Lorraine."

"That is a drug!"

My mother stood up from the table, chucked her plate into the sink like a frisbee, and charged out of the kitchen.

"Please," he said, grabbing her arm.

All I could hear was the sound of the plate wobbling in the sink until it came to a stop.

"I guess it's all okay with you, is that it?"

"Honey, it's not okay, but you could be overreacting."

"She's flunking out! She's taking drugs!"

"She's hardly the first kid to try marijuana."

My mother glared at him, then me. "Nice talk," she said, "in front of the girl."

❧

Our mother invented a pretext to get Ollie out of the house, knowing she would never agree to see a psychiatrist. I felt guilty for not warning my sister. As they backed out of the garage, Ollie called out, "Don't touch my shit."

As soon as the car was out of sight, I gathered all the stuff I needed for one of my favorite games, Cobbler. I was fascinated with my father's electric shoe-shine machine, a capsule resembling a fuzzy caterpillar that buzzed like a table saw when a shoe touched the bristles. He told me it nearly took off his finger one time and warned me not to touch it. Unlike Ollie, that was enough for me. I was not the kid who was going to touch a hot stove or stand too close to a ledge. I put on an old apron, arranged the shoe creams, and lined up my father's loafers and wingtips. I was meticulous as I pretended to shine and buff the shoes. At fourteen, I knew I was too old to indulge in these make-believe scenarios, but they were familiar and soothing, little worlds I lorded over.

Home alone, I did something I'd never done. I flicked the silver switch on. The bristles sprang to life, whirring fast. I turned the machine off with a satisfying click, and it slowed to a halt. After doing this a few more times, I put one of my father's loafers into the spinning bristles and watched the dull leather come to a shine. Pleased with the result, I reached over to get some shoe cream, and the machine suddenly grabbed a clump of my hair. With a nausea-inducing wave, my scalp began to rip. Hot tears stung my eyes as I tried to pull away. The machine made a screeching sound like tires skidding, then miraculously clicked off. My nostrils were filled with the sickly, sulfurous smell of burning hair, and I gagged.

The only way to get free was to cut the hair caught in the machine's core, wound as tight as thread on a spool. I had to contort my body to reach into the little drawer on my father's bedside table, where I blindly felt around, praying for scissors. I found a toenail clipper and frantically chopped at my hair until my head came free. If Ollie had been there, she would have laughed her ass off. There was a cartoon version of what had happened, my hair sucked in the way a retractable cord swallows itself. In my hand was a divot of my scalp with my hair attached. On the side of my head, a soft red penny of blood spread to the size of a silver dollar.

As my panic subsided, the pain became more intense. I quickly put away all the shoes, creams, and brushes, frantically trying to erase the evidence, as if I were wiping off the fingerprints at a crime scene. I yanked out the clump of hair still wound around the machine, wrapped it in tissues, and buried it in the outdoor garbage can. Testing the limits of my stoicism, I touched the tender spot on my head and coolly inspected the watery blood on my fingertips. I peered into my mother's magnifier mirror, pushing my hair away from the wound, then dabbed the blood with a cotton ball and nearly fainted as the tiny fibers, like capillaries, filled with blood.

Afraid I would pass out, I lowered myself onto the bathroom floor. I'm not sure how long I stayed there, but when I stood up, there was a bloodstain on the mat, so I rolled it up and stashed it under my bed. I combed my hair into a side part to cover the bald patch and found a barrette in Ollie's old room to keep it in place. Very little had been touched or moved since she'd decamped to the basement. The scissors on her desk lay open, like a girl with her legs splayed.

Our sister rooms, connected by a shared bathroom, had cabbage-rose wallpaper and matching furniture trimmed in pink, with identical coverlets and accent pillows. Ollie's bed had an old-fashioned canopy that I coveted, but she preferred my sleigh bed. She loved to jump on it, grabbing imaginary reins and making a getaway in her stagecoach after she'd robbed a bank and killed the teller. As little kids, we'd race between the rooms; in all of our games, Ollie always cast herself in the dominant role. Only later was I struck by how sadistic it all was: me in the role of Curious George, Ollie as the Man in the Yellow Hat trapping me under the hamper and sitting on it as I wailed to be set free. Ollie played the murderous Bill Sikes from *Oliver*, chasing me all over the house with a kitchen knife. I'd lock myself in the bathroom, and she'd wave the blade beneath the door. And yet I returned for more.

After the psychiatrist appointment, Ollie stormed through the house, stuffed some clothes into her knapsack, and took off for Ben's.

"That went well." My mother wasn't usually sarcastic.

Grabbing a hanger from the front hall closet, she glanced over her shoulder at me as if checking for passing traffic.

"What's different?" she said, eyeing me up and down with the same X-ray vision she used to tell if I had cleaned behind my ears or brushed my teeth.

I was terrified she would detect the bald spot under my hair, but she was distracted by her anger.

"Amy, I'm not guessing." She said this as a threat even though I hadn't asked her to try. Under normal circumstances I loved making my parents guess: how many deer lived on the planet (approximately 25 million); the name of the chimp that went into orbit (Ham); the number of spokes on a bicycle wheel (thirty-two on average).

"I don't have any time for this."

"I changed my part," I said quietly.

My mother scrutinized my head and said with no emotion, "I guess you did." She hung up her coat with extra conviction, rattling the hangers, and announced she was going to take a nap.

"It looks terrific," Dad said, holding out his thumb and squinting one eye as if I were a model that he was about to paint.

My eyes filled up and tears spilled over.

"I really do. I love it."

My father rubbed my shoulders.

"What is it, Bunny?"

I was mute, the scarlet coin burning on my scalp. He tried to kiss me on the top of my head, but I squirmed away, afraid the barrette would slip. The next day while I was at school, my mother found the bloodstained mat under my bed and was thrilled that I had my period at last. "Sweetheart, it's nothing to hide." I didn't have the heart to tell her that I was bleeding from my head.

That April, in what would be our last attempt at being an intact family, my parents planned a trip to our nation's capital. Ollie refused to go. By now my parents realized they couldn't force her to do anything, so they bribed her with a motel room to herself, which meant that I would have to sleep in a foldaway bed in my parents' room. Even with that concession, Ollie complained up until the minute we packed up and took off. In the car, she was distant, wrapped up in herself. Uncharacteristically, she turned down a handful of Mini Chiclets, small as confetti. Usually Ollie would swipe the little packet from me and tilt the whole thing into her mouth.

The trip was built around an exhibit my mother wanted to see at the Smithsonian: "Steuben. Seventy Years of American Glassmaking." She'd first encountered Steuben glass when, as a girl at the 1939 World's Fair, she wandered into what she described as a crystal forest. Number one on my list was going to the National Zoo to visit Ling-Ling and Hsing-Hsing, the giant pandas who had recently arrived as a gift from China. My father, obsessed over the timing, had planned the trip to coincide with cherry-blossom season. He called our trip a pilgrimage, and while I tamped down my excitement in front of Ollie, I couldn't wait.

Welcome to Delaware. We pulled into a rest stop to have lunch. Ollie was the first to reach the picnic tables.

"There's bird shit all over these."

She ran from table to table, slapping each one as if playing Duck, Duck, Goose. "Shit," "shit," "shit."

The tables weren't nearly as soiled as Ollie made them out to be, but my father's attempt to clean the bird poop with his handkerchief only made it worse, spreading the white paste.

"Ugh, gross!"

Mom sat down at the picnic table and declared it one of these make-the-best-of-it situations, pouring coffee from a thermos. Ollie continued to pace around the table as we unwrapped our sandwiches. I began my ritual of peeling off the bread crust in a single unbroken piece. It was a small but significant pleasure, like peeling the skin of an orange in one go or sharpening a pencil without breaking the ribbon of shavings. Ollie couldn't stand the slow, painstaking way I approached my beloved projects: spending long afternoons on card houses and jigsaw puzzles, growing a gum-wrapper chain link by link. Her intolerance wasn't about impatience; her mind just ran faster and more furiously than mine. Sometimes her leg would jackhammer under the table, or she'd crack her knuckles as if releasing excess energy.

Just as I reached the tricky crosshatched stretch of crust at the bottom of the slice, Ollie grabbed my sandwich, squeezed it into a ball, and threw it into the scrub.

"You annoying piece of shit."

Before any of us could react, black birds erupted from the bushes and dive-bombed the bread. Ollie had awakened a murder of crows, and she called back to them: "Caw! Caw! Caw!"

Another family arrived and started to spread a tablecloth over their poop-stained table; when they heard Ollie, they fled as far away from us as they could get. The curtains had parted, and our family was yet again in the middle of a play we hoped no one else could see.

Ollie raced off toward the parking lot, where the crows had gathered. She flapped her arms and cawed loudly, and the birds lifted in unison, a black cape snapped into the air. My mother corralled us to the car, while my father picked up our brown bags and tinfoil and threw them in the garbage. He tried to take a last swig of coffee before closing the thermos, but my mother waved him back to the car; she was intent on getting away. I expected her to reprimand Ollie but she commanded my father to drive, and he pulled the car back onto the highway.

"Mom!" I whined.

"What could they possibly think of us?" was her response.

I pulled my blanket over my head and fumed. Then I heard Ollie quietly singing a line from a Pink Floyd song about people leading lives of quiet desperation, and of course she was referring to us, to me. She wanted a worthy opponent, and I folded too easily, never giving her the fight she was spoiling for. This time, though, filled with as much rage as I've ever felt for my sister, I emerged from under my blanket and lunged across the back seat, grabbing clumps of hair on either side of her head, and pulled as hard as I could. She reared back and screamed so loud that my father jerked the car over; a van in the next lane swerved to avoid hitting us, and that set off a chain reaction of cars veering and drivers blaring their horns. My father lost control of the car as it started to rock and careened off the road. My mother covered her eyes. Then, without any warning, Ollie stretched out her powerful leg and karate-kicked me twice, first in my stomach and then in my hip. I folded into the well of the back seat. When my father slammed hard on the brakes, my head cracked against the car door.

We landed on the side of the road. A guy in a truck gave us the finger and yelled "asshole" as he drove by. Ollie gave him the finger back.

"Olivia!" my mother screamed.

My father turned off the engine, his head bent forward. For a wild second, I imagined him dead. Then he sat back up.

"Lor, are you okay?"

She held her head in her hands as if to make sure it was in one piece and nodded.

I thought he would ask us too, but he hooked his elbow over the seat and glared. "Do you want to get us all killed?" The anger in his voice scared me, and I temporarily forgot about my own pain and the injustice of it all. Dad, so slow to anger, was seething.

"If you cannot stop fighting, I will turn this car around. Is that what you want?"

My mother was excited by his ultimatum, a rare expression of patriarchal power. She had been waiting for him to step up and take control.

"Olivia? Amy? Do you hear me?"

Ollie, under her breath, "Fine by me."

"What did you say?"

Olivia folded her arms over her chest in a perfect braid of insouciance, dismissiveness, and disgust. "I didn't want to go in the first place."

"Fine," he said and turned the key. "We're going home."

4

We called it The Place. My mother would say, "Let's go to Italy after Olivia gets out of The Place," or, "Parking around The Place is abysmal." Olivia was eighteen the first time she was hospitalized in a locked ward for people with psychiatric problems. It was a medium-to long-term facility in New York City, where patients stayed for three months up to three years. My parents dutifully went to the hospital on Saturdays to participate in mandatory family therapy. Dad gave up his golf game, my mother a day of shopping or tennis. She would pack freshly laundered clothes, extra floss (Ollie wound the string around each hand as if she were a boxer taping her fists), and two cans of Pringles.

The bags had to be searched by the nurses, a protocol my mother found excessive and "for show." She assumed that the confiscated items likely wound up in the nurses' own bags: razors, nail clippers, emery boards, and Q-Tips. She also said that Ollie didn't want any visitors, including me. I suspected that my mother didn't want to expose me to whatever Ollie had, as if it might be contagious. I didn't like being left behind, but I was also scared of seeing my sister locked up. Before they left for the hospital, my father would pull me in for a sideways hug, his arm hooking me like the long cane in a vaudeville act. Ever since I had started developing, he had stopped hugging me full on. I'd stand in the doorway and watch as he backed the Chrysler out of the garage, slow as a cruise ship, onto the driveway and out of sight.

I read a bunch of books, trying to understand what was happening to my sister. They all had a girl on the cover, brunette and brooding. *Go Ask Alice, Lisa, Bright and Dark, The Bell Jar.* None of the girls reminded me of Ollie. *They* didn't jump into convertibles and unfurl their ponytails to feel the wind in their hair. They didn't dive off cliffs and come back up to the surface, slapping the water with crazy energy, ready to go again.

Ollie's absence was more suffocating than her presence. The chair she always sat in, the music she blasted, the window she slipped out of on cold winter nights. Ollie had agreed to go to The Place only to placate Dad after he persuaded a judge, an acquaintance from Running Brook, to keep her out of the juvenile detention system and thus wipe her record clean.

It had been the first party of the school year, and Ollie, along with a bunch of other kids, had descended on a house where the parents were away. They set up a keg and plugged in an amp that thumped the bass through the house. When the police arrived, some kids hid in closets, others took off through the woods. Pure adrenaline. According to Ollie, that was half the fun.

"It isn't epic unless the pigs show up," she said.

All of the kids were interrogated when it was discovered that the mother's mink coat and eight spoons forged in Paul

Revere's workshop, possibly made by Revere himself, had gone missing. When the police came to our house, Ollie looked like a Merit Scholar. She sat between our parents, knees pressed together, hands folded in her lap, her glorious hair pulled into a ponytail. She answered the officers' questions, made eye contact, and gave the impression that she was fully cooperating.

"Yes, officer, I was at the party."

"Yes, sir, I had been invited."

"I've known Bobby since elementary school."

"Yes, I knew his parents were away."

"Yes, there was marijuana at the party."

"No, I don't like marijuana."

"Yes, I did have two Heinekens."

The older policeman asked to see Ollie's room, apologizing at the same time for the intrusion. I trailed behind as they followed our dad and Olivia down the steps to her basement room, awash in black light, the posters glowing purple and green, the white of Stevie Nicks's teeth shining. When the young officer switched on the overhead light, the room was revealed as a junkyard of discarded furniture, old mirrors, posters, makeup, dirty clothes, a mountain of shoes and boots, a stereo, vinyl records and their jackets in disarray.

The older officer respectfully asked if he could open the dresser drawers, check inside the closet. Ollie didn't object. She was so cool that day. He pulled open the top drawer, extended a retractable probe like the antenna of a portable radio and pushed her underwear and bras around. It was embarrassing, especially for Dad. The younger officer shined his flashlight under the bed. Illuminated in its beam were dust bunnies, scattered journals, textbooks, dirty plates, more clothes. Just then Ollie became a little aggressive, a wobble in an otherwise perfect performance.

"Okay? Are you done?"

He snapped off his flashlight. My father put his hand on the doorknob, ready to show them out, but then the younger officer circled the bed again, sweeping his flashlight like a lighthouse beam through the fog.

"That's enough," my father said. "She doesn't have them."

Ollie moved closer to our dad, and he put his arm around her, protective and proud.

"Holy moly," the young officer called out, yanking the mink coat out from under the bed and holding it up by a sleeve. Inside the pockets were the eight silver Revere tablespoons, worth, we would discover, more than $60,000. The older policeman said he had to take Ollie in.

"Couldn't we just return the items?" my father asked. "Have the coat cleaned?"

"I'm sorry," he responded, sounding genuinely contrite. "I have daughters myself."

Our mother would say that she had two heart attacks that day, first as the red and blue lights flashed through our windows and then as Ollie was escorted into the back seat of the squad car.

Before the night of the party, Ollie had been running away more frequently and for longer periods. With every disappearance, my parents recalibrated the idea of normal as it shifted beneath us. They no longer called around to her friends, her teammates, her coach, the police. Ollie would eventually come home, and her routine would resume. For a day or two she would shut herself in her room and eat out of the refrigerator in the middle of the night. One time she left a milk bottle out on the counter with the cap off. In the morning, I watched as my mother turned the bottle upside down in the sink, her back rippling with anger. Our household had become a filling station, a place where Ollie refueled before taking off again.

When my mother's antique diamond ring from her grand-mother disappeared along with the tennis bracelet Ollie had given her, my mother fired our cleaning lady. But the suspicion lingered: would Ollie really have taken the jewelry? My father went to as many pawnshops as he could find in a sixty-mile radius. He came home empty-handed, bereft. He couldn't shake the image of all that stuff in those stores: wedding bands, retirement watches, cameras, a bugle. He said it broke his heart, imagining people breaking off parts of themselves to survive. He briefly considered buying a pair of bronze baby shoes mounted on bookends.

"Imagine having to pawn your child's baby shoes?" he said.

"They're using the money to buy drugs," my mother countered. "I wouldn't shed any tears."

My father's kindness and even keel had always been my mother's ballast. Now those same qualities inflamed her. She wanted my father to react, to share her emotion, feel her indignation and frustration. Of course, he was heartbroken that his beautiful daughter was locked away in a loony bin. For as long as he could, my father would rescue Olivia, bail her out, wire her money, take her to a different hospital, bring her home.

"How's that big sister of yours?" Dr. Salinger asked me.

"She's great," my mother said, jumping in. Until now, Ollie and I had come for our annual check-ups together. The doctor asked my mother if she wouldn't mind waiting outside for a few minutes. He'd been our family pediatrician for my whole life, and this had never happened.

"We have some grown-up things to talk about."

"Oh! Okay," Mom said, too brightly.

Dr. Salinger wore enormous orthopedic shoes with little leather mounds stitched on to house his bunions. He'd tap my knee with a rubber hammer and jump a little as if testing his own reflexes. I was bursting to tell him about The Place, what Ollie had done, and how my parents argued constantly about her in the long days when the fumes from all that secrecy and shame filled the house.

I felt I could trust him, but my mother had strictly warned me not to say a word to anyone. Plus, I knew she would grill me in the car the way a cop worked over a suspect, and I'd crack.

Dr. Salinger asked if I was sexually active. "Um, no." Was I menstruating? "Not yet." He made a few marks on an index card, worn around the edges.

"What about your grades, still top-notch?"

"Yup."

"Friends?"

I knew he wanted me to say yes, and I obliged. No one really wants to hear that you can't find a way to fit in. He summoned

Mom back into his office and invited me to pick out a stuffed animal from the vast collection of Steiffs in his bay window. Although I was not one for stuffed animals, I appreciated the Steiffs' realism: they were as hard as pincushions, with mohair fur and glass eyes. The little silver buttons in their ears, smaller than a thumbtack, showed proof of authenticity according to Mom.

"That's okay," I said, declining his offer.

"Take one, Amy," he said, as if he intuited that I needed a friend.

I knew they were inanimate, but how could I remove one from its family?

"That's okay," I said again.

"Please," he said. "It would make me happy."

While he and my mother spoke, I settled on the smallest one, a white mouse. I checked the tiny ear for the button. It was real.

Dad finally convinced our mother to include me in family therapy at The Place. "This is a mistake," Mom said, as we cruised along the Merritt Parkway on our way to the city. She didn't want to expose me to the other patients, some of whom were "certifiable."

"They're sisters, Lor. We're her family."

"Amy has better things to do."

I was studying for the PSATs in the back seat.

"Dr. Simon says it's important we all go," Dad said, defending his position.

"And here we are all going." She took a tube of lipstick out of her pocketbook, lowered the visor, and reapplied color to her lips.

At The Place, after our bags were searched for contraband, we were buzzed into a big open space known as the Community Room, strewn with shabby furniture and a muted TV advertising QVC jewelry. The nurses' station was partitioned off with thick glass walls reinforced with chicken wire. It had a pass-through medication dispensary and a poster of a cat hanging by its paws that read "Hang in there."

Other families started to trickle in. A custodian wheeled in a cart of folding chairs and arranged them in a wide circle. In ones and twos, patients started to emerge through the huge stainless steel doors. Mom told me the dorms were back there and said Ollie was always the last to arrive, needing to make an entrance. I started to worry that I wouldn't be able to recognize my sister or that she wouldn't recognize me, even though she'd been at The Place for only a few months. Small flowers of panic erupted inside me.

One girl was wearing short shorts and a cropped top. Another had a T-shirt with a peeling decal of Garfield the cat. A boy with a bowl haircut wore a Girl Scout uniform and sash, without any pins or badges, and enormous Puma sneakers. They joined their families around the circle, exchanged cautious hugs and muffled hellos, and took their seats. Ollie finally emerged, and my anxiety dissipated: she was the same. She was herself. Tracksuit, flip-flops, Ray-Bans atop her beautiful curls.

"Hey, that's my barrette. Who said?"

I wrapped my arms around her waist and held her tight.

"Hey, hey, I missed you, too."

I tried not to cry.

"Where have you been, Acorn?"

I hugged her harder.

She plopped down on one of the chairs and pulled me onto the seat beside her. Closer now, I saw that her mouth was dry and her lips were cracked in the corners. The hair around her part was flaked with dandruff, her cuticles bloody. Her feet were filthy.

The therapists and social workers entered in a line, carrying clipboards and manila folders. Ollie leaned over and whispered, "the Seven Dwarfs." Last, a man entered wearing leisure slacks with a cream turtleneck, a gold chain with a chai symbol dangling from it. Dr. Simon was the hospital director. "The man is an egotist," my mother had declared after their first session. They had returned home, exhausted, with a bucket of chicken, a treat reserved for the rare night when Mom didn't cook supper.

"What's the difference between an egotist and an egoist?" Dad innocently asked.

"You know what I mean," my mother snapped.

A few weeks later, Mom implied that Dr. Simon was "doping up" the patients. The doctor had explained that psychiatric medicine was an imperfect science, that trial and error were involved, but medication alleviated suffering. Did she want Ollie to suffer? My mother didn't like his tone and accused Dad of not sticking up for her.

"He talked to me as if I were a child. You were there. You heard it."

"He was trying to explain how it works."

"Half of them look like zombies!"

My mother didn't believe Ollie was suffering. She always maintained that if Ollie had gone to a detention center after her arrest, she would have straightened out. All this therapy was just a way for privileged kids to avoid legal consequences for their bad actions. Ollie had been caught stealing, and we, her family, were suffering on account of it. Dr. Simon was also a proponent of family systems therapy. He believed that what happened to Ollie happened to all of us. If we wanted her to get better, we also had to examine ourselves.

"How dare he!" my mother said. "How dare he pin this on us."

From the way my mother had characterized him, I imagined Dr. Simon would be large and imposing, but he was small for a man with a large head that pitched forward and bounced like a bobblehead doll. He sat down, hiking up his pants, and introduced himself as the director of the psychiatric ward. I couldn't help but look at his crotch. I was both interested in and repelled by male anatomy. But in the case of Dr. Simon there appeared to be nothing at all, his junk, as Ollie called it, invisible in the creases of his slacks. Another mystery of male anatomy I couldn't comprehend.

Dr. Simon surveyed the circle, making meaningful eye contact with each patient and family member. When he came to me, he stopped.

"And you are?"

Ollie came to my rescue. "Amy. My baby sister."

"Welcome, Amy. Let me put you on the spot. Do you know why your sister is here? There are no wrong answers."

Judging from my classmates, I knew that there were lots of wrong answers and plenty of stupid questions.

"Amy," he repeated the question more slowly, "can you tell us why Olivia is here?"

All eyes were on me.

"I hope she's okay," was all I could manage. The social workers and staff started snapping their fingers. I would come to learn that finger-snapping was the highest form of praise on the ward; you received a chorus of snaps for one thing alone: being authentic. My father joined in, snapping with one hand as if keeping a jazz beat. My mother's arms were firmly folded over her chest.

"Thank you, Amy," Dr. Simon continued. "You are all part of this process. We are so glad you are all with us today. We are here because your sons and daughters are fighting for their lives. Some are addicted to drugs, serious drugs, some have stopped eating, some are reckless." A dramatic pause. "Some have tried to kill themselves."

He let that sink in.

"We need you," he said, "because families are dynamic systems."

"Here comes the part where he blames us," I heard my mother whisper to my father.

Ollie took a lollipop out of her shirt pocket, snapped off the cellophane wrapper, and popped it into her mouth. She yanked it in and out rapidly, and I could hear it tapping against the back of her teeth. When she bit down on the lollipop, it sounded like glass crunching in her mouth.

I suspected that therapy was never going to cure Ollie. She would just learn how to game a new system. She wouldn't overdose or stop eating, but by refusing to participate and failing to comply, she kept adding more time to the length of her stay. She called Dr. Simon the original Dickless Wonder, and I wondered if she too noticed that his thing had disappeared in the creases of his polyester pants.

In the afternoon, we were invited to visit the art room, the gym, the library, and the cafeteria, where complimentary coffee and cookies were served. I wanted to see the art therapy room. "I'm sort of on their shit list," Ollie said. She had pretended, or so Ollie said, to stab the art therapist with baby scissors and had been sent to her room for the rest of the day, her television privileges revoked.

"Fucking baby scissors!"

At the next art session, she drew a coffin on a piece of construction paper and wrote "Rest in Peas." This time they took away her smoking privileges.

"These people!" Ollie said. "No fucking sense of humor."

Dr. Simon believed that all comments and gestures were important, especially jokes. He said people used humor to deflect pain. Ollie said it was all bullshit, but it sounded kind of true to me. My mother said, "All they care about is covering their own arses."

The art room was festooned with patients' pictures, like clothes on a line. The art therapist struck me as a well-meaning person, with her shiny brown hair, Laura Ashley smock dress, thick tights, and clogs. No wonder Ollie had taken an immediate dislike to her. The tables were set up with cookie tins containing crayons, sponges, plastic pots of tempera paint, the kind we had used in elementary school. Paintbrushes were banned. According to Ollie, one of the patients had pushed the stick end of a brush through his eye socket. "That is whack," Ollie said. I tried to picture it, but it was too gruesome. "One guy hung himself with a sheet," she added. "Now that's dedication."

We were invited to use the supplies to make a "special card" for our loved one. I sponged a red heart on a piece of yellow paper. Inside I wrote *Come home* and then scribbled over it. Normally I would have taken a new sheet of paper, having no tolerance whatsoever for mistakes or cross-outs. But there was no time to start over, so I wrote the first thing that came to mind: *This sucks.* Late that night, after we had gotten home, Ollie called. She loved my card, she said, starting to cry. Ollie had never cried before, or at least I hadn't witnessed it. "You're the only one telling the truth," she said. I listened until she calmed herself. Then another patient hollered through the phone, "Time, Shred!"

I went down into Ollie's room and switched on the black light. The room glowed, illuminating the frets of her guitar, the lint on her blanket looked like a sea of luminescent algae, and the stars she had glued to the ceiling, a birthday gift from me. They were meant to be in the shape of Aries the Ram, the constellation for her zodiac sign, but Ollie couldn't be bothered to follow the instructions and had randomly scattered the stars across the ceiling.

5

I made myself invisible. I hid behind my long brown hair and concealed my underdeveloped body in loose-fitting clothes. The high school was three times the size of our junior high, and my goal was to blend in. To that end, I stopped raising my hand and no longer sat in the front row of the bus or any classes. As in all teen movies, the cool kids took up residence in the back rows. I secretly named them the FAA, Future Assholes of America, but I was smart enough to sniff out my own envy.

Most of all, I hoped the bullying would stop, but within the first weeks, streamers of flaming toilet paper came spiraling down into my bathroom stall. Thankfully, the thin strips burned out before they came too close. Girls flicked lit cigarette butts at my feet. I wouldn't have survived without my battery of defenses and deflections. *I'm smarter than they are. I'll go to a better college. I'll win a Nobel Prize in molecular biology.*

Early in the semester, my biology teacher asked me to stay after class. He had a swirl comb-over and his fingers were yellowed from years of chalking the board.

"You're Olivia Shred's sister?"

"Yes."

"Boy, you two couldn't be more different."

I felt defensive about Olivia, even though he meant it as a compliment. He wanted to know why I wasn't raising my hand; it was clear from my work that I knew the answers. "You don't need to be shy, Amy."

He opened his desk drawer and pulled out a box of bright yellow marshmallow Peeps. I couldn't tell if he was being nice or was in fact the pervert my mother had warned us about, the man in the car with his junk in his hand.

"For you," he said, pushing the candy toward me. I was massively confused; I thought the polite thing to do was to take the Peeps, but I was afraid to. When the bell rang for the next class, I grabbed the candy and dashed out of the classroom, awash in shame. Had my biology teacher singled me out because something repellent in him sensed something repellent in me?

For the first time in my life, I skipped my next class and hid out in a bathroom stall in the gym. I opened the cellophane and peeled off a Peep, slowly letting it melt in my mouth, the treacly sugar mixing with my saliva. I heard a couple of girls enter the locker room and stuffed the rest of the Peeps into my mouth, as if the yellow blobs were contraband. Suddenly my eyes bulged, and I started to gag. I was drenched in sweat. The sandpapery skin of the chicks lodged against the roof of my mouth. Then my ears started to buzz, my eyeballs bulged as if about to explode. I hooked my index finger into my mouth, but the wad of Peeps wouldn't budge. When the girls heard me gagging, they went silent. Then one said, "What the fuck was that?"

With my legs tucked up under me on the toilet, tears streaming down my face, I held on to the sides of the stall to steady myself, trying desperately not to gag and give myself away.

"Whatever," one of them said as they closed their lockers and left, the sound of cleats mercifully clicking away on the cement floor. Whatever spit I was able to manufacture had loosened the marshmallow, and with one strong push, the ball of Peeps flew out of my mouth, hit the stall door, and plopped down on the floor like a shivering yolk.

When I took first place at the annual Science Fair, my parents and I celebrated at the Golden Door. I had made a model volcano that erupted every three minutes, operated by a miniature hydraulic pump I'd built and hooked up to a timer. Lots of kids and parents had gathered around to watch it erupt. Some stayed to watch a second and third time.

The koi pond at the restaurant was being cleaned. Drained of water, the once shimmery black pool now looked cracked and chalky.

"I'm not going back to school." The words just came out.

"What are you talking about?" my mother said. "You took first place!"

"I want to go to boarding school."

"Both my daughters away—I don't think so." Mom squashed it.

"Then private," I said.

"Bunny," Dad said. "Talk to us. What's going on?"

I couldn't speak.

"Can you tell us what's wrong?" His tone remained gentle, expecting that whatever I said would be something he could fix.

"Talk!" my mother said, impatient. "What is it now?"

What is it now? I hadn't made a fuss. When I was in middle school, she had finagled invitations to birthday parties and cajoled parents into including me in sleepovers. Now, in high school, I told white lies about having friends to eat lunch or study with. It was easier to keep up a façade than face my mother's disappointment or risk her interference.

Recently, a bunch of boys had played hot potato with my brand-new calculator before the teacher arrived.

"You want it, robot? Come get it."

I tried to grab it, but they outnumbered me. I sat down at my desk and contained my anxiety, praying that they wouldn't drop it and full of rage for being so utterly defenseless, and beyond that the feeling most difficult to manage: humiliation.

"This is your celebration, Bunny. Let's get eggrolls?" Dad said.

"I can't, I can't!" I started to cry, covered my face with my hands, and ran to the bathroom. Less than a minute later, the door opened. I hoped it was my mom come to soothe me, but it was a woman with a little boy who hid his face in her crotch. When I returned to the table, my father announced that if I could finish out the term, we could investigate private schools for the fall.

"Really?"

"Yes, really," Dad said.

"Can we afford it?"

"Not to worry, A."

"What about you, Mom?"

"I agree. You've earned it."

I don't know what my dad had said to convince her in those few minutes, but it didn't matter. It was all the promise I needed to get through freshman year. After that night, Mom transferred a lot of her energy to helping me. Finding the right private school became her new project: making calls, getting applications, arranging campus visits. Many years later, she admitted that she should have sent me to private school from the outset.

For the rest of the semester, the three of us formed a polite triangle. We each had our jobs around the house and performed them without complaint. Occasionally we'd have a big laugh, like the time Mom dropped a steaming casserole of baked ziti on the floor. But the laughter felt hollow. Ollie had left us in a holding pattern. Then Dad announced she'd be coming home on a weekend pass, and if it went well, she might return over the summer.

Dr. Lucie, the youngest doctor on staff, was probably the first and only man whom Ollie couldn't seduce. She had therapy with him three times a week, and Ollie admitted to me that she woke up extra early to shower before their early morning sessions. She wanted her hair to look amazing. During her allotted phone time, Ollie would relay those sessions to me. I felt privileged to be on the receiving end of her calls. I also realized that for all her popularity at school, Ollie didn't really have close friends. Ben had moved on, and of course, she acted as if she didn't care.

She scrutinized everything about Dr. Lucie: the flare of his nostrils, his knit tie, skinny as a ruler, his penny loafers with the slot empty. His body was lean like hers. She wondered if he was a runner. Over the course of their sessions, Ollie regaled him with tales of her sex life. She bragged about how much she loved giving blow jobs and how expert she was at it. She loved having sex outdoors, under the bleachers, in the parking lot, on the beach. According to Ollie, he never flinched or flirted back, just scratched notes on his pad. As a game, she'd talk fast to make him write faster, as if she were the puppeteer and he the puppet.

During one session, the spare pen he kept in his shirt pocket had leaked, the ink staining his shirt like a Rorschach test. *Rabbit, potato, penis.* She knew Dr. Lucie was married; his wedding band was his only accessory. Over the course of their sessions, Ollie's attachment to Dr. Lucie developed into a full-blown obsession. She confessed her love for him in her journal, writing his name over and over, starting to believe it was mutual. When Dr. Lucie asked her what she was feeling, she was shocked he couldn't read her mind.

Around that time, Ollie begged an orderly to leave two doors unlocked so she could sneak out. She had made out with a night nurse who played bass in a band and wanted to see her perform at CBGB, the downtown punk club. When she slipped out into the night, Ollie told me she felt like an animal being released into the wild. It was intoxicating, exhilarating. All that air! On the subway to the club, she wondered if people could tell she had busted out of a loony bin. Then she said the good thing about New York is that no one gives a shit.

It turned out she had the night wrong and the nurse's band wasn't playing. She didn't care. The club was loud, chaotic, rebellious. The walls were graffitied many times over, the music was deafening. From the minute she heard punk rock, it became her church of choice. When Ollie went to the bathroom, the drummer from the warm-up band followed her inside and fingered her.

"Aim, it was incredible."

She hadn't planned where she would go or what she would do after the concert, but her wild night ended abruptly. The security camera at the hospital had caught her leaving, the orderly had "ratted her out" in exchange for a "slap on the wrist," and the hospital van was waiting outside the club.

Dr. Simon summoned my parents and Ollie for a private meeting. He offered the theory that Ollie felt safe within the confines of the ward; subconsciously, she wanted to stay. Why else would she continue to break the rules and thereby extend her time there? She had been at The Place for ten months; Dr. Simon was recommending another year, so great were the consequences of her transgressions.

"I was only going out for the night," Ollie pleaded in her defense. "I was going to come back." Her trial visit home was called off. Dad's dream of having her there for a summer of sailing and cookouts was off the table. On the phone to me, Ollie wailed about the injustice as if she were a prisoner and Dr. Simon her warden.

"I know my rights," she sobbed. "They can't keep me here against my will."

Had she gone to juvenile detention, Ollie would probably have been released. Or, as she was famous for saying, "Do the crime, do the time," as if she were a hard-bitten inmate. Now her high school class would be graduating, while she embarked on her second year at The Place. She was officially a ward of the state (and, by proxy, of Dr. Simon), and he alone would determine the terms of her release. She had the greatest disdain for the patients known as Lifers, especially a woman named Cathy, who lived to please Dr. Simon and the staff.

"Where does all that ass-licking get her?" Ollie said. One night, as Cathy was sleeping, Ollie ripped the orange pom-poms off Cathy's beloved Turkish slippers and threw them in the toilet. Ollie laughed. "They looked like little turds someone forgot to flush."

Everything came to a head during Ollie's next session with Dr. Lucie. She was still reeling from her punishment. "At first I didn't say anything, and we just sat there." Ollie often described the start of her therapy sessions as if they were staring contests. "Of course, I made him blink first," she boasted as if it was a major triumph. "Then he asks me what I'm feeling. So fucking original. And he starts writing something down, only I didn't say anything." Her agitation heightened. "I told him to put the pen down. I said he didn't have permission to write about my life. It's *my* fucking life!"

I didn't know what to say to that.

"Are you still there?"

"I'm here."

"I'm never going to get out," she wailed.

"You will," I offered.

"He just kept writing." Then Ollie got quiet.

"I thought he loved me," she said. "That's when I lost it."
First she heard the words feed through her brain: *Runners take your mark.* Exploding as if out of a starter's gate, she lunged at Dr. Lucie and slapped the clipboard out of his hand. The pages fluttered to the floor. Before he could react, she stood up, lifted her chair over her head, and threw it against the window. Instead of shattering the glass, it boomeranged back into the room and caught Dr. Lucie in the side, knocking him down as it crashed to the floor.

An orderly down the hall heard the noise and ran to the room. He saw Dr. Lucie on the floor, grabbed Ollie and restrained her, securing her wrists with zip ties. Adrenaline pumping through her body, she went into a rage and was put in the Quiet Room to cool off for the rest of the day. She was forced into a restraining jacket to keep her from harming herself. Her already reduced privileges were further stripped: she would no longer be allowed outside. Not on the front steps to smoke and not in the rat hatch, a caged area on the roof where patients played kickball with a partially deflated ball. Ollie never accepted responsibility for her behavior. According to her, these punishments were a mind fuck, Dr. Simon's power trip. She also lost her phone privileges, and our nightly calls ended abruptly. Her next review for possible release was some undetermined time in the future. And until further notice, the Shred Family was no longer required to come to family therapy.

❧

That spring we toured Carlson Academy, a private day school two towns over. We fell for the beautiful ivy-covered brick buildings, the quad where kids played hacky sack, the clusters of study groups dotting the perimeter, textbooks open on the grass.

"It's a miniature college," my mother proclaimed. All the moms wore jeans with skinny belts, some of the dads were in Bermuda shorts and Topsiders. But not the Shreds. Mom wanted us to make a good impression, Dad in a seersucker suit, she in a Lilly Pulitzer shift, garish in pink and green flowers. She agreed to let me wear pants as long as they weren't jeans. I wore khakis and threaded a rainbow belt of Ollie's through the loops.

One of the seniors, dressed in the school uniform (a pleated plaid skirt, white shirt and blazer) showed us around. A lanyard swung from her neck with a laminated badge of the school's mascot, a great horned owl, and in neon green the words Tour Guide. She took us through the quad walking backward and delivering a steady patter of facts. On the way to the gymnasium, she backed into a water fountain and said, "Oops! Occupational hazard." The parents laughed. One of them asked where she would be going to school in the fall.

"Harvard." She blushed.

On the way home, my mother called our guide the total package: pretty, smart, well-rounded, and charming. Check, check, check, check.

❧

Carlson Academy proved to be a positive change. Uniforms were mandatory, so I no longer melted down in front of my closet every morning before school. Getting good grades was a priority; admission to a top-rated college was the universal goal. No one would bully me for raising my hand. On the contrary, Carlson students tried to edge each other out in the classroom as well as on the playing fields. I thrived on the competition, especially with Roland Braff, the school's smartest student. When tests were handed back, the girls would cheer in solidarity if I had the higher grade.

Another advantage of Carlson: it had a mainframe and three terminals. I signed up for computer class, eager to learn rudimentary coding. My mother pushed me to join the theater or the newspaper instead. "You're not going to make friends hunched over a computer," she said.

On the day of auditions for the winter play, I slipped into the auditorium and watched from the risers as students sang, danced, and recited the monologues they had memorized. I had the profound sense that if I tried out, blood would pour from my mouth. Instead, I signed up for stage managing and enjoyed wielding a clipboard and wearing a headset. I was promoted from assistant to stage manager when the girl who held the position came down with mono and dropped out of the play. The drama teacher said I was a natural at the job. I mostly hung around with the tech guys, who had a million in-jokes and loved splicing wire and running cables. They called me Shred Head, and it felt more affectionate than taunting.

Toward the end of the school year, during a rehearsal for the senior play, *Gypsy*, I headed up to the lighting booth, my forehead clammy, with a cupcake for Rob, a senior and the head lighting designer. I knew it was a risk to bring him a cupcake, since he usually demanded I evacuate any space he occupied. I knocked lightly. No answer. I pried open the door to find Rob making out on the floor with Gina, the wardrobe assistant. I froze.

"Get out!" Rob yelled. "Now!"

I stayed away for the next two rehearsals until my sense of duty reeled me back in. Until I climbed those steps to the lighting booth I didn't really know that I had a crush on Rob. There were girls at Carlson who hiked up their tartan skirts and wore thigh-high stockings. They spent forever in the bathrooms applying eyeliner and smoking. I was still wearing knee socks and a training bra. I never made eye contact with Rob again. From that point on, I carried out my stage-managing duties with grim solemnity, nothing more than a dust mote suspended in a lantern's high beam.

The play was a huge success. Cast and crew dined on a buffet of Chinese food on closing night, and I watched as Rob fed Gina, his now public girlfriend and prom date, some lo mein with chopsticks. The actors had changed into jeans and sweatshirts, eye makeup sweating down their faces, laughing and hugging, arms around each other, singing snippets from their favorite numbers. The girl who played Mama Rose, her arms filled with flowers, tossed a pink boa around her neck and laughed her full-throated laugh; Juilliard bound, she was loved by all. At the end of the night, she gave each member of the cast and crew a gift wrapped in gold paper.

She thanked me for all I had done and kissed me on both cheeks, mwa! mwa!

"Open it," my mother urged, driving home after the show.

"I'll open it later."

"Open it now."

I made no motion to pick it up.

"Hand it here," my mother said.

"Let her be," Dad said.

Alone in my room, I lay down on my bed, my head swirling from the emotion of closing night and the end of the school year at Carlson.

I finished the year with some newfound confidence. I'd been invited to join the Mathletes, and we competed all over New England. Though only a sophomore, I helped lead the team, mostly upperclassmen, to victory at Nationals. I was allowed to elect yoga as my sport, and it was a relief to stay off the climbing ropes and playing fields. The instructor was in awe of my flexibility and complimented me on my body. I'd even been invited to a few parties. And my parents, for the most part, had resumed their lives.

I opened the gift. It was a key chain with a gold star engraved with the message *You are a star!*

Ollie's release coincided with my last day in tenth grade. Mom thought I should attend classes, but Ollie's release was a big deal, and I wanted to be there. She had been at The Place for nearly two years. I'd mostly stopped visiting, blaming my absence on Carlson—the homework, AP classes, my clubs. Ollie's phone privileges were eventually reinstated, but we no longer talked every night the way we had. And when we did talk, Ollie was different. Her reports were no longer urgent; sometimes she'd even apologize for being blah or getting off the call before her allotted time was up. It was as if she had run out of gas.

My parents reported that Ollie was finally compliant with Dr. Simon's medication regimen. She took the nightly cocktail he'd prescribed: an antidepressant, an antipsychotic, and a mood stabilizer. My mother, once so adamantly against medication, now agreed that it was the right course. Ollie was a more manageable, acquiescent version of herself. She had a new therapist, a woman, who she said was helping her. She played cards or Sorry with the other patients in the afternoons and shelved books in the hospital library on Sundays. Slowly she earned back her privileges and started studying for a GED.

As a final requirement for discharge, patients had to make a "declaration" in front of the staff, patients, and families. We three piled into the car for what would be our last trip to The Place. I recognized most of the staff, but there were a lot of new patients. They all gathered in the Community Room for Ollie's speech.

"I need to thank Dr. Simon and the staff. I know I wasn't the easiest person." The group laughed a little. "I've never met a rule I didn't want to break, and this place has a lot of them." More laughter. "I've come to learn that there are better ways of expressing myself."

Ollie thanked the other patients, calling them out by name and saying something touching or funny about each one. She called out Siobhan, her favorite nurse, for her good Irish wisdom. Siobhan winked at her as if they shared some sexy secret. She gave a salute to Jimmy, the orderly, who had always been there for her with a light. "That's right, baby girl," he said, holding up his lighter, flicking it on as if he were at a rock concert. She even bequeathed her pink Adidas jacket to Cathy, the girl whose slippers she had clipped, the only patient who'd been there longer than she.

The one person missing was Dr. Lucie, who had taken a job in the Midwest. He had tried to say goodbye before he left, but Ollie refused to come out of the dormitory. She saved us for last. She thanked Dad for always being there, Mom for putting up with her and bringing clean clothes, floss and Pringles. A little more laughter and a sprinkling of finger snaps. She walked over and draped me in an enormous hug—lots of finger snapping then. Ollie took a bow. I suspected, perhaps we all knew, that it was the performance of a lifetime.

6

My parents agreed. No frantic calls would be made, no search parties dispatched. Ollie had taken off in her car with some clothes, boots, and the new Nikes with the red swoosh that Dad had bought as a welcome-home gift, as if she were still running track. Add to that the cash from Dad's wallet, Mom's purse, and my stash of silver dollars.

Forever after, she would maintain that the real theft was the time taken out of her life while she was at The Place. She would never forgive my parents for locking her up. I asked if she got anything out of being there, and she said, "Not a fucking thing." After being home for two months, she'd flushed her meds and left without saying goodbye. As my parents saw it, they had spent the better part of two years shuttling back and forth from the hospital, bailing her out of trouble, trying to help her. They'd had it.

"So that's it," I said. "She's gone and we don't care."

"That's not it, Acorn," Dad said.

I grew frantic, imagining Olivia homeless, walking up and down a city street screaming obscenities or getting picked up at a bar and strangled in an alley.

"Then what?"

"She'll be twenty-one next year," he said.

"It's up to her," Mom said, "if she wants to be part of this family."

Over the next few years, Ollie would surface from time to time. None of us could forget the four a.m. calls when the sky was streaked with charcoal, your feet not yet touching the floor, knowing some terrible news about to be delivered, and the magical belief that it might go away if you didn't answer. Ollie would call from a holding tank, or a shelter, or the security booth of a department store, having been caught stealing again. Or squatting in a decrepit warehouse in Portland, El Paso, Detroit. When a phone rings in the middle of the night, the news is never good; nothing prepares you for the simple, terrifying question: "Is this the Shred household?"

Also terrifying was how quickly we resumed our routines and roles. Mom returned to her bridge and tennis games, Dad to work and golf, though he was away a lot more now. Mom complained about his absences, but her protests were hollow: each of us was comfortably siloed. In the beginning, I couldn't grasp how it was going to work. Were we never going to talk about Ollie? Sometimes I guiltily hoped she would die; our grief would have an end point.

Most of the time, I doggedly pursued my single-minded goal: to graduate at the top of my class. Roland Braff edged me out by a percentage point and became Carlson Academy's 1978 High School Valedictorian. I didn't want to go to graduation, but Mom said skipping was out of the question.

"We haven't paid a pretty penny all these years to miss out on the big day," she said, pulling together a bright ensemble paired with her summer pearls. "We already missed one graduation. I'm not going to miss another."

"Please don't make me go," I begged.

"The Shreds are not sore losers," my mother proclaimed. "Now get dressed."

Seated among America's future lawyers and investment bankers, I listened to Roland's canned speech. I was headed for Columbia in the fall and had lined up a summer internship at a biology lab. My real life was about to start. My only wish was that Ollie would appear, watch me get my diploma, put her arm around me under the big tent, where graduates and families gathered, taking pictures, shedding gowns, lots of hugs.

After a glass of iced tea and a chocolate-covered strawberry, I insisted we go home. I didn't know it then, but the last picture of the three of us was taken by a guy wearing a neon vest directing traffic in the parking lot. He motioned for us to stand closer together. "Say cheese!" The heat of the day and the solemnity of the occasion conspired to make us heavy, wincing more than smiling. None of us mentioned her, but she was there, shadow sister.

Two days before I started college, my parents sat me down and told me they were divorcing.

"Great timing," I said, my voice catching.

"We wanted you to finish high school, have your summer," Dad said.

"What's going to happen?"

"This wasn't my idea," Mom said.

"Nothing," Dad said. "We're all going to be fine."

I had believed that it was Ollie who drove them apart, but now I saw that she was the fulcrum of their marriage. Without her the union collapsed. Lawyers were retained, divorce papers signed, all of it handled discreetly. "That's all I ask," my mother said, though she got to keep the house and receive generous alimony payments. Dad would pay for my college; that wasn't a question. On the day that officially ended our life as a family, we also made a pact to let one another know if Ollie surfaced. For a long time, we began our calls the same way: have you heard from her? Eventually, we stopped asking.

I emptied my room of all personal effects, hoping to erase any trace of who I had been. I threw out my four-foot-long gum chain that took years to assemble. I threw away the snow pants that made me look like a giant Kotex pad, or so Ollie said. I threw away my Rubik's Cube and my gemstone collection from the Museum of Natural History. Ollie had taken the aquamarine. "It's my birthstone," she had said, as if that gave her the right. The only thing I kept was a collection of assorted trinkets stored in a shoebox: the clarinet cap that had belonged to the boy who died of leukemia, the key chain with the gold star, my Steiff mouse from Dr. Salinger's menagerie. And nestled in a white handkerchief with my father's monogrammed initials was the little polar bear my mother had brought back from the fjords, which I had taken from Ollie's room. She never missed it, as I had suspected.

⚜

Tina Valore, my freshman-year roommate, decamped to her boyfriend's dorm within weeks of our arrival. With her departure, my hope of finding a best friend dissolved. Alone in our dorm room, I'd hear kids partying, music blasting from behind closed doors. I desperately wanted to join in, make new friends, sway to the music. Instead, I'd return from the library to an empty room and continue to study late into the night under the glow of my gooseneck lamp, mindlessly cracking pistachios between my front teeth.

Jen, my Resident Assistant, saw it first, or perhaps she was the only one to say something about it as we rode up in the elevator.

"Your mouth is a little green?" she said, and my hand flew to my lips. The second she mentioned it, I knew what it was. I had somehow fooled myself into thinking the ghostly green aura around my mouth was too faint for anyone to notice.

"It's pistachios," I said, shame creeping through my body.

"Oh, thank goodness. I was afraid it might be typhus!" She laughed. We arrived at our floor, and Jen insisted I come in for a cup of tea.

Her room was a mix of art posters: Monet's lily pads, the Rolling Stones, Arbus's twins. Jen had a large assortment of teas and a big box of Kleenex. She was a psych major and played intramural volleyball. She told me that being an RA came with room and board and a stipend, but quickly added that she would have done it for no pay.

"I want to be an adolescent psychologist," she explained.

"So, we're your guinea pigs," I said, trying to be funny.

"We're all just figuring stuff out," she said.

Jen put loose tea in a pot and filled it with boiling water from her electric kettle. The smell of chamomile filled the room. She cupped her hands around a mug and asked if I was homesick. "A little," I said, though that was a lie. It was a relief to be away from New Haven and our lonely, half-empty house.

"How are your classes? Are you keeping up with schoolwork?"

"Yes." All I did was study.

"Friends?"

"Some." Another lie.

"Do you ever have thoughts of harming yourself?"

It was then I realized that these questions were a checklist. "No," I answered. "Not really." I didn't want to harm myself, I wanted to be someone else. But I guess my hesitation was enough to set off Jen's alarm bells. She convinced me to let her make an appointment with a counselor at the mental health clinic.

"It's good to talk to someone," Jen said.

My mother believed in marriage the way some people believe in the Declaration of Independence. By faithfully doing her duties, she thought she would be rewarded with the dignity accorded wives and widows as they navigate the empty nest, retirement, and old age. She would take my father to be fitted for orthopedic shoes with Velcro straps when the time came. She would make sure he received enough morphine at the end, and she'd empty his locker at the country club after he died.

She was the only one in her group of friends whose marriage foundered and never recovered; for her, divorce was a multilayered exercise in humiliation. Growing up, she understood that her parents' partnership was loveless, bound by duty and economic hardship. They owned a dry-cleaning business; her father was embittered by the backbreaking work, her mother's fingers were prematurely gnarled and arthritic from buttoning and unbuttoning shirts all day. My mom loved poking through what her parents called the left-behinds, the items people neglected to empty from their pockets: keys, earrings, money clips, lipsticks. Racing forms, lighters, phone numbers, buttons. Over the years they collected hundreds of dollars in change, which they kept in five-gallon water jugs they called piggy banks, also known as their retirement fund. Once a year her mother would donate the abandoned clothes to Goodwill. Mom never said as much, but it explained why she hated Ollie's shopping at the Salvation Army.

She had been determined to marry for love and had found in my father everything she could have wanted: a breadwinner, the ideal father to her children, tall and handsome, a gentleman. They'd met at a dance and talked all night. My mother said a jolt of electricity shot up her arm when he dropped her at home and touched her elbow. "That's when you know," she said.

They were married six months later, and Ollie was born a year after that. When I came along, they moved from an apartment into a house in a suburb known for its one-acre lots and good public schools. Dad transformed the sleepy lumberyard into a bright showroom with the help of Anita

Wormer, a design consultant he met at a trade show in Boston. Do-it-yourself was the fastest-growing segment of the home-building business, and Anita Wormer was in the vanguard, constantly scouring manufacturers and designers for new ideas and materials. I loved to play in the brightly lit model rooms she'd assemble and gussy up with curtains, throw rugs, and potted plants, like a life-size dollhouse.

My parents had never expected to do so well. They had enough money for my mother to hire a decorator. She spent hours contemplating wallpaper and fabric swatches. With Anita's help, she installed a tasteful slate patio. They became friends and would often share a joke at Dad's expense. He couldn't remember people's faces! He was all left thumbs! He could put an entire soft-boiled egg in his mouth!

After the divorce, my mother stopped seeing her women friends; she didn't want to be pitied. She despised being a third wheel and refused invitations from couples. She was determined to tackle the day-to-day alone: paying bills, doing taxes, changing lightbulbs, but mostly filling the empty time. Her days began with a two-mile walk, rain or shine, followed by errands and doctor appointments, opening the mail, Phil Donahue, the news. At five p.m. she allowed herself a single scotch on the rocks. It eased the transition from late afternoon to evening, now the saddest part of the day. She had always said late afternoons were the happiest time, as she watched the light drain from the sky, peeling potatoes or carrots at the kitchen sink, gazing at the trees in winter, burnished by the copper sun. She called it the "almost time." Homework almost done, dinner almost ready, Daddy almost home. I called my mother most evenings around five. She called it "check-in," but I wasn't clear who was checking in on whom. Maybe it was also the way we siphoned off anxiety about Ollie's unknown whereabouts.

"I wish I could start college all over again," she'd say from time to time.

"Why don't you take a course or two?" I'd venture.

"It's too late."

"Maybe try doing something new?"

My mother didn't want to try anything new. She wanted her life to be exactly as it had been. Half the time she was barely listening to me as she finished the crossword puzzle from the morning paper. "Bun, what's a five-letter word for 'strike up the band'?"

Looking back, I place the beginning of Dad's affair with Anita Wormer on my last day of seventh grade. It was a half day at school, and Dad had promised to take me to lunch, just the two of us. But I gleaned that Anita was joining us when she approached the car, wearing a chiffon blouse with a matching scarf knotted around her neck like a stewardess, pocketbook dangling from her wrist, a cardigan draped over her arm. I grudgingly gave up the front seat. Dad told me to be a good sport, even though I had already jumped into the back.

Louie's Lunch, housed in a small, run-down brick building with a red door and red shutters, was famous in New Haven for having invented the hamburger. It was always packed with customers. There was a wait, but Dad and Anita agreed it was worth it. When my father remembered that they only took cash, Anita pulled out her purse and said, "He always does this." *Always?* As we ate, some hamburger juice dribbled down Dad's chin and I watched Anita blot it with her napkin. There was the rest of the afternoon to fill before Dad and I headed home. He sat at his desk looking over projects, with Anita perched on the edge, feeding him pieces of paper to sign. The business had quadrupled after she came on board, and Dad chalked it up to her energy and creativity. "The woman is a workhorse," he'd say, "and a visionary!" Anita asked if I wanted to see the new window treatments, but I declined, parking myself on a stool behind the register. I opened my book, *Great Expectations*, which I was reading for the third time.

Manny, one of my dad's truck drivers, pushed through the Employees Only door. He told me I was going to wear out my eyes. *Ha ha.* I knew that Manny had gone to prison for stealing from the lumberyard but my dad had given him a second chance. "That's the kind of man your father is," Mom would say proudly. He had paid for his secretary's cancer treatments. When one of the salesmen was in over his head at the racetrack, Dad floated him an interest-free loan to cover his debts. And when one of the drivers tragically lost his five-month-old baby, Dad paid for the funeral, went to the cemetery, and watched the tiny coffin lowered into the ground. I had regarded my father as a god up until the day Anita Wormer wiped hamburger juice from his chin.

Manny asked if I wanted to help him wash his truck. I was glad to get out from under the fluorescent lights and my wretched mood. The truck was piled high with two-by-fours secured by enormous belts. The mud-encrusted tires were as tall as Manny. Another driver walked by and asked if I was

Manny's new girlfriend. I blushed deeply. He unspooled an industrial-size hose, turned on the spigot, and aimed the water on the tires. The force was explosive, clumps of mud flying off in all directions like a meteor storm.

Manny asked if I wanted to try.

"That's okay," I said.

"Come on, give it a try."

The force was a million times more powerful than our garden hose at home, and it jumped out of my hands, spraying water in all directions. Manny wrapped his arms around me and helped me get control of it. My top was soaked, and I was terrified that he could see the training bra under my shirt. Together, we aimed it at the big clumps of mud the way you shoot water into a clown's mouth at the county fair—a game Ollie never lost. She'd take her place on the stool, slap her dollar on the counter, dig her heels in, and never move. That was the secret. She didn't flinch, and I'd beam with pride as her buzzer went off and the carny declared "We have a winner!"

Something hard was pushing into my back, insistent and uncomfortable. The yard manager happened to come out and saw Manny with his arms around me. Mike was one of the many young men in search of a father who, over the years, would attach themselves to Dad, a man without sons. He cut the water and pushed Manny away. "You okay, sweetheart?"

Manny's boner was the first but not the last time a man would push his erection into my back. When I was older, it made me laugh, as if someone were knocking at the door. Mike rushed me inside, and I dried off as much as I could in the ladies' room.

When we got home from the lumberyard, my mother interrogated me about my dirt-spattered clothes. I told her that Manny had invited me to clean his truck. She scolded me to never, ever go off with him or any man; suddenly my father's largesse in hiring him back seemed foolhardy. Dad was pouring his evening drink and had no idea why Mom was making a fuss. He defended Manny as one of the most hardworking and decent men on the planet.

My mother made me change immediately and take a shower. She tried to retrieve my clothes, but I made her wait outside the bathroom.

"I don't know what all this modesty is about."

She knew exactly what it was about. I had never seen my parents in their underwear let alone naked. She wore a housecoat over her nightgown at all times and he wore a bathrobe over his pajamas; a body was something you covered up. Ollie thought nothing of taking off her top at the beach. In the communal dressing room at Loehmann's, she would shimmy out of her jeans, even if she wasn't wearing any underwear. You could tell the other ladies were made uncomfortable by her naked body. Ollie didn't seem to notice or care.

I came into the den in my pj's, hair combed. My mother patted for me to sit beside her on the couch. "That's better," she said. "Clean as a daisy." Dad had told me not to mention Louie's; it wasn't her kind of place—no salads! And I gathered he meant not to mention Anita either. Years after the divorce, and after my own marriage would crash Mom admitted that the worst thing for her was imagining my father and Anita laughing behind her back as they conducted their affair. When it came to infidelity, my mother always insisted that if a wife didn't know, she didn't *want* to know. As it turned out, she was the one who buried her head in the sand. And as a result, she was left with a chasm of unanswerable questions and suspicions: Did they diminish her so they could feel justified? Did they pity her? Did they go to cheap hotels on the Merritt Parkway? Or Anita's garden apartment? All the while she ran the household, cooked our meals, and laundered our clothes with impeccable care, soaking stains, pressing pleats, folding underwear, balling the socks. Particularly galling to our mother was the fact that Anita Wormer was only a few years younger than her. Anita wasn't prettier, though she was softer. Couldn't he have had an affair with a younger woman, the way other men did, and then come back to her full of remorse, begging her forgiveness? My mother said more than once that she would have found it in herself to take him back.

Anita and Dad became a team, expanding the business, updating systems, installing a database at Anita's behest. He said she dragged him kicking and screaming into the twentieth century. According to my mother, she also dragged him into her bed. In the last few years of their marriage, Mom told me that they slept back to back on opposite sides of the bed. He would immediately fall asleep, while she lay awake, quietly grinding her teeth. On the rare occasions when they did have sex, he acted different in bed.

"After twenty years, you learn a person's ways," she said. "Out of nowhere he starts biting my lip, he wants to do it sideways."

"Mom, gross. Please."

"You're the one who wanted honesty."

"I don't want to hear about your sex life with Dad, or anyone. Please, it's gross."

After the divorce, Dad moved out, taking two suitcases of clothes as if he were leaving for a vacation. My mother donated the rest to Goodwill. In his top dresser drawer, she found the left-behinds: a retired wallet thin with wear, golf tees, single cuff links, Father's Day cards and birthday cards, tins of shoe polish and waxed shoelaces. The next day, Mom had the patio that Anita designed ripped out.

Suzanne Valley had a white-noise machine that was supposed to block outside sounds, but I often heard students raising their voices or sobbing in the warren of offices at the mental health center. That would never be me. I'd withdraw or go blank rather than show my feelings, and people assumed I either had no emotions or was snobbish. A girl in my dorm once asked if I thought I was better than everyone else.

I told Suzanne about my parents' recent divorce. She said it was not uncommon for parents to wait until their children went to college before splitting up, believing they had stayed together "for the sake of the children." Instead, many newly arrived freshmen were confused and destabilized by their parents' split.

"I see it all the time. The rug pulled out from under them."

Suzanne blamed my parents for the problems I had adjusting to college. I didn't correct her. How could I begin to talk about Ollie?

"Would it be insulting if I recommended having a little fun? That's a pretty heavy workload," she said, eyeing my transcript.

I wanted to believe that Suzanne was there for me, but of course she was being paid to be there. Sometimes she'd share stories from her private life, more like a big sister or a friend. She described being the target of some mean girls at riding camp: "They filled my helmet and boots with manure." She let the nightmare of that sink in, but then she turned the anecdote into a life lesson: "After that, I started preemptively pushing people away, afraid I'd get hurt. Does that sound familiar?"

I didn't answer.

"Amy," she said, "I'm not going to let you push me away." Her brand of caring turned me off, but Suzanne Valley unlocked a question I've never satisfactorily resolved. Had I been pushing people away, or was it the other way around?

At the end of my freshman year, Suzanne landed a job at Duke in North Carolina, running the undergraduate mental health services. She told me this with muffled pleasure; I could tell that she felt bad about leaving, but also that she was thrilled. She blurted out that she'd bought a house. Even though she wasn't leaving for another few weeks, I stopped showing up for our appointments. Suzanne left a few messages saying she was holding my hour, and I pictured the Salvador Dalí clocks at the Museum of Modern Art sliding off branches and over ledges. She said it would be good to have closure, but I had given up on that idea, thanks to Ollie.

On the day that would have been my last session with Suzanne, someone slipped a manila envelope under my door. I had fallen asleep at my desk with my physiology textbook open. Inside the envelope was a wooden hoop covered with twine woven in the shape of a spider's web. A few pieces of string with feathers were attached like the tail of a kite. I had no idea what it was, but something about it made me recoil. Suzanne's note inside explained that it was a dream catcher made by the Hopi tribe to welcome good dreams in and filter out bad dreams. She hoped I would fulfill my dreams. She left her number and said I could call her. *Not in a million years.*

I had put off visiting Dad for over a year. We spoke on Sundays. He was thrilled with his new life, and I bluffed my way through our perfunctory calls. As our conversation wound down, he'd always ask if I needed cash and would try to pin me down for a visit. I found excuses: classes, exams. I'd volunteer to take care of the lab rats and mice over the holiday break. The real reason was a combination of loyalty to Mom, my disappointment in him, and his decision to move over a thousand miles away and marry Anita Wormer. By the middle of sophomore year, I'd run out of excuses.

Each lawn in their gated community was mowed to exactly two inches. Each stand-alone home had a kidney-shaped pool in the back and a tasteful border of plants and succulents flanking the driveway. Beyond lay a golf course, as plush as a carpet and contoured with moon-crater sand traps. Dad forgot to leave my name with the security guard at the gate, so I had to wait until he finished his golf game. The guard, a shabbier version of Richard Gere, apologized for not letting me through.

"Where you coming from?" he asked.

"New York."

"I used to live in the city. Queens," he said.

"Cool."

"How long are you here for?"

"Just a few days."

"That's too bad."

I wasn't sure if he was flirting. I still didn't have a handle on that. I feared that people could tell I was a virgin, which was somehow worse than *being* a virgin. It was as if everyone had boarded a boat and taken off for a distant land. Ollie had called me Miss Purity and Forever Virgin. One time, in middle school, waiting on a movie line, I couldn't stop staring at a couple nipping at each other's noses and pawing each other as if they were baby tigers on a nature show. I wasn't aware that I was gaping, trying to decode their intimate language, but the woman caught me. "What are you staring at, little girl?" she said, loud enough for everyone on the line to hear.

Richard Gere asked if I wanted to wait in the security hut, get out of the sun. He took out a Fresca from the mini fridge and put the cold bottle to his forehead. His armpits were soaked with sweat. I couldn't tell how old he was. I wanted something to happen, and I was afraid of something happening.

"Oh! Look who's here," he said. Dad pulled up in a golf cart with a fringed top. A mini license plate read *Hole 'N' One*. He wore plaid golfing slacks with a salmon-colored polo and sported a new haircut with too much on top.

"Welcome to paradise, kiddo." *Kiddo?*

"Hi, Dad."

"Hop in!"

Richard Gere put my suitcase on the back seat. "Enjoy sunny Florida."

"Thanks," I said.

"No problem, Miss." He tapped the top of the cart, good to go.

Parked in my father's driveway were two white BMWs side by side. A sedan for her and a convertible for him. Until Anita came into our lives, my father was a Chrysler man. But Anita convinced him that a successful businessman should drive an impressive car. Together, they had built the lumberyard into a mini gold mine, and Anita had seduced our dad with a series of glossy brochures, each one holding out the promise of a new life. First, a BMW brochure turned up on his desk, then one for a trip to Capri, and last, a gated community in Southern Florida with a golf course, pool club, and tennis courts.

The place was pure Anita: the coral-colored stucco, the potted palms, a welcome mat that said "Welcome" in three languages. The way I saw it, my father didn't want a new wife so much as a new life. With Anita, he no longer had to face my mother's accusations, her anger, frustration, and hopelessness. He could escape all those painful days, especially holidays and birthdays, when we'd wonder if Ollie might show up or call, her absence more glaring and sadder.

The first year she was gone, a cheap cut-out valentine card arrived without a stamp or a signature. It showed a girl with apple-red cheeks holding a heart that said *Luv U*. We never knew for sure that she had sent it, but Dad perched it on the windowsill over the kitchen sink. Though I'd come to Florida for only a few days, Dad continued to play golf in the morning while Anita did water aerobics with two friends. Between futile attempts to study for finals, I grazed on all the food in the cabinets: Triscuits, Wheat Thins, Planters peanuts, a bag of chocolate chips, making sure not to make too much of a dent in any of them. I went through my father's drawers, an old habit. They were as orderly as a store display: polo shirts crisply folded and color coded. A whole drawer of pressed handkerchiefs. My mother had always ironed his handkerchiefs on Sunday night for the week ahead, fishtailing the iron into the corners.

We did a little sightseeing and had a few meals out. I asked if we could go to the beach, but Anita said it was too sandy. The amount of small talk she could generate was impressive and doggedly upbeat. It was almost as if my father had stopped thinking for himself. She ordered meals for him in restaurants, picked out his clothes, filled his prescriptions, and dropped the pills into a weekly organizer, marveling at her own industry and efficiency.

On the last morning of my visit, with Anita jumping around in the pool, Dad and I went to the clubhouse for breakfast.

"Any time for boyfriends?" he asked with a wink.

"Not really," I said.

"There's plenty of time for that."

When a waiter came to take our order, Dad said, "You gotta try the short stack. And the orange juice."

"Sounds good," I said.

He wanted to know about the campus, the lab, how it felt to live in the greatest city in the world. I was leaving in an hour, and this was our only time alone together.

"Dad," I said, "I feel like you know where Ollie is."

PART II

The Almost Time

7

The Rotunda. An upscale mall in downtown Baltimore. A *Help Wanted* sign in the window of Swarovski beckoned. Ollie waited until lunch hour, when the store was crowded and the salespeople were busy helping the influx of customers, to inquire about the position. This came to be her MO over the years—waiting for a distraction before taking what she needed or wanted. If caught, she'd pivot to Plan B: make a scene, act untethered, and be taken to a hospital instead of a holding cell. She had learned well that acting crazy was the equivalent of a Get Out of Jail Free card. Her parachute. The trick was knowing when to pull the cord.

Ollie called Dad from the Johns Hopkins ER. She had been accused of stealing crystal bracelets from a display case, had convinced the police that she had gone off her medication and needed help. They took her to the hospital. When Dad arrived, the ER receptionist said that no one had been admitted by the name of Olivia Shred. "Then it came to me," Dad told me, "Addie Loggins! Can you believe I remembered that from *Paper Moon*?"

Many years later I realized that they were both playing a part: a father-daughter duo on the lam, conning judges, law enforcement, psychiatrists, themselves. Another Academy Award–winning role for Ollie. Only now Dad found her wearing a hospital gown, sedated, staring at the curtain that separated her from another patient. She was released two days later. Anita found an "alternative" residential treatment center for Ollie called Roxbury Workshop, often shortened to Rocks, on an estate near Boston, with porches and walking paths. Patients stayed on the top floor in rooms previously used by the servants who worked on the estate. Over the next decade, as arranged by Anita and bankrolled by Dad, Ollie would drop in for a spell at Rocks the way other people would go to a spa or, in an earlier century, the sea for rest or respite. The patients were called citizens, and they were there on their own recognizance. Therapy was optional, medication was optional. The Roxbury philosophy maintained that unless a person participated of their own volition, any treatment was futile. It was the antithesis of The Place: no rules, no restrictions.

Dad took Ollie shopping before their flight from Baltimore to Boston. He bought her two Adidas tracksuits, new Nikes, Frye boots, and a Walkman. At Victoria's Secret, he gave her his credit card and waited outside the store. They had pizza at California Kitchen and went to see a midday showing of the movie *Top Gun*. The theater was nearly empty. Ollie loved it: the fighter pilots' moxie, the idea of an elite squad, and their motto, "The need for speed." In the middle of the movie, she went to the bathroom and never returned. "All the shopping bags were there, so I was sure she'd be back," Dad said, still mystified. He searched the other theaters in the complex, spoke to the manager, retraced their steps.

Ten days later, Anita received a call from Visa. Dad's credit card had maxed out at $10,000. The charges were traced from Baltimore-Washington International Airport to LAX. A first-class flight, a week at the Beverly Hills Hotel, a rental car. At Anita's urging, Dad reluctantly put a stop on the card. By then I knew that cutting Ollie off was like cutting off his own supply of oxygen.

Dad confessed that it wasn't the first time he had rescued Olivia. She had called from Dallas after a man she was living with locked her out, leaving her essentially homeless. And he had bailed her out in Seattle after she was caught stealing from the till at a Starbucks.

"Why didn't you tell me? We promised each other!"

"You were in school. We didn't want to derail your studies," Dad said.

"We?"

"Anita thought it would be a bad idea."

"What does she have to do with it?" My voice rose.

"Bunny, it's not so simple."

"I have a right to know about Ollie," I said. "Does Mom know?"

"On a need-to-know basis."

"I can't believe this," I said.

According to Dad, and it pained him to say, Olivia made her way mostly via men, some married, some not, drawn by her beauty, who fell for her and stayed for a cycle or two of her dazzling energy. If you were looking for fun, danger, or magic, if you needed to blow up your marriage, your job, or your life, Ollie could help you out. You could call it a pattern, though it was more of an algorithm: Ollie would steal something, smash something, cause a disturbance. She would get caught, cause a scene, crash.

I finished my undergraduate degree in three years and was accepted at the Zuckerman Institute on the Columbia campus, where I'd spent hours shadowing the scientists and caring for the lab animals. The institute specialized in research on the brain's effects on mind and behavior. I would get to design my own experiments. A massive body of neurological research had been done on the "fight or flight response" but I'd become obsessed with the lesser reaction known as "freeze" or "reactive immobility."

Over the next two years, I experimented on more mice than all of the grad students and postdocs combined. I was the Himmler of the lab: more dedicated, more determined, more driven than my colleagues. Mom said I needed to get a life. I believed this *was* my life, and I was proud of my work. My research required patience and diligence, the two qualities I had cultivated since childhood.

Our lab had a wall of western windows with views of the Hudson River and New Jersey. Sometimes the researchers and assistants would gather to watch the spectacular sunsets, the craggy cliffs of the Palisades bathed in golden light. I'd hear the pop of a bottle of wine being uncorked, the hiss of air escaping a beer can. One evening, as the group gaped over a particularly beautiful sunset, one of the researchers came over and said, "Shred, you gotta make time to smell the roses."

I continued to prep my mouse.

He walked away. "Suit yourself."

I saw myself in sharp relief: the sum of my pristine lab reports, more hours logged than any of the other researchers, my name on a few papers in scientific journals charting the neurons of tiny animals that had not volunteered to have their small skulls drilled and probed.

I opened my hand and saw that the mouse was dead, a tiny jacket of fur.

That night, alone in my tiny room, I couldn't stop crying. I had opted for international graduate housing; Mom saw this as an opportunity for me to make friends with people from all over the world. Only the international students kept to themselves, cooked by themselves, shared in-jokes in their native languages, and coopted the common rooms on every floor. All that time they spent watching TV together, I spent working on my grants.

Early April. On campus, the buds on the magnolia trees were beginning to emerge in tight fists. In anticipation of warm weather, students were prematurely stripping down to shorts and flip-flops. I was never ready to shed my layers and expose my skinny arms and flat chest with the arrival of spring. Then the letters began to arrive. The rejection from the National Science Foundation was as warm and personal as a bank notification: "Funds for this project have been declined." The rest followed: the Rockefeller Foundation, the National Science Foundation Research Fellowship, an MIT graduate fellowship.

A student must have heard me heaving in the restroom and called the department secretary, Kira Banerjee. She was beautiful, dressed in brightly colored saris with red high-tops, her wrists loaded up with bangle bracelets, and was relentlessly upbeat. Kira urged me out of the stall and patted my back. "Sweetie, grants get turned down all the time. You tweak them and turn them around for the next application cycle." I couldn't acknowledge her or take in what she had said. "Come on," she urged. "Let's get out of here." Then she put her arm around me. She said she was used to the Type A personalities at Columbia and especially at the lab. "They should be more like me, Type C!" She laughed at her own joke. "I just want to have fun."

As we walked along the river, she told me about the boy she was supposed to marry. She believed on some level that her parents knew what was best for her and that arranged marriages could be more lasting than love marriages. She had known Ari (short for Arjun) since they were in kindergarten. She had made him eat bugs in grade school and dared him to steal his sister's vibrator in junior high. He was more like a brother or cousin than a boyfriend.

"Now he has a full beard and is quite hairy. Too hairy!" Kira laughed.

On the plus side, Ari had an exciting job at a computer start-up. Much to his parents' unhappiness, he had turned down a job at IBM.

"They don't even know what a start-up is," she said. Kira liked this rebellious and risk-taking streak in Arjun. On the con side, he always deferred to her, agreeing to whatever movie or restaurant she preferred.

"I know he wants to make me happy," she said. "I'm such a bitch."

She stopped at a hot dog vendor. "Hungry?"

We sat on a bench overlooking the park and the river beyond, eating our hot dogs and passing a can of soda between us. Kira knew other girls would kill for someone as generous and kind as Ari, but he provoked a meanness in her she couldn't explain. She said she might be able to love him and come to believe that he was the one for her; the only problem was she couldn't stop fucking Kurt James, an undergraduate star of the rugby team who, she said, went down on her for miles.

Kira called a few weeks later, ostensibly to check in on me. Since receiving the raft of rejections, I had stopped going to the lab. Then she confessed that she really needed to see me; she had no one else to call.

"I've done something really bad," she said.

I met her at a noodle shop on Broadway, loud and filled with students. Kira did a quick survey to make sure no one she knew was there.

Kurt's team had come back to campus victorious after a match. "He comes over totally pumped from scoring the winning goal, and we go for it. Like totally."

"Okay."

"I lost track of time." She lowered her head. "I forgot Ari was coming over."

"Oh no."

"He called off the marriage. He won't return my calls. I went to his office and his apartment. I'm dead to him."

"You don't know that."

"My friends won't talk to me. My parents want to kill me."

"Maybe you didn't want to marry Ari," I said, trying to be helpful.

"It's my karma," she said.

"There's no such thing as karma," I said, "scientifically speaking."

She disagreed. "It's definitely karma. My karma."

I tried to soothe Kira, but she had humiliated her family, she had humiliated herself. One of her hoop earrings had come undone and she fixed it by feel, turning the hoop through the fleshy part of her ear.

"What about Kurt?" I asked.

"He just wanted to fuck a brown girl."

I couldn't bear to return to the lab and face my fellow researchers embarking on their internships at labs in Lucerne and Silicon Valley. I couldn't face another round of grant applications and possible rejections, or drill into the skull of another mouse, attach an electrode to its brain, and record the results. Maybe my research was bogus, the data nothing more than an exercise in hubris, as if the human mind could be understood as a series of brain waves and electrical pulses responding to external stimulus. I had put all my faith in science, in the fact-based world: the logic of molecular structures, the beauty of predictable patterns in nature. *Broccoli, artichoke, nautilus, pinecone.* I sought fairness. I sought symmetry and reciprocity. Where did any of that get me?

Maybe Ollie was right. I was nothing more than a grind, with no flare, no originality. "You're so predictable," she'd say cruelly. In every way the opposite of her, I complied with rules, met or exceeded expectations. Now, all the scaffolding holding up my rule-abiding, single-minded self crumbled. And in the end I guess that, too, was predictable.

I was sitting on the steps of Low Library, the magnolias now in full plumage like fat ostriches, watching the campus empty out. I hated being alone in my apartment. Though relieved to finally have my own place, I didn't realize how small and suffocating it would feel. A wiry man with curly dark hair plopped down next to me. It was warm out, but he was wearing scuffed brogues, a leather jacket two sizes too small, with duct tape covering the cracks, and cuffed dungarees.

"Are you depressed?"

I wasn't sure he was talking to me.

"I'm Josh."

I marveled at people who could introduce themselves at a party or gathering, walk up to a stranger and say I'm so-and-so. I took him in more fully. I guessed he was a few years younger than me, maybe twenty to my twenty-three. I had no idea what to make of this man-boy, but I found myself drawn to him. I could have told him a million different things: that I had a sister who haunted me, that I'd never been kissed, and that science, the religion I prayed to, had excommunicated me.

"My grant was rejected."

"For what?"

"Dopamine D2 receptors and the mediated circuits that regulate fear in the amygdala."

"In English."

"It has to do with fear," I said.

"Are you hungry?" he asked, as if we were already friends.

"I am."

"I'm famished."

I would learn that Josh was always starving. He'd been living on scraps like a city rat, plundering half-finished trays in the dining halls ever since he had dropped out and his meal plan was canceled. We went to Tom's on Broadway, a popular diner near campus, and he ordered for both of us: grilled cheese sandwiches and Cokes from the soda fountain. He took a long pull through the candy-cane-striped straw and declared the syrupy cola the nectar of the gods.

Josh said he had dropped out of school to become an actor, believing he possessed the innate talent of a Marlon Brando. He was obsessed with Brando, saw his movies over and over and read all the books he could find about him. He admitted he bought his leather jacket after seeing *The Wild One.*

"How tall do you think Brando was?"

"I don't know."

"Guess."

"Six feet."

"Ha! That's because of his towering presence. Guess again."

"Tell me."

Josh stood up straight and thumped his chest. "He's five foot nine, same as me."

Reaching over to finish my fries, he admitted that he hadn't exactly dropped out; he had flunked out. He successfully kept it from his parents until a termination letter arrived from the dean's office, along with a bill for some overdue books. "It was for eight fucking dollars and change."

I paid for lunch that day, having surmised that Josh was broke. I also guessed correctly that he didn't have a place of his own and was crashing with friends and acquaintances for however long he could. For a time, he lived with a girlfriend, Mary Kelly, until her roommates ganged up on him. "They didn't think I was good enough for her! They objected to my music! It was the Talking Heads!" Josh said in his defense.

Over the next weeks, we'd meet on campus, get a hot dog from a cart or sandwich from a deli, and take walks through Morningside Heights and into Harlem. Josh pointed out the original location of the Cotton Club on Lenox Avenue at 142nd Street. He knew all about its whites-only policy and about the Black musicians who had performed there, Louis Armstrong and Count Basie, the Duke Ellington Band. We walked down Striver's Row, home to many of the artists and intellectuals of the Harlem Renaissance. Josh had read Langston Hughes and W. E. B. Du Bois. I had never heard of them. When he found a book on the street about Gustave Eiffel, he became obsessed, pointing out intricate wrought iron details on buildings and bridges all over the city. I happily trailed behind, listening to his soliloquies on design and beauty. He called himself an autodidact. I had to look up the word.

There was a certain intensity in the way he moved, his body pitched forward as he walked, as if something exciting were just around the corner. Josh showed me a side of New York I didn't know existed: a cupcake bakery painted pink, black-box theaters, and the flower district at dawn, where long wooden crates resembling caskets were unloaded, revealing white lilies and the long sleek arms of pussy willows. Josh was the king of discovering discarded furniture, Basquiat graffiti in hidden alleyways, Italian cafés that roasted their own coffee beans and baked cookies with pine nuts. Like Ollie, he loved the Salvation Army and Goodwill. He'd show up in a navy blue sailor shirt with a bib, a Nehru jacket, a Borsalino fedora from Italy. Josh wore his leather jacket all summer and purple Converse high-tops without socks. He had a heavy beard and often had to shave twice a day, which he boasted was a sign of manliness.

He befriended a group of homeless men who congregated in the philosophy section at the public library, in a remote part of the building where the security guards left them alone. He named them the Socratic Club and said these were the real people, not the coddled jack-offs who passed themselves off as professors at Columbia. I both admired his lack of prejudice and worried that he was romanticizing a group of troubled, broken men.

When Josh started to stay over, he assured me it was temporary. My tiny one-bedroom apartment was in a gracious brownstone on Riverside Drive; the steep steps led up to a grand mahogany door with rippled glass that evoked an earlier century. A highly polished brass directory listed the tenants' names beside a row of buzzers. My name had a typo that I never bothered to have corrected: Shed. Inside, the once grand rooms had been subdivided into tiny studios. To save space, I'd bought a single bed. It had "monastic" written all over it, which I fully comprehended only when Josh became my first official male visitor.

"That's where you sleep?" was all he said. *Yes, Sister Amy slept here.* My only indulgence was a green velvet couch with maple claw feet that I found at a flea market. Everything else came from Walmart, including a rattan hamper that snagged my clothes. There were thick black bars on the window, and the sash only stayed up if I stacked textbooks beneath it. The kitchen had a half fridge and a stove with a single working burner. For most of the winter, I lived on soup and what Ollie used to call hobo food—anything from a can. I hated going to restaurants by myself.

I couldn't say exactly when Josh moved in, but the apartment filled with books on art and acting, a folk art painting he found in the street, thick restaurant mugs and plates from Oscar's Salt of the Sea where he briefly worked as a busboy. After we went to the Van Gogh exhibit at the Met, he painted the kitchen wall azure blue and filled a pitcher with sunflowers. He found an auctioneer's podium on the sidewalk outside Christie's, gave it a faux-marble finish, and turned it into a dictionary stand. And every morning, he made a show of folding the sheet and blanket he used on the couch.

I encouraged Josh to take acting classes. He'd heard of an experimental school run by a man named Arthur English, a self-proclaimed iconoclast who was willing to trade classes for work at the school. Arthur believed you had to break down your ego to act authentically, and he took the students through a series of exercises that included rolling on the floor, primal screams, and getting naked. It sounded questionable to me, but Josh insisted Arthur was the real deal and the classes transformative. "It's about really getting naked," he said, "not just naked."

For my birthday, Josh took me to see the Whirling Dervishes at City Center. I offered to pay, but he insisted. "This is on me, Shred. I owe you!" It was the first time there was any mention of the financial imbalance between us, and it caught me off guard. I never felt taken advantage of; I supplied the money (well, Dad's money) and he changed my life. "These are the best seats," he said as we climbed to the last row of the balcony. "You can see the whole stage."

The dervishes moved slowly, gaining speed as they whirled. I felt my body lifting, as if there were a warp in the universe, zero gravity—as close to an out-of-body experience as I could imagine. When it was over, I was in a stupor and couldn't move. The audience stood for multiple ovations, stomping and screaming bravo, Josh hooting and wolf whistling. When the lights came up, he sat back down and put his hand on my neck. I flinched as if I'd been bitten by a horsefly.

Back at the apartment, somewhere in the middle of the night, Josh came into my bed and curled his naked body around me. I wanted to unfurl myself like the great white skirts of the dancers, but I was afraid of changing the terms of our friendship, and I was afraid of losing my virginity. I was aware that

I'd grown more brittle. When I was still working in the lab, I overheard one assistant telling another that I needed to get laid. The comment, hurtful and obnoxious, was also true. I remembered a radio interview with a woman who had been in the French Resistance and had had many affairs. "What else is life for?" she said in a knowing, world-weary way. "Never making love is returning a present unopened." *A box wrapped with gold paper and gold ribbons shimmered in a dream tree.*

I turned to face Josh and confessed my secret.

He laughed. "You're kidding, right?"

"Don't laugh."

"No, come on. I thought you'd had a hundred lovers."

"No, you didn't."

"It's not a big deal," Josh said. "We don't have to."

I was suddenly flooded with the suspicion that Josh had never gone to Columbia, that there was no Mary Kelly, no Arthur English. What kind of phony name was Arthur English? And what were we playing at? Josh wasn't my boyfriend. He was what my father would have called a freeloader. Past humiliations flooded back. *Eat shit, Shred.* Josh retreated to the couch. I turned to face the brick wall, pitted, pocked, mocking me.

Kira and I had been meeting every other week or so at the Hungarian Pastry Shop, a cafe on Amsterdam. After her engagement imploded, Kira started having what she called revenge sex, sleeping with one of Kurt's fellow rugby players, a married professor in the Classics Department, and a woman she met on a checkout line in D'Agostino's. She said it was liberating, fucking people you weren't that into.

I asked if she ever considered therapy.

She laughed. "I'd rather drink myself to death,"

I took a risk and said what I felt: "You seem really unhappy."

Kira's bravado deflated. "Yeah, I ruined my life for some douchebag."

Ari had stopped by to return her keys and a few other things. "It turned out to be every gift I ever gave him." She started to tear up. "What is wrong with me?" Her voice was thin. She ran her fingers beneath her eyes to keep from crying or messing up her makeup.

"You'll get back with Ari," I said.

"Really?" she asked, her eyes widening as if I were a fortune-teller running my hands over a crystal ball.

"Yes, but on one condition."

Kira's face was expectant; she would do anything.

"Go to therapy."

"Ha! You got me. What the fuck, maybe I should."

When the bill came, Kira grabbed it.

"It's on me," she said.

"Let's split it."

She refused and reached into her handbag. "You're a lot less expensive than a therapist." She took a twenty from her wallet.

"Thanks," I said.

"Now, what about you?" she asked.

"What about me?"

"When are you going to get laid?"

9

On the bus to Leonia, New Jersey, we held hands. It was Josh's sister's graduation party and his first visit home since he'd been kicked out of school. He was squirming long before we arrived. His sister had already landed a high-paying job at a consulting firm, and his cousins had good jobs selling insurance, importing car parts, making instructional videos. I built Josh up, reminding him that he was the only one doing anything where creativity and passion were involved.

I brought a pink geranium in a clay pot and pastries. His mother cooed with approval and hugged me. I'm sure she imagined we were boyfriend and girlfriend since we were living together. His father didn't get up from his lounger. He had called Josh a girl when he grew his hair long, called him a fag after he pierced his ear. And now, since Josh had flunked out of college, his father called him a bum.

Josh's sister looked like a female version of him; they could have been twins. "We're complete opposites" was all he'd said about her, and "She's a bitch."

Josh said he'd be back in a minute and disappeared into his childhood bedroom. His mother plied me with questions about my family. I explained that my father lived in Florida and my mother lived in Connecticut, but at present she was on a bridge cruise around Cape Horn.

"They're divorced?" his mom surmised.

"Yes," I said and felt a small black mark go against my name.

"That must be hard at holiday time."

"It's really nice to be here," I said, wishing Josh would come back.

"Do you have any siblings?"

"Just me," I said. I felt squeamish about lying to her. Having said it out loud, I half expected Ollie to jump out from behind the couch: "Not so fast, sister!"

I turned the doorknob of Josh's bedroom, now also home to a sewing machine and a box of bright-colored spools of thread. Splayed out on the bed, he patted the spot beside him. I flopped back and we both stared at the ceiling. There was a stain the color of weak tea. Josh turned on his side and traced his finger around my face, like the sweep of a second hand.

"Thank you for coming," he said.

"You disappeared on me!"

"I hate him," Josh said.

I turned my body toward him, saw the defeat written on his face. We stayed like that for a bit when Josh reached out and slowly followed the curve between my breast and hip with his hand. I felt warm, my chest filled with air. The door opened a crack and I gasped. The family cat walked in and then walked out with a whiff of disapproval. I closed my eyes and we kissed. Maybe because we appeared as a couple, maybe because being in Josh's high school bedroom felt illicit, as if we were in high school, we kissed again, rubbed our bodies together. I could feel Josh's erection through his pants, and I took off my sweater. He locked the door, then pulled off his shirt and my boots.

"Is this okay?"

I nodded, and he yanked off my tights, nearly falling backward in a pratfall. Then he took a condom from his dresser. Now Josh was full of purpose and concentration. He touched my breasts and groaned. He kissed them, kissed my stomach, hoisted himself above me, fingered me, and entered me. My back arched, my shoulder blades reaching toward each other. I imagined myself as Winged Victory, a headless figure with enormous broken wings. I wanted to hold Josh inside me no matter how much it hurt. I wanted him to be the rough waves I would swim against for the rest of my life. Josh gently pushed himself off me, kissed my eyebrows.

"What do you think, Shred?"

Josh and I should have stayed friends. It was as if we had become a married couple overnight, bickering about doing the dishes, capping the toothpaste, making the bed. Sometimes we caught ourselves and could laugh about it. After sex, if Josh asked if I came, I didn't know what to say; honestly, I had no idea.

I needed to get a job. I needed Josh to get a job! Some days I wished for my own place back; it felt claustrophobic with both of us in my tiny space. Josh had amassed a considerable amount of found stuff: clothes, a lamp in the shape of a crane, a juicer that didn't work.

I also had to either return to the institute or officially resign. I was cashing my father's monthly checks and had not yet divulged, either to him or to my mom, that I had basically dropped out. Months had passed since all of my grant applications had been rejected, and I was floundering. Josh came home with cartons of Chinese food and the *Village Voice*. We sat on the floor to eat, the Help Wanted ads spread out around us. After we circled a bunch for Josh and exactly zero for me, Josh put on Van Morrison, and we slow-danced to "Crazy Love." I surprised myself by starting to cry. I had a premonition that we had reached our end. He pulled me close, our bodies pressed together, arms draped over each other's shoulders, barely moving, like teens at a high school dance.

The song finished, but we continued to hold each other up, foreheads mashed together, unable to separate.

Josh landed a job at the Empire Diner washing dishes and met a waitress named Ellen. She also wanted to be an actor, and she was impressed that he had taken classes with Arthur English. She knew about auditions and encouraged him to try out. They'd wait in line for hours to get a few minutes in front of a casting director. Josh would come home filled with horror stories about the process. He said it was a cruel version of *Groundhog Day*. For him the rejection was paralyzing, while Ellen had this crazily positive midwestern attitude. She believed that affirmations were the key to success. Going into an audition, you tell yourself over and over that you're going to get the part. Ellen was also disciplined. She ran four miles a day, did home facials, took tap and singing lessons if she'd had a good week tip-wise. In the face of Ellen's determination and commitment, Josh wondered if he should give up trying to get acting jobs. I reminded him that it had only been a few weeks of auditioning, that no one gets discovered overnight. "Brando did. Well, basically."

"You shouldn't quit," I said, even though I had no idea if Josh had any talent; he struggled to memorize monologues. Influenced by Ellen, though, he started running in the park, doing a hundred sit-ups and push-ups in the morning. He was spending more time away from the apartment now, hanging out late at night with new friends from the diner, all aspiring actors and writers living on tip money and extravagant hopes. Though I mostly relished having the place to myself, it made me gloomy and anxious when he didn't come home until two or three in the morning, reminding me of Olivia escaping through her bedroom window and returning at dawn. I tried to keep busy, combing the Help Wanted listings, weeding out books to sell, defrosting the tiny freezer's ice-encrusted mouth. I had my boots reheeled and my eyes checked by an optometrist; I picked out small round gold frames for my new glasses. Josh complimented them.

"They're a cross between James Joyce and John Lennon."

"High praise," I said.

"And you picked them out without me."

"You haven't exactly been around," I said, and instantly regretted it.

A few weeks later, Josh called from an audition; he had something to tell me. He sounded excited, and I hoped it might be his big break. We met at the Brasserie, one of Josh's favorite haunts, with its wide wooden bar and toasted chickpeas in small clay bowls. Josh downed his drink and finished the chick-peas. When the bartender asked if we'd like another round, Josh dug into his pockets and pulled them inside out, his boyish way of displaying that he was broke.

"What's going on?"

Josh looked down. He couldn't meet my eyes.

At last he blurted it out. Ellen had won the part of Laura in *The Glass Menagerie* on Broadway. He confessed that he'd gotten drunk when they went out to celebrate and had stayed over with her.

"And you slept with her."

"I guess so."

"You've been sleeping with her."

"Sort of."

"So, you're with her now?"

Then it all came out. Ellen had quit her job at the Empire and started full-time rehearsals; Josh was moving in with her.

He said he didn't know how to tell me.

"Well, now you have."

"I never meant to hurt you, Shred."

"You didn't," I said, sounding meaner than I meant to, trying to absorb the news.

Josh turned the little chickpea bowl upside down and moved it around the bar like a shell game. I didn't want to appear pathetic, and on some level I was happy for him. I knew we weren't good together that way. We vowed then to always be there for each other, the way lovers promise to remain friends. Josh gently took my glasses off as if he were going to kiss me, but instead he breathed on the lenses and wiped them clean.

✦

I officially withdrew from my program at the institute with about as much fanfare as canceling a credit card. The next evening I went to the lab, knowing it would be empty then, to collect my personal effects and turn in my ID and key card. Inside, I heard the familiar sounds of nocturnal life, scuffling and scratching. Jack, one of the undergraduates who cleaned the cages and fed and watered the rodents, had fallen asleep on a molded plastic chair, his head pitched back, mouth wide open. Hearing me enter, he jumped up and apologized, saying he'd just closed his eyes for a second. "Sorry, sorry, sorry."

"It's okay. I probably fell asleep once or twice myself," I said.

"Thank you. Thank you."

"No problem."

"I can't afford to lose this job."

I realized then that he was afraid of me, the taskmaster, the cold bitch who needed to get laid. "You can relax," I said. "Your secret is safe with me."

"I appreciate it."

"No problem."

"Is it true you're leaving?" he asked. I wasn't sure if it was widely known in the lab that I had flamed out, the Great Amy Shred knocked off her perch. I had told myself I didn't care who knew or what the official word was, but now, face-to-face with Jack, it fully registered that I was walking away from everything I had worked toward. I had nothing left to lose.

"What's it to you," I said, a touch flirty.

When he ran his fingers through his hair, it fell back perfectly into place. If Kira were here, she would already be having sex with him on the lab floor, with the rats and mice cheering from their cages, Dr. Simon and the staff snapping their fingers.

I packed up my moving box. All of my personal effects fit neatly inside: lab coat, goggles, notebooks. I took my nameplate, my electric kettle, and a mug Josh gave me with a stencil of Madame Curie.

"Do you need help?" Jack asked as we stepped into the elevator. I said I was okay.

"Are you sure?" He took the box from my arms anyway. "Do you want to get a beer?" he asked.

"With you?"

"I'll take that as a yes."

After a few drinks at a local dive, we went to his apartment and started making out. He took out a never-opened box of condoms.

"You're getting a lot of use of those."

He handed me the box to open. "I don't have any nails."

His boxers looked three sizes too big, his legs as skinny as sticks, his chest concave. He managed to remove my glasses and put the condom on while I slipped out of my bra and panties. So this is what I've missed out on, I said to myself: stupid, fumbling, half-drunken late-night encounters with college boys. I realized that I was actually more experienced than he was, and I helped him slow down. Then we did it again. This time Jack was more confident, and I felt freer, more daring.

"You're amazing, Shred," he said, and fell asleep.

I left his room with all the artifacts of my former life. I couldn't wait to call Kira. She'd insisted that I needed to have sex with someone new as soon as possible after Josh left; it was the only way to get over a relationship. That sounded ridiculous to me, but it turned out she was sort of right. We met at what we now called "our bench" in Riverside Park and I told her about my night over bagels and coffee.

"You did the nasty with Lab Boy!" she said and raised her paper coffee cup for a toast.

10

Ollie showed up at our mother's house with a yoga mat and a backpack. By then Mom, about to turn fifty, was living in a two-bedroom condo, claiming to love the place, but she seemed lonely and vulnerable most of the time. Though who was I to judge; I was still casting about months after Josh moved out.

All Ollie told Mom was that she had been living in Denver with a naturopathic doctor and she had left after he became too serious.

"How do you know he didn't break up with her?" I asked my mother.

"Well," Mom said, "I guess we'll never know."

"So she's living with you now?"

"For the time being."

"I thought you said you wouldn't let her."

"For the time being, Amy." End of discussion.

In her first few weeks at Mom's, and at her behest, Ollie agreed to see a dentist, a dermatologist, and a gynecologist. She reported that she had no cavities, and my mother acted as if she'd won the Fields Medal. She took Ollie shopping for clothes and didn't say a word about her new tattoos: a lightning bolt on her knee, a rose on her shoulder, and a spade on her lower back. My mother hadn't exactly mellowed, but something in her had shifted. After losing her daily sparring partner, her dukes had come down.

Ollie loved Clinique cosmetics, with their medicinal pale green packaging and dermatological approach. Mom, too, was impressed with the paraben- and fragrance-free products and indulged them both in a buying spree at Saks. They received a complimentary case with miniature samples inside that Ollie put aside for me, having remembered how much I liked miniatures.

"Wasn't that thoughtful?"

My mother needed me to get on board with her fantasy that the world had returned some new and improved version of Ollie, one that wouldn't hurt or disappoint us. She cooked healthy meals, introducing our mom to tofu, tempeh, hummus, and green tea. "It takes some getting used to," Mom said, but declared that she was a new person thanks to Ollie's diet of greens and legumes.

Ollie found a part-time job baking bread at a health food store in New Haven and became known for her yeasty sourdough boule. At night they watched Turner Classic Movies on Mom's bed and ate apples with peanut butter from the natural foods store. You could grind the peanuts right there! They started walking together in the mornings, Ollie waking up "bright and early" to join Mom. They talked about a walking tour of the Lake District, and in anticipation my mother started reading Wordsworth and Coleridge. Ollie was interested in taking psychology classes at the University of New Haven. Maybe criminology. I did a spit take when I heard that.

I told myself it wouldn't last, as if I didn't *want* it to last, and that made me feel punky and small. I didn't want to bet against Ollie, but I couldn't put my money on her either. She wasn't in therapy, wasn't on medication. My mother was now fully on board with meditation and the various concoctions Ollie made with ginger, turmeric, and St. John's wort.

Mom had also been reading up on Chinese medicine. "It makes a lot of sense," she said with the conviction of a convert, condemning Western doctors for their tunnel vision.

A month into her stay, Ollie heard about a foreclosed bakery in a once-thriving but now struggling part of New Haven. She dragged our mother there.

"It has potential," Mom admitted.

When they went back a second time, Ollie persuaded Mom to call the realtor.

"He explained the history of the place; it used to be the premier Italian bakery in New Haven," Mom told me with pride, and I could see the train leaving the station, fueled by Ollie's grandiosity. She had a zillion ideas for renovating the space and the inspiration to call it Dough, which our parents (Dad now on board) agreed was incredibly clever; Mom was already hunting down period fixtures.

It was easier for Dad to write a check than dig too deep into the details. He was busy sending golf balls into the Floridian horizon and following up with an extra-spicy Bloody Mary to "wake up" his veins. During our weekly call, I suggested that the bakery might be a bit ambitious, expecting him to agree with me, but he said it was a promising idea and potentially a solid investment. Anita had coincidentally discovered sourdough bread at their local Publix.

"That's not exactly market research," I countered.

"Your sister needs a shot," he said. "She's good at this."

Dad needed to believe that Ollie was rebuilding her life. To further convince himself, he added, "And she's a born salesman."

No shit, Shred.

Four months later, Ollie made off with my father's $70,000 investment. My mother was flattened. She had gotten way ahead of herself: choosing tiles and fixtures, ordering fifty-pound bags of artisanal flour milled in Vermont, red-and-white bakery twine from a distributor in the Bronx, and aprons with "Dough" embroidered in pink. Ollie left it to Mom to deal with the building, the landlord, and all the equipment that had to be returned or sold. Mom had to cancel the permits, insurance, and the health department inspection, then auction off the brand-new cases and cabinets. The pink neon "Dough" in loopy letters was not returnable. In a fit of pique, my mother was going to throw it out, but I stashed it in the back of her closet, where the fluorescent tubes would gather dust. After Ollie left, Mom threw out the powders and capsules and yoga mats and the handcrafted Himalayan singing bowls.

How could she do that to us? How could she do it to Mom? For a long time, I was convinced that Ollie was responsible for everything that went wrong in our family. At random moments, I'd find myself having one-way conversations with her in my head. I saw her everywhere: standing on a subway platform, in line at a movie or crossing a street. When a woman with Ollie's blond ringlets stepped into an elevator, I waited for the next one. One time I saw her exact double harassing a deli guy for giving her the wrong pack of Marlboro's; she sounded so much like Ollie that I froze. I continued to watch her out on the sidewalk as she struggled to light her cigarette, throwing match after match on the ground. When she finally lit it, she took a drag so deep it seemed to stir her soul.

Then, after weeks of seeing Ollie everywhere, days would go by without my thinking of her at all.

After Ollie disappeared, I fessed up to my mother about my half-hearted attempts to find a job. She insisted I make an appointment with Rena Adler, a career counselor she met on one of her bridge cruises.

All the furniture in Rena's office was Scandinavian. There were two enormous ficus trees and a crystal pendant hanging in the sunny window that threw prisms of light, tiny rainbows that danced on the walls. She had two framed degrees. On closer inspection, I saw that they were certificates, one from a place called The Learning Center, the other from EST, a trendy course in self-actualization.

Rena herself was a version of my mother, only she had proudly taken control of her life after taking the EST seminars: "Those two weekends changed my life." Rena had dropped her "mask" and "confronted" herself, she told me. She also fell in love with one of the facilitators, left her husband, found an apartment in Kip's Bay, and trained to become a life coach.

She drilled me with questions: education, hobbies, goals. What would I say were my strengths and weaknesses? Was I comfortable speaking in front of people? Was I a problem solver, a team player? She said she would "crunch the data," and we would meet again in one week.

"I don't have a magic wand; it's going to take work," she warned, handing me an EST pamphlet (in case I was ready for personal transformation) and reaching for a book on her shelf. There were multiple copies, the spine a gentle wash of rainbow colors. It was *What Color Is Your Parachute?* by Richard Nelson Bolles.

"This is our bible," she said, handing me a copy. "No extra charge!"

My mother had left four messages on my machine. She wanted to hear all about the session with Rena, but more than that, she was excited to tell me she had met someone. A widower at her condo, Al Gottfried. They were both taking in their garbage cans and he waved to her. "I invited him in for a cup of coffee, and now we're going to a movie!" she exclaimed.

"Mom, that's amazing."

"I keep telling you, you have to put yourself out there!"

That night, I opened the book Rena had gushed about. It was filled with dated illustrations and sidebars of clichéd advice, but I found myself taking the quizzes, wondering what job I might be able to get, which skills were transferable. What color *was* my parachute? If I even had one?

At my second session with Rena, she could hardly wait to pounce. "Magazines! Have you heard of *Scientific American*? *Omni*? *Smithsonian*?" She had proudly done some "research" on my behalf and saw editorial work in my future. "You have the science. They need women. Come on, Amy, let's fire up the resume!" She schooled me on my attire, suggesting that my mother should take me shopping for two suits and some mix-and-match shells. She said a little heel wouldn't hurt, given my slight stature. Rena prided herself on telling it like it is.

"Maybe I'm stepping over a line, but you seem a little depressed to me," she said, handing me a business card for a therapist.

In closing, Rena said, "Have you given any thought to your hair?"

I turned the card over in my hand many times before calling Paul Weiss, MSW. Mom and I were shopping at Ann Taylor when I mentioned that I had made an appointment with a social worker. "How is a social worker going to help you? You're not on welfare."

"He's a therapist social worker," I said.

"You'd get more out of joining a gym, at least you might meet someone."

"Please stop."

"I don't know what good therapy did Ollie." It was the first time Mom had mentioned her since the bakery debacle. "Sometimes I wish I had mental illness, then I could do whatever I want."

"She doesn't mean to hurt us," I said.

"She doesn't mean to hurt anyone. That's the problem."

Mom paid for my suit. The salesgirl started to shove it into a shopping bag, and my mother demanded a garment bag. "For goodness' sake!"

Paul Weiss worked out of his apartment. He had sectioned off half of the living room with a partition; it had a leather couch, a well-worn Eames chair, and was filled with large hanging spider plants, some sprouting new shoots with babies dangling from them. The apartment was overheated, permeated by the smell of last night's meal and a coffeepot too long on the burner. Paul had the empathic face of a noble Saint Bernard: deep-set eyes, and gentle jowls; I could see him carrying stranded people down a snowy mountain. He wore gray slacks, a V-neck sweater, and paisley socks.

He started every session by crossing his legs and clasping his hands together in his lap. I worried that I wouldn't have enough to talk about during our introductory meeting, but then the fifty minutes were over. Paul asked if I'd like to come back, and we set an hour for the following week.

As I left Paul's office, I asked if I should leave the door open or closed.

"Either way," he said.

"Which do you prefer?" I said, my hand on the doorknob.

"Either way is fine," he said again.

I paused in the doorway; surely he had a preference. How could I get a gold star if I didn't know the rules? Over the next few years, whenever I asked about the door, Paul, benevolent sphinx, maintained that it was up to me.

❖

Never give up on your hair. I'd been seeing Paul for almost a month when I noticed the sign outside a hair salon.

I felt Rena Adler's invisible hand push me through the door. A young man at the reception desk asked if I had an appointment.

"I don't," I said.

"No problem." He jumped up and led me over to a chair. I saw that the place was empty and instantly regretted going in. He put his hands on my shoulders and asked what I had in mind. I couldn't lift my head to look at my reflection. He massaged my shoulders a bit, and I tensed more. Then he came around and raised my chin.

"Would you mind taking off your glasses?"

I folded them in my lap.

"You're pretty," he said.

Then he felt the texture of my hair. "What do you say we clean this up? Bring it up to here," the heel of his hand touching my neck. I nodded yes.

"What about some color? Perk you up."

Two hours later I left the salon with auburn hair and a bob with bangs. Walking down the street, I couldn't stop glancing at myself in the storefront windows, happily surprised each time I peeked.

Walking by Mattress World on Broadway, I made another rash decision: I needed to get a double bed right then. Inside, a small crowd had gathered around a man in a suit who had fallen asleep on one of the display mattresses. He was quietly snoring, blowing out little puffs of air, and a thin line of spittle escaped his mouth. The knot of his tie was loosened, the top button of his shirt undone, and his wingtips were scuffed. What if a pea was buried beneath the mattress? What if he was my prince? My fantasy life was full of such encounters. Men on subways, at the cash machine, buying a baguette at Dean & DeLuca. Any one of them might have been my husband.

Perhaps emboldened by my new hair, I touched the sleeping man's shoulder. He twitched. I shook him a little harder, and he roused himself awake. Still slightly disoriented, he swung his legs around and sat up.

"Jesus, I'm sorry."

Show over, the circle of gawkers moved on.

"Are you okay?" I asked.

"I've been working around the clock."

He stood up, took a handkerchief from his pocket, and wiped his mouth. "Oh god, that's gross. I'm so sorry. I'll buy the mattress."

"I don't work here."

"Jesus. I'm sorry."

"It's okay."

"Was I snoring?"

"More like blowing bubbles."

"Oh, god."

"It wasn't that bad."

"You're too nice," he said.

"I'm actually not that nice." A combination of my new look and my overwhelming attraction to this man made me bold—more flirtatious and available than I had been in all my twenty-four years.

"I'm Marc," he said.

"Amy."

He asked if I wanted to get a bite; had I ever been to Eisenberg's, an old-fashioned deli nearby. We were wedged in at the counter, our thighs touching. He had taken off his jacket, undid the top button on his shirt, and loosened his tie. A single curl of chest hair escaped the collar. My world boiled down to watching his Adam's apple bobbing as he talked about college, LA, where he was from, and wanting to get a dog.

"I just don't think it's fair in a one-bedroom," he said.

"Totally."

Marc wondered what I did, and I explained that I was transitioning from grad school. I was sending my resume around to publishers and science magazines. In fact, I hadn't yet sent a single resume.

He insisted on paying and took out his credit card. I saw his full name, Marc Charles Goodyear.

"Are you related to the guy who invented rubber?"

"I am." He seemed impressed. "Not too many people put that together."

"Science geek. Well, former science geek."

I nervously yammered on about vulcanization, the process that kept rubber from hardening in the cold and melting in the heat. "It was genius."

"He was a royal screwup when it came to the patents. He died broke and left the family destitute." Marc explained that the present day rubber company kept the Goodyear name, but the family-owned company had been sold long ago. "My grandfather and father became patent attorneys!"

"And you?"

"Yup, I'm a lawyer, well, a litigator."

"Wow."

"It's not like on TV."

"Are you good at it?"

"Yeah, not to brag, but I am."

"What makes you good?"

He took a few seconds before answering: "Because I can be a real prick."

I knew I was meant to laugh, but I saw it in the set of his jaw, his perfectly pared nails.

"I'm kidding," he said. "Well, sort of."

"That's good," I said. "Self-knowledge."

We headed toward the subway. The light was changing, the air cooler. Marc checked his watch and said he had to get back to the office, he was working on a big case and would probably pull another all-nighter. Only we wound up sitting on a bench in Union Square for another half hour, and he mentioned a friend from high school who worked at a major publisher. He said he'd call her; she might be willing to give me an informational interview, and we exchanged numbers.

Five days passed and I still hadn't heard from him. I called Kira for her take. She said he'd call. "Men need to make you suffer."

"It's almost a week," I whined. "Should I call him?"

"Absolutely not. Throw away the number if you're so much as tempted."

Eight days later, when the call came, I acted a little distracted to cover my excitement. "Oh, hi."

Marc had spoken to his friend Courtney, and she agreed to meet with me. Though happy for the contact, I was also a little crestfallen. Then Marc asked if I liked sushi.

Courtney took me under her wing. She was the youngest senior editor at Rogers & Rogers. She had a knack for signing celebrities just as their careers were taking off. Dressed in designer jeans, a man's button-down shirt, fat pearls, and Belgian slippers, she seemed much older than her twenty-nine years, a blend of Mae West and Kathleen Turner from *Body Heat*.

We met at an outdoor café near her office. She commented on businessmen and messengers alike as they walked by, declaring them fuckable or not. If she saw a woman in a great outfit, she'd say, "Love that." She and Marc had gone to the same high school, went to prom "as friends," and had drifted apart until their paths crossed in the city.

"He's too busy for me," she said. "Hell, I'm too busy for him. I hate this city."

I would learn that Courtney had her "spots," restaurants where she regularly schmoozed with the maître d's and waiters. "The key to success is being able to get a great table." She laughed.

She turned to my resume.

"Well, you're a smarty-pants."

I tried to deny it.

"No, no. This is good. We've been looking for a science editor."

A few days later, the publisher's secretary called to set up an appointment. I put on stockings and the Ann Taylor suit Mom had bought me and modeled it in the mirror. Then I took it all off in favor of a miniskirt, tights, and Doc Martens. I'd swapped out my wire-rimmed glasses for Buddy Holly frames. Courtney called them "nerdy-chic" and approved. I recalled Ellen's advice: go to the audition telling yourself you'll get the part. I took the subway to Midtown, rehearsing my lines.

The publisher's office had sweeping views of Manhattan. An entire wall was filled with books, the credenza behind the desk piled high with manuscripts. Crammed in were photos of what must have been his family in the Caribbean, going by the color of the water, and on ski trips out West, by the color of the sky. He was tall with slouching shoulders and a full head of salt-and-pepper hair. I noticed that his wedding band was loose on his finger, resting at the knuckle. He put his feet up on the coffee table between us and asked if I'd like a Diet Coke. He'd been trying to find someone to edit science books, "popular science, the stuff that sells, not that dry academic crap. I'd give my eyetooth to find the next Carl Sagan."

I had read science books almost exclusively, for school and for pleasure, and I mentioned a few possible reasons why some became popular and others didn't.

"I like the way you think," he said, and then, "What kind of a name is Shred?"

"A mix," I said. "Mostly German."

He asked if I was afraid of long hours, explaining that editors did their reading on their own time. I said I put in twelve hours a day at the lab. He wanted to know why I quit graduate school.

"I'm done with research," I said. "I can't fry any more mice brains." He clapped his hands and said, "Ha!" He asked where I grew up, went to college, what I wanted to be when I grew up. I blanked on the last one, and he said that's okay: "I'm still trying to figure that out!" Then he stood up, signaling the end of the interview.

I was prepared for him to say that he'd keep my resume on file, that it was nice meeting me. But he took me in his sight and asked, "Why should I take a chance on you, Amy Shred?"

"I'm a good bet."

"Good answer."

I walked out of the office with the title of junior editor, a low salary, health benefits, a small windowless office, and a new friend in Courtney. I also had a second date with Marc.

11

"She's in California." I could hear the hope in Dad's voice. It had been almost a year since Ollie had fled New Haven, the bakery scheme, and Mom. She was living in LA with a movie producer.

"He sounds like a solid guy," Dad said.

"What about the money she stole?"

"Bun, let me worry about that."

"Seriously?"

"Why don't you visit her? I'll buy the ticket."

"I'm not doing that."

"It would be good for her."

What about me? I knew better than to say that.

"What about my new job?"

"Go for a long weekend."

"How do you know she even wants me?"

"Because she said so."

She picked me up at the airport in a Mustang convertible. Olivia was breathtaking. Her hair, her signature Ray-Bans, skinny jeans, a fitted T-shirt. She jumped out of the car and waved me over.

"I love these," she said, mussing my bangs, giving me a quick hug, grabbing my suitcase.

"Thanks."

"I mean it, you look really good."

"I changed my hair."

"It looks great, I love it."

Her approval caught me by surprise.

"Really?"

"And your glasses, damn."

On the drive to the house, negotiating the highways like a formula racer, Ollie disclosed how she had met the producer Hunter Gray. There had been a long line of women with blond hair on the sidewalk of Melrose Avenue, applying makeup, rehearsing monologues, putting hair up in messy buns, then taking them down. It was an open-call audition for a Ridley Scott movie.

"I had just come from the beach, and I figured why not." She told me she was channeling Jodie Foster in *Taxi Driver*, wearing cutoffs, a bikini top, flip-flops. The casting director's assistant asked for her head shot, and she pretended she'd run out of them. They asked for her agent's name, and she said she was between management. Ollie hadn't even realized that the audition was starting when the casting director asked if she had any special skills. She told them she could run faster than anyone and never got caught shoplifting.

"I could tell they loved it."

She egged them on with stories of stealing tins of caviar and thousand-dollar jeans.

"You have no idea how easy it is to impress people here," she told me. "They love gangsters."

Reader, she got the part.

One big problem: Ollie couldn't act. A week into rehearsals, it was clear that she had bluffed her way into the job. She kept missing cues at the table read, coming in too late or too soon. Worse, when they started filming, she kept staring into the camera.

"Acting looks so easy," she said, turning in to a driveway as the gates automatically opened.

The director had asked her point-blank if she had any acting experience. Possibly for the first time, Ollie didn't have a comeback at the ready.

"You're gorgeous, darling, but we have a movie to make."

Hunter Gray, the producer, took her to lunch and said how sorry he was, that she was the freshest face they had seen in ages, and they wished she had more experience. Within the week, Ollie had moved in with him. Could she stay for a few days while her condo was being renovated?

Hunt had a craftsman house with a pool in the hills behind Chateau Marmont. She stayed in the guesthouse at first and soon moved into his bedroom. Hunt enjoyed having her on his arm at premieres and industry functions. Ollie was never impressed by actors and directors, was never starstruck or fawning the way most people acted in their presence, and that impressed Hunt. They established routines: Hunt swam laps in the morning before work, Ollie went back to running five or six miles. They shopped together at the Hollywood Farmer's Market and went to the beach on weekends.

I marveled at her life as we lounged by the pool, sipping cucumber lemonade and snacking on seaweed chips, a pile of well-thumbed scripts flagged with Post-its on a nearby table. At night we draped ourselves over the cushy chair in Hunt's screening room and watched movies. Ollie, remembering that Milk Duds were my favorite movie candy, had a stack of mustard-colored boxes waiting for me.

I visited LACMA and the Getty and drove up to Malibu that weekend, all on my own because Ollie said she had scripts to read for Hunt. He highly valued her opinions, including her knack for casting ideas. They joked that no picture would get made without Ollie's green light. She was his secret weapon. Hunt said she had the best bullshit detector of anyone he ever met. *Oh my god, this poor man.*

In Malibu I stopped at a small shack on the pier and ate fish tacos while gazing out at the Pacific. I couldn't tell if any of it was real. Had my sister been spat out by a great whale, or was she the whale?

Our last morning together by the pool, I applied sunscreen to Ollie's back. I could make out the razor-thin scars from the day she collided with our living-room window. We dangled our feet in the pool, the water warmer than the air.

"Hunter's great," I said. He had arranged for a car service to take me to the airport and gave me a huge hug before he left for work. He said that Ollie really missed me and I was always welcome.

"Are you sure we're talking about Ollie?" I joked.

"Don't be a stranger," he said.

Ollie dunked under the water, then held on to the side, flutter-kicking.

"A, can I tell you something?" she said, looking around

to make sure we were alone, though we had heard Hunt's car leave.

"What?" I thought it would be about the bakery, taking off with Dad's loan.

Instead, Ollie confessed that the audition was a story she and Hunt had cooked up.

"So how did you meet?" I asked.

"I was doing sex work when I first got to LA."

"What?"

"Trust me, it's not a big deal." Ollie claimed that in LA people called sex workers as casually as if they were ordering takeout.

"Hunt doesn't want anyone to know. I mean, that's fair."

"Was it safe?"

"In the grand scheme of things." Ollie paused but didn't finish the sentence.

"Did you do it a lot?"

"Not so much."

"That's good."

I had a million more questions, but I knew I couldn't ask them: how did she know what to do, how did she handle herself? What if the man was gross? Or dangerous? How much money did she get? Did she have a madam or a pimp; did she walk the streets like Jodie Foster?

"Don't tell anyone," she said, and I knew she meant Mom and Dad, as if we were teenagers and she'd stolen vodka from the cabinet.

I asked her how serious it was with Hunt.

"Who knows."

"You seem attached."

"Whatever that means." She dunked under the water.

"*We're* attached," I said, lowering myself into the pool and holding on to the wall next to her. "Aren't we?"

"You're here," she said.

"Don't thank me for coming, or anything," I said.

"Don't worry," she said, and dunked again.

"Welcome to editorial row!" Courtney introduced me to the editors, an eclectic group whose offices lined the north wall of the building. Outside each office was a cubicle for an assistant, usually a recent graduate hoping to climb the editorial ranks. Fiona, who had been an assistant for three years, was pissed off that I'd been fast-tracked. According to Courtney, Fiona had expected a promotion when the editor she worked for went on maternity leave and then decided not to come back. She was polished, professional, played softball on the Rogers & Rogers team, and had a degree in art history from Haverford. Courtney called her "Eve" and said I should watch my back.

"Take her to lunch and blow smoke up her ass" was Courtney's advice.

"Really, I have to do that?"

"Take her somewhere nice."

I let Fiona choose the restaurant, and she booked a table at Michael's, known for its power booths, where media giants, captains of industry, and B-list celebrities mingled. The day of our lunch, Fiona showed up for work in a crisp, tight-fitting suit with heels and pearls. If she was trying to intimidate me, mission accomplished. I must have looked like her assistant, in my now customary miniskirt and Docs. She scanned the restaurant for famous people, pointing out news anchors, magazine editors, and aging stage actors.

"How do you know all this?" I asked.

"You just know."

The waiter asked what we'd like to drink, and I said tap water would be fine, but Fiona overrode me and said we'd prefer Perrier with lime. She ordered the sole meuniere, the most expensive entrée. Toward the end of the lunch, she shared her five-year plan. "By the time I'm thirty, I plan to be a senior editor, married, one child, one on the way. We'll probably move to Westchester or Montclair and get a starter house."

"Are you engaged?" I asked.

"I'm pre-engaged," she said confidently. "What's your five-year plan?"

"I don't have a five-minute plan," I joked.

"I'm not afraid of hard work," she said, "so long as it's recognized."

"It doesn't always work out that way," I said. Everything about her, including her hot-pink patent leather Filofax, turned me off. I wondered what would happen if life wrapped its cruel arms around Fiona and dropped a starter house on her head.

A plaque with my name was mounted outside my office door, giving me immeasurable pleasure every time I crossed the threshold. The editorial meetings hooked me. I loved hearing the editors pitch projects and learning about the business side of publishing. Coming from academia, I believed that this was the *real* world. Courtney taught me which agents to curry favor with, how to put together an offer, and how to edit even the most recalcitrant authors: "Pepper their pages with compliments, and they'll be putty in your hands."

If Courtney wasn't wooing a writer or lunching with an agent, we'd meet in the corporate dining room. She'd save a seat at a table near the windows. "Sit!" she'd say, and I happily obeyed. During our very first lunch, she relayed the story of her disastrous high school romance, which ended when she became pregnant a month before graduation.

"Is this too much?" she laughed, suddenly self-conscious.

"No, no."

"I'm an oversharer," she said, the way some people announce their zodiac sign. On the day Courtney was scheduled to have an abortion, her boyfriend Danny drove her to the clinic, shoved two hundred dirty, crinkled bills into her hand (caddying tips), and took off. She had expected him to stay with her and was already crying as she approached the door.

"This fucking woman appears and shoves a picture at me of a fetus attached to an umbilical cord saying, 'Don't kill your baby!'"

Courtney said she must have been hallucinating, but the woman appeared to her as a witch with a withered face drawing her into an oven. The woman blocked the door and shoved the picture in her face again, an alien with a giant floating head. Courtney tried not to look at the tiny hands, the five fingers like a tiny translucent glove. A security guard pushed the door open for her and admonished the woman to vacate the premises.

"That's horrible," I said.

"Shit happens," she said.

"I'm so sorry."

"And now you know my secret!" she said, "so you're my official new best friend, Amy Editor."

Courtney and I got together on most weekends. We went to sample sales, where she'd work her way through a rack and pluck a designer jacket or dress buried among the "rags." She insisted on treating me to my first manicure and pedicure. At this I balked. I had never painted my nails.

"Humor me," she said. "Keep me company."

I kept fidgeting as the woman scraped at my heels, clipped my cuticles, and massaged my hands, locking her fingers with mine.

"Relax," Courtney said. "Pampering never hurt anyone."

It became part of our routine, meeting up on Saturday mornings, two queens on our manicure thrones, manuscripts in our laps, gossiping about colleagues, making plans. Sometimes she would cook dinner at her apartment, her "famous" tuna casserole with potato chips crumbled on top. One night she confided that she had dreamed of jumping off a building in those weeks and months after her abortion and before college, which she called the Dark Ages. She assured me she was never serious, having come to the decision that jumping was selfish because you could kill innocent bystanders.

Courtney also wanted regular updates about Marc and me. She'd tap her fork on her plate and say, "So, tell me."

Marc and I had gone out to dinner a few times, had hung out in the East Village. The one time he invited me to his apartment, we chastely watched a movie, ate takeout, and drank wine sitting on opposite ends of his couch. After the movie ended, he waited with me by the elevator, the long awkward seconds before it arrived filled with tension, at least for me. But I needed him to make the first move. When he didn't kiss me, I worried that Marc only wanted to be friends.

"He likes you," Courtney said.

"Did you talk to him?"

"No, I would tell you."

"Then what?"

"It's just a feeling," Courtney said, but she sounded sure of herself.

"He's probably dating other girls," I said. "I mean, he's allowed."

"He works a zillion hours," she reminded me.

That was true.

Over the summer, Marc and I began to spend more time together. A long day at Jones Beach, another at the Brooklyn Botanic Garden. One afternoon we secretly bought each other a book at the Strand after poking through their open stands. Marc picked out Lewis Thomas's *Lives of a Cell* for me, and I bought him *The Portable Machiavelli*.

Courtney couldn't believe we hadn't slept together in the six weeks Marc and I had been dating. She was sure she had ruined most of her chances with men by sleeping with them on the first date, but she insisted she couldn't help it.

"I'm horny," she announced, "why should I apologize?" Plus, the sexual double standard infuriated her. While she claimed she was impressed with my restraint, she couldn't fathom it.

"I would have jumped his bones."

"I know."

Around that time, Marc and I started playing a game whenever we passed a couple, guessing their relationship status based on body language and other intangibles. Soon after, we started holding hands, leaning into each other, forging body language of our own. On the night that Marc's new mattress was delivered, he invited me over, and something told me that this was going to be it. Courtney had insisted I buy lingerie for the big night, which had never occurred to me.

"Men love it," she said.

"Come on, isn't it kind of a cliché?"

"They're really all the same. Trust me."

"Marc isn't," I said.

Two days later, I found myself going into a lingerie store I had passed a million times on Columbus Avenue. There were no bras on display, and I wondered if I had wandered into the wrong place. A woman emerged from the back, parting two curtains. A tape measure hung around her neck, and a tissue was stashed up her sleeve. She spoke with an Eastern European accent as she inched the tape around my back and closed it around my chest.

"Thirty-two A. Very small but perfectly shaped breasts."

I was ridiculously proud of this pronouncement. She disappeared into the back of the store and came back with three see-through bras in pink, coral, and cream that shimmered like mermaid shells, the small iridescent ones Ollie and I used to collect at the beach. Girls like black these days, the woman said, but with my pale skin, I should stick with pastels. She pointed out the workmanship and the hand stitching on the bras, which she paired with matching panties, a delicate pink bow sewn into the waistband. I couldn't believe how tiny they were, and she mentioned that I might want to get a trim. The total was over three hundred dollars, and I blanched. She took my credit card, wrapped up the bras and panties in tissue paper, and slipped them into a bag with the word "Dream" in silver glitter.

As a gift, I brought Marc a set of sheets, then panicked that it was too presumptuous, too obvious, possibly creepy. I considered dumping them in the garbage, but they were expensive, and I had carried them all the way from the West Side. I worried about the color, the thread count; I was unraveling with each step. I was also fifteen minutes early, so I walked around the block three times. No matter how I tried to adopt the New York posture of showing up "fashionably late," it went against every grain and I could never pull it off.

I had worked up a sheen of sweat on my forehead, and the crisp shopping bag with the sheets had wilted by the time the elevator reached Marc's floor. I felt faint and wanted to flee. Was this happening? Then the doors opened, and Marc was there to greet me.

When he opened the shopping bag, he said he couldn't believe it: the sheets were the most thoughtful gift anyone had ever given him. Before we finished pulling the fitted sheet across the mattress, we were all over each other. With him leading, his certainty, I shed a lot of my inhibitions. I had only been with Josh and Lab Boy, but I knew this was different. After, staring at the ceiling, Marc confessed that he'd thought about kissing me the day we first met, but something told him to take it slow. Also, he said, he wasn't sure if I felt the same way.

"You're mysterious, Amy Shred," he said. At last my reticence was interpreted as allure. We did it again and again and again, and forever more we'd refer to that night as our personal best. From that night forward, we were a couple. Almost all of the anxiety I had felt over my sexual inexperience dissolved. With Marc my body responded. I didn't have to worry. And best of all, I didn't have to think.

12

Long before I was engaged, my mother knew which wedding planner she wanted to hire: a woman named Candy Barr out of Westport.

"Mom, you've got to be kidding. That's not a real person."

"She books out a year or two in advance. We'd be lucky to get her."

All of Marc's friends at the firm were married, and some of the wives were pregnant or already had a child. One junior partner had a picture of his baby's sonogram as his screen saver. Marc had said more than once that he wanted to have a family. He thought we should move in together, hinted about sizing his grandmother's ring. I wanted to wait; it hadn't quite been a year. I was also falling in love with my new career, befriending colleagues, bonding with some of the authors I was editing.

I'd call home, and my mother would register a touch of disappointment if it wasn't "the big news." She'd say, "There is no right time to do it!" and "You're not going to do better than Marc." She also said it was a miracle that I'd "nabbed" him.

"Mom, can't you just be happy that I'm happy?"

"Of course I am! Just don't let him get away."

I introduced Marc to my mother six months into our relationship, meeting for Sunday brunch at a restaurant in the city. She was a vision in camel-colored separates, her hair done, black patent heels and bag. Marc jumped up to shake her hand and pulled out her chair.

"Oh my," Mom said. "A gentleman."

Sitting down, she set a black box on Marc's place mat. She said she couldn't help it, having found herself back in one of her favorite places, the men's shop at Barneys with its cool ambience, slim salesmen in monochromatic clothes, merino wools and cashmere. My mother used to love picking out ties and matching pocket squares for Dad, assessing the quality as she rubbed the fabric between her fingers.

"For me?" Marc asked, confused.

"It's nothing."

"You didn't have to do that."

"It's not every day Amy introduces me to a fellow."

"Mom!"

"Go on, open it."

What was she doing? My emotions ramped up, convinced that whatever was in that box would either humiliate me or destroy my relationship with Marc. I was so sure of it that I grabbed the box from his plate, pulled off the top, and clawed through the tissue paper and cotton batting. At the bottom of the box were two gold blobs. Marc reached in and held up the cuff links: a tortoise and a hare.

"Oh, wow! They're great," he said.

"You mix and match. They have all kinds of pairings, dog and cat, lion and lamb, moon and star. You can exchange them for any ones you prefer."

"These are perfect. Thank you, Mrs. Shred."

"Call me Lorraine, please!"

"Thank you so much!"

"Marc," she asked, "would you say you're more tortoise or more hare?"

Walking back to Marc's apartment, I wrapped myself in a shawl of sullenness.

"Babe, what was that?"

"She's so fucking manipulative."

"She was charming."

"Charming?"

"I mean pathetic, sure."

I hated hearing him call her charming, but I felt wounded when he added pathetic. The traffic light hadn't changed, but no cars were coming.

"Can we walk?"

"Are you mad at me?"

"I'm mad at my mother," I said, but I was upset with Marc too.

"I call it the way I see it," Marc said, pinching my elbow.

It was a phrase he was fond of using, certain of the way he assessed people. It helped explain why he was so good as a lawyer, not getting emotionally embroiled. When we started dating, I found Marc's conviction intoxicating. There was right and wrong, good guys and bad guys, and it wasn't hard to tell which was which. His life philosophy followed suit: if you wanted something, you worked hard for it. Make a decision and stick with it. Sometimes I'd equivocate about a decision for too long, and he'd say, "Life ain't that hard, Aim." Mostly, I persuaded myself that Marc's temperament was enviable, perfect for me. I admired his clarity. I wanted to be more like him!

We had a couple of hours back at his apartment before Marc left for the office. He spent every Sunday afternoon at the firm, preparing for the week ahead.

"Come here, Babe," he said, and pulled at my sweater.

"I'm not going to bed with you right now."

"Is this about the cuff links?"

"It's not the cuff links."

"Then what?"

"Do you not see what I'm talking about?"

I should have been happy. Marc and Mom had genuinely gotten along. He had passed her test, and she had charmed him. I wished I hadn't torn open the gift box.

Marc tried to kiss me, but I turned away.

"Okay, I'm taking a shower." He had indulged my churlishness for long enough. "At least we don't have to deal with *my* mother!" he said, closing the bathroom door and turning on the water.

Marc's mother had left the family when he was eight years old. I asked how he felt about it, and he gave me a one-word answer: bad. But he didn't believe there was any point in dwelling on it. At a librarians' conference in Portland, Maine, she had fallen in love with another librarian and followed her to San Francisco.

Marc's father kept the truth from Marc and his brother and refused to let her visit. His mom returned almost a year later, her hair cut short, and Marc mistook her for a man. As he told that part of the story, his tone betrayed the pain of a young boy whose world was suddenly and completely altered. His mother called faithfully and sent birthday cards and Christmas presents, which Marc threw in the trash in imitation of his even angrier older brother, no matter how much he wanted to open them. At night his brother warmed up TV dinners for them both, while their father built a fortress around himself. The living room was choked with yellowing newspapers, foil trays, and piles of plastic containers. After his brother left for college, Marc worked two part-time jobs, saved his money, graduated a year early, and left for Princeton the following fall.

Marc came out of the shower and asked if he could change my mind.

"I'm a nice clean boy," he said, pummeling me. It was like being pounced on by a golden retriever. Putting up resistance had become part of our mating ritual. I'd push Marc away, and he would plow into me, I'd scream and laugh, and he would shush me and get us to concentrate. Sometimes the sex was so pleasurable, I'd forget who I was for a while. After, I'd watch Marc get dressed; I loved the way his thighs filled his trousers, the slight sag in the seat of his pants, the way he felt around for the loops and threaded his belt through them. Only this time I pushed him off me.

"What did you really think of her?"

"Are we back to your mom?"

"Just be honest."

"You can let her have the win from time to time," he said.

"The win?"

"You know what I mean."

One of Marc's friends from the firm had said, and it stayed with me, that the person with the most money at the end of their life wins. We were at the Princeton Club, a place that cultivated and reified winners, with its vaulted ceilings, forbidding portraits, dark leather couches, and enormous chandeliers. Marc and his friends considered themselves winners, and they gathered there on Friday nights, connoisseurs savoring small-batch bourbon and imported cigars.

His lovely wife shoved him. "It's the person with the most love at the end of their life who wins, you idiot." Then his friend put me on the spot. "What do you say, Amy, love or money?"

"Oh, money," I said, my tone blasé and world-weary. My answer was met with laughter, and I knew I had passed some unspoken test with Marc's friends.

Riding down in the elevator, Marc kissed me and said he would call later, maybe grab sushi if it wasn't too late.

"You're not mad at me?" I asked pathetically.

"Parents are fucked-up people," Marc said. "You have to get over it."

When I returned home, the light on my answering machine was flashing: three messages, all from my mother, eager to debrief after brunch. Delete, delete, delete.

Hunter was frantic. He'd come home from a shoot in Vancouver and Ollie was gone. He called friends, the LA hospitals. He drove around at night, cruising after-hours clubs and VIP lounges. He called Dad, Mom, and me. Sometimes twice or more times a day. We tried to convince him, as we had convinced ourselves, that she'd be back. Ollie couldn't help it. Her leaving didn't mean she didn't love him.

"How do you know?" Hunt asked me.

"She always comes back."

Two weeks passed, and his calls tapered off.

"She's a cunt," he said on our last phone call, then apologized for his language, his voice filled with a mix of anguish, rejection, and worry.

"It's not personal," I said, understanding well how cruel Ollie's actions could feel, how heartless. "It's hard to separate the person from the illness."

Hunt was quiet.

"You do know she's ill," I said. "She's not stable."

Quiet again.

"She's manic most of the time except when she isn't."

"She's manic depressive?" As Hunt formulated the question, I could hear him struggling with the realization.

"Or something. I mean, she's *something*."

We didn't really know what she was. After The Place, Ollie never stayed anywhere long enough to be properly evaluated, never stayed on any medication long enough to give it a chance. She found men to support her mania or buy into it: the sex, the adventure, the excitement, the disruption of their routine lives. And in the low periods she'd cool out at Roxbury from time to time, take yoga classes, go on long walks, help out in the kitchen. In South Dakota she found a sanctuary for wild

mustangs, where she worked in exchange for riding. She had
stayed with Hunter longer than with any other man.

"You matter to her," I said.

"I'm such an idiot."

"Please don't give up on her."

Marc offered to help me pack up my apartment. It reminded
me of dismantling my childhood bedroom, and I wanted to go
through it myself, say goodbye to my solitary life, sad as it was,
safe as it was. My downstairs neighbor took my beloved couch. I
put my futon, lamps, and assorted appliances on the street; they
disappeared before I brought out the next batch. All my clothes
fit in two suitcases and a duffel bag. I limited my books to three
boxes and sold the textbooks back to the university bookstore,
but not before inking out my name on the inside cover.

On the top shelf of the closet, I found my childhood box
of treasures. I considered throwing it out but instead wrapped
it with packing tape, the way we created time capsules in fifth
grade for future generations to find. I stuffed the box in my
duffel along with the Roseville vase Josh had bought for five
dollars at a tag sale and filled with sunflowers. Before leaving,
I swept the place, and something under the bed tugged at the
broom. I toed it out with my boot: a manila envelope covered
in dust. Inside was the dream catcher.

Marc had cleared out an entire closet and half his dresser
for me. I placed my high school graduation picture of Dad,
Mom, and me on the bedroom dresser next to a photo of
Marc and his college buddies holding beer cans out in front

of themselves. I couldn't decide whether to unpack the one picture of Ollie I'd kept. I had shared with Marc only the minimum: I had a sister, she was mentally ill, she had an on-again, off-again relationship with an LA producer.

Marc didn't push for more; since she wasn't in our lives, he couldn't imagine that she could have much impact on us. In the photo, taken at my father's company picnic, Ollie is smiling broadly, her arms around two of the drivers, her long legs tan, in denim cutoffs and a macrame belt. After vacillating for a while, I showed it to Marc.

"Do you think she's beautiful?" I tragically asked.

"She definitely has something."

I'd been in therapy with Paul for a year by the time I moved in with Marc, who did not understand why I, of all people, needed it. "There's nothing wrong with you," he said when I first told him about my sessions with Paul. I knew he thought it was a crutch; he had said as much about other people and psychiatry in general. "But, hey, if it's helping you," he also said. I feared the real me would emerge, a friendless girl who concocted Cobbler and Tupperware games to play alone. The girl who went to the movies with her dad on prom night, who drowned her disappointment in Milk Duds, letting the little caramel turds melt in her mouth before swallowing them. I was desperate to shed her. "Am I supposed to accept who I am or change who I am?" I'd challenge Paul. "Am I ever going to stop being her?"

If he didn't answer, I'd taunt him. "Which is it? Do you even know?"

Sometimes I remained quiet in those long sessions as the sky darkened. I'd stare for so long that the teardrop shapes on Paul's paisley socks started to swim like amoebas. Other times, I'd provoke him further, spewing insults and accusations: Maybe I should see a woman therapist? Do your other clients figure stuff out? I grew paranoid, accusing him of knowing things about me that I didn't know. He'd remain calm, acknowledge that change was hard to come by, but he wasn't keeping anything from me.

"Then what are you actually doing? Can you give me a clue?"

Paul, who rarely offered an opinion or suggested a path, surprised me during one such session. "We need to talk more about your sister." What was there to talk about? Ollie was ill. That's what we told ourselves, what I'd told Hunt. We couldn't hold her accountable. Worse, I wasn't able to quell the occasional fear that if she did return, Ollie would drag me down into the muck and ruin everything.

Marc worked late most nights, and I'd hear him arrive home before I saw him: key in lock, tumbler turned, briefcase plopped on credenza, mail riffled. He'd call out, "Amy, Amy, Amy, where's my girl?" He knew I was either on the couch or in bed with a manuscript. He'd join me, and I loved watching him devour his takeout directly from the carton, his tie loosened and shoes off. With a mouth full of noodles, he'd describe taking a deposition. I marveled at his confidence. He never wondered or worried about what people thought of him. I'd ask for a bite, and he'd hold out the noodles on the end of his chopsticks. I had flashes of Carlson Academy, the boy I fancied feeding the girl I envied. Only now the girl I envied was me.

We got engaged on our one-year anniversary. Marc slid the ring on to my finger, and we flapped our arms, too excited to kiss. We went out for dinner at our local Italian place and shared our news with the waiter, who insisted that dessert was on the house. I fed Marc a forkful of tiramisu, as I would feed him a piece of cake six months later at our wedding.

"Let's practice," he said back at the apartment, swooping me up in his arms and carrying me over the threshold.

Marc's inner circle of college friends would stand up for him as groomsmen. His older brother would be his best man. They would plan a trip to Vegas, they would make long, hilarious toasts at the rehearsal dinner and again at the wedding. Marc either didn't notice or was too polite to mention that I didn't have a close group of friends who would do the same for me. Knowing that I could never count on Ollie, I asked Courtney to be my maid of honor.

As her first official duty as maid of honor, Courtney arranged a picnic for the two of us in Central Park, complete with wicker basket, sandwiches from a gourmet food shop, two flutes tucked inside, and a small bottle of champagne to celebrate.

"I can't believe you're marrying little Marc Goodyear," she said, holding up her glass for a toast. I didn't care for the diminutive, but I knew Court was jealous on some level—the younger friend getting married before the older. She had been seeing the CFO of our company, who claimed to be separated from his wife but spent weekends with her and their kids in Sag Harbor. She pretended it was fine, but I could tell she was upset and lonely, and it made her a little meaner. I asked what Marc had been like in high school.

"Dorky."

"That's all?"

"I mean, he was on the debate team," she said, waving away a gnat.

"Okay."

"I mean he was sweet."

"What about the prom?" I knew Marc had been her date after the whole debacle with Danny and the abortion.

"I always knew he had a crush on me. I mean, he was a sophomore; it was cute. He showed up at our house in his rental tux with a corsage, and he waited in our living room with my parents for an hour. I could barely get dressed. We didn't even take any pictures. Thank god, because I looked like shit."

When I asked Marc about it, he confirmed her account: "I wasn't so much a prom date as a shoulder to cry on."

I called Kira and asked her to be my one bridesmaid, even though we'd hadn't seen each other much since I'd moved in with Marc. When she answered the phone, I could tell something was wrong from her voice.

"I did something really stupid the other day," she said. After some prodding, she revealed that she had taken a lot of pills when she found out Ari's parents were making arrangements for a new marriage. "I woke up the next morning on the bathroom floor."

"Oh no, Kira, are you okay?"

She said it was a cry for help that no one heard, and she laughed. "You know, like a tree in the forest."

"I'm coming over," I said.

"No, please don't. I'm okay. I have to go to work."

"Let me find you a therapist," I said.

"It's not going to change anything. I'm not getting him back."

"In case you change your mind," I said.

"Thanks, Shreddy," she said. "We'll see."

We booked the Princeton Club for our engagement party. Gifts arrived from family, friends, and colleagues, many in Tiffany's robin's-egg-blue boxes. Marc placed the empty boxes inside one another like a set of nesting bowls. I saved all the white ribbons in a heart-shaped tin. They were heady days, and I felt transformed by this beautiful man who sang in the shower, who sat naked on the edge of the bed and without any self-consciousness clipped his toenails, the crescents falling on a towel. We loved all the same TV shows (*Twin Peaks* and *X-Files*), shared the same opinions about film directors (Hitchcock and Scorsese). We loved REM and danced around the apartment yelling the lyrics to "The One I Love," stabbing the air with our index fingers.

Around that time, Hunter called with news of Ollie's return. His emotions ran the gamut: relieved, angry, confused, happy. He reported that when she first showed up, she mostly slept. She wouldn't say anything about why she had left or where she had been. After a few weeks, he called again to report on her progress.

"She seems better now. Really good."

"I'm so glad," I said.

"She's up to four miles!" he said, as proof.

"That's really great," I said.

He'd let Ollie back into his life on her terms, as he would continue to do again and again, suffering her abrupt departures and accepting her unapologetic returns. He'd become one of us.

"If she could just settle down" was Dad's refrain. He believed that a good man could fix her, protect her. He wanted Ollie and Hunt to come to the engagement party so he could meet "this Hunter person." Mom was still fuming about the bakery, and she had to deal with Anita Wormer at her own daughter's engagement party. I warned Marc not to fall for Ollie; he said not to worry. He prided himself on having a finely tuned bullshit detector.

The groomsmen were charming. Three of them had been in the Tigertones, one of Princeton's a cappella groups, and they sang "Can't Help Falling in Love," as Marc wrapped his arms around me. Courtney made a surprisingly touching toast, free of innuendo and cynicism. "Let's raise a glass to the two sweetest people on the planet. To a lifetime of taking care of each other and loving each other as much as you do today!" The assembled lifted their glasses.

After all my worry, introducing Marc to Ollie was a non-event. Ollie was on good behavior; Hunt normalized things and anchored her. Marc and Ollie found some points in common, namely the club scene in LA. Marc boasted that he had seen the Ramones at the Viper Room. Ollie said she loved the Ramones. Back at home, Marc said he couldn't believe that the Ollie he had met was the same woman I had feared might ruin the night. "And Hunter's a great guy."

I wanted to explain how wrong he was, but I decided to leave it there. It was easier, and I was tired, coming down from the party, and massively relieved no one had made a scene. Anita had been warm. Mom was civil. We had pulled it off.

"What did she say about me?" Marc was poised for a compliment. We were getting ready for bed.

"She said you were okay."

"Just okay?"

In bed we repeated our origin story: Marc on the mattress, a prince long asleep in a grove, awakened by my touch. I called him Mighty Oak and Bear. He called me Squid and Little and Baby. We made love in a quieter register. The need to show off, to have Olympian sex, subsided, and that felt good, too.

Marc was made junior partner at the firm, and I was promoted to full editor, which we saw as signs that our union was good. We were flourishing.

As the wedding date drew close, I grew more anxious. Marc would cover me with his body, a human compression blanket, until my tension dissipated beneath the weight and heat of his body. He'd make my favorite comfort foods: meatloaf, mac and cheese. And he expertly fielded most of the calls from my mother, limiting my exposure to her outsized need to control every detail of the wedding.

One evening on the way home from work, I let myself linger in front of a children's clothing store on Madison Avenue, admiring a tiny pale pink dress made of raw silk, with white smocking and tiny white florets. Those six months were the happiest of our life as a couple. *The almost time.*

13

A week before the wedding, I thought I spotted Josh in Washington Square Park. We hadn't spoken since he moved in with Ellen, and I wasn't 100 percent sure it was him. His head was shaved, and his body looked sturdier, less wiry. But as I watched his forward gait, he was unmistakably the person who had helped me through the lowest time in my life.

I wasn't sure he recognized me, and I feared we would pretend that we hadn't seen each other. New York was like that, plenty of fish to throw back into the sea. Only Josh ran up to me, and we hugged hard. He said he loved my glasses, my hair. I touched his head, fine sandpaper. We walked to Café Dante, where we used to go, and settled on a table at the back. The place, with its checkerboard floor and pressed-tin ceiling, hadn't changed; an espresso machine, shiny as a new car, hissed from time to time.

"You start," I said.

"No, you go."

"No, you."

Josh said Ellen had moved back to Wisconsin in disgrace after *The Glass Menagerie* was canceled. She had forgotten her lines twice on opening night, hordes of people left during intermission, reviews were savage. "It was opening-night jitters, but she never recovered, they shuttered after two weeks." I could hear the resignation, the injustice. "I quit acting after that, too, in solidarity."

Josh had found a job at a theater bookstore in Midtown and spent his days reading plays and suggesting them to actors in search of monologues. "The owner never even asked for a résumé—we totally hit it off." He'd let Josh crash in the basement on a cot and take bird baths in the utility sink until Josh saved enough to find a place.

I went to the bathroom and washed my face. I knew I had to tell Josh about Marc, but I didn't want to admit that I lived on the Upper East Side, was marrying a lawyer, and often spent weekends with his fancy friends at their country homes. I was embarrassed about how safe it seemed. I feared he would judge me for being conventional, for giving up on my research, but he was eager to hear about my new life as an editor, the writers I plucked from obscurity.

"You're a genius," he said.

"I'm lucky," I said.

"You're brilliant. Believe it."

Sinatra's "Fly Me to the Moon" came on, an old favorite of Josh's. He leaned over and sang into my ear; his breath was warm and close. It took me by surprise. It had all ended so abruptly between us, and I didn't know how to account for this rush of sensations: attraction, fascination, danger.

"Ellen wants to get married," he said, when the song ended.

"Isn't she in Wisconsin?" I tried to sound confused, but I felt stung. I had no claim to Josh, but I suddenly didn't want Ellen to have him either.

"She licked her wounds in Wisconsin," he said. "Moved back and got her realtor's license."

"Oh," I said.

"She's the top earner at her firm."

"That's great."

"She wants to have babies." Josh told me she was older than us by a few years and her biological clock was ticking.

"Oh, wow. Are you ready for that?"

"Probably not. I don't know. Maybe."

"You'd be a great dad," I said, and I meant it.

"That's what she says. She just made a bid on a brownstone in Harlem, a fixer-upper."

"Wow. What are you going to do?"

"Let's run away," he said, pushing the bangs from my forehead.

"Ha ha."

"I'm serious." He put his foot on my foot. "Run away with me."

"I'm getting married," I blurted.

Josh tilted back in his chair. "Married, married?"

"Yes. I know. Me."

"Shred. No."

"The wedding's next weekend," I said without thinking and invited him. Josh asked if he could bring Ellen.

"Of course," I said.

"Who's the bum, by the way?" Josh asked.

"Just some guy I picked up."

"I hope he's good enough for you."

"I think so," I said.

"He'd better be," Josh said.

"What are you doing home?" I was surprised to find Marc on the couch while it was still light out.

"I live here," Marc said, half joking, half put out. When he asked where I'd been, I suddenly felt guilty. "I ran into an old friend."

"Who?"

"Josh, I've told you about him."

"Who is he again?" Marc asked. "How do you know him?"

"From college. Well, he dropped out."

"What does he do?" For Marc, a person and their profession were one and the same.

"He was an actor, or he was trying to be."

"That gets kind of old, don't you think?"

I had no idea how to explain Josh. We hadn't exactly been boyfriend and girlfriend; the term "best friend" was beside the point. I didn't tell Marc that I had invited him to the wedding. I knew he'd be angry after all the cutting we had done to the guest list. And it would throw my mother into a tizzy with the tables. She spent many evenings in the "war room" moving place cards around the way generals plot military maneuvers.

Marc lost interest, fanning out the collection of takeout menus we'd amassed. "How about Thai?"

My mother insisted I try on her wedding dress. She had made a big deal of it, inviting me to the condo for lunch, getting the dress out of storage. She lifted it from the delicate tissue paper and held it out like a newborn ready to be baptized.

"Oh god, I wonder if it still fits," she said.

"I thought we were seeing about me."

"Let me have my fun," my mother said and carefully stepped into the dress.

"Zip me." I worked the zipper up her back, and with each inch I could feel my mother draw in her breath.

"My, my," she said, admiring her figure. "A lot of women just let themselves go."

She slipped out of the dress and handed it to me. "Okay, your turn."

Mom plopped down on the chaise, suddenly distant, her victory hollow. Her slim figure wouldn't win Dad back.

The dress swam on me. "It's not worth taking in," my mother stated. She couldn't see "destroying" the lines on the dress to fit my boyish figure.

"There's no point saving it for Ollie," she said, then laughed at herself. "Ollie getting married! That's a good one."

Marc and I had decided to stay apart the night before the wedding, and he had taken a hotel suite with his groomsmen. In lieu of a wedding shower, which I didn't want, Courtney gave me a wicker basket filled with chocolate penises, Astroglide, a butt plug, and assorted magazines: *People, Penthouse, Vogue*. She had booked appointments for us at a deluxe spa for a massage, facial, and a mani-pedi. After, I went back to the apartment steamed, scrubbed, and exfoliated. The phone rang, but the caller hung up when I answered. It rang again, and I figured it was one of the groomsmen pranking me, but then I heard Josh's voice.

"Can I come over?"

I knew it was a bad idea. It was after eleven p.m. when Josh arrived. He appeared stoned and hyper at the same time. He said he'd sent a case of champagne as a wedding gift, but it hadn't arrived. It never did arrive.

"Fancy," he said, surveying the apartment, taking a step and peering into the kitchen and bedroom. He took off his jacket, his armpits dark with sweat. Then he sat on the couch right next to me. Too close.

"Come here."

"What?"

"Come here."

"I'm right here. What's going on?"

He stood up, and I felt weirdly frightened. Then he perched on my lap like a ventriloquist's doll and robotically said, "You-are-making-a-big-mistake-Amy-Shred."

"You're fucked up."

"It-should-have-been-us."

"Stop it!" I said, my voice harsh.

"Stop it," he parroted back.

"What are you doing?"

"What are you doing?"

"Stop it." I tried to stand up, and Josh pitched forward. "I'm getting married tomorrow. Please stop."

Then he dropped the puppet voice. "What happened to us?"

"You found Ellen. Remember? I'm with Marc."

He took my head in his hands and held me there, brushed his lips across my lips, covered my mouth with his mouth. How can I say this? He was so hungry. I thought he would swallow me. I'd never experienced anything like that impossibly endless forbidden kiss, and I responded.

The phone rang, and Marc's voice bleated out of the answering machine. I jumped up and grabbed the phone. I could tell he was a little drunk. I could hear the boys in the background, messing around.

"Hi, bride," he said.

Josh sat up, covering his crotch with his hands. I was terrified he was going to say something or make a noise, and I covered the mouthpiece with my hand.

"Are you there?" Marc asked.

"Yes."

"What's happening?"

"You're drunk."

"I love you, bride."

"Good night, groom," I said, "sweet dreams."

"See you tomorrow, bride," Marc said.

"See you tomorrow, groom," I said and hung up.

Josh took a step toward me. "I'm sorry."

"That didn't happen."

"Amy."

"What are you doing?"

"I'm jealous. I'm a jerk."

"That's not good enough."

"I'm really sorry."

"Just go."

Josh pulled on his jacket and asked if he could hug me. I folded my arms across my chest and stepped back.

"Please go."

I thought he was going to cry. After he left, I locked the door, straightened the cushions, showered, and changed into my nightgown. I knew I couldn't fall asleep after what had happened. I spotted Courtney's basket of goodies and picked up *People* magazine, flipping through the pages. Apparently, Valerie Bertinelli had learned to love herself.

My mother knocked and peeked into the bridal suite.

"Anyone home?"

"Come in," I called. Courtney was out getting us breakfast sandwiches. I was still in my jeans.

"It's your big day," Mom said. "How does it feel?"

"I don't know yet," I said. "Unreal?"

She sat down on the bed and patted it for me to sit beside her. Then she took an oxblood leather jewelry box with a gold clasp out of a tote bag and handed it to me.

"You know," she said, "this was supposed to be for Ollie. I always assumed she'd marry first."

"Why don't you save it for her?" I put the box on the bed and started to get up.

"No, no, no," my mother said, trying to take it back.

"You know I'm not Ollie, right? I would have gone to City Hall. This is all for you. You're aware of that."

"Oh, honey. You're nervous. Weddings are stressful."

"And I'm sorry I couldn't fit into your wedding dress."

"Oh, Amy, don't be silly. I don't care about the dress."

"I can't take her place." I fought back tears.

My mother tried to speak in her own defense, but I was not completely in control.

"I know you wish this was Ollie's wedding. But it's mine. Are you ever going to stop punishing me for not being Ollie?"

"Did your therapist say that? Is that what he teaches you?"

There was a soft knock on the door, a knuckle.

"Mrs. Shred?"

"What is it?" My mother was harsh, her tone meant to get to the point.

It was Candy Barr. "The florist is here and needs a word."

Mom frowned, as if this were an unwelcome intrusion, but she jumped up.

"I'll be right back," she said. "Don't open it."

I opened the box the moment she left. Inside was a three-strand necklace of pearls, held together by a butterfly clasp with four yellow marquise-cut diamonds. I knew the necklace had been her grandmother's. Mom had put it in a bank deposit box after her jewelry started to disappear.

Courtney returned with my last request as a single girl. "Your Egg McMuffin, princess." I was in a fetal position on the bed.

"My god, what happened to you?"

I couldn't move. Hadn't I complied with everything my mother wanted? Marc was Jewish, a lawyer, tall, and charming. Check, check, check, check. We were having the big wedding she had dreamed of. Guests would be filling the hotel's banquet room, a many-tiered cake would be assembled by a French couple with a trendy bakery that my mother had discovered in Greenwich, and my maid of honor would scratch the soles of my wedding shoes with a penny before I walked down the aisle.

I sat up and gave Courtney the short version; she pried open the box.

"Holy shit, girl, this is stunning."

"I'm not wearing it."

"I would. And I'd keep it."

We ate the sandwiches.

"These are actually really good," she said.

"I told you."

She rolled the wrappers from our McMuffins into funnels, opened the window and lit them on fire. They briefly shot into the air, yellow and blue flames mixed, before whirlygigging down to the city street below.

"I wish you were my sister," I said.

"I know," she replied.

Then I told her about Josh.

Courtney said it didn't count. "Technically, you didn't fuck."

"It was bad."

"Anyway, you're allowed to sleep with previous lovers. You just can't sleep with someone new; that's cheating."

"Who said?"

"It's common knowledge." She was so certain of this unspoken rule, and all the other rationalizations and justifications she had acquired along the road of her life, that I half believed it. "Come on," she said. "Let's get some makeup on you."

⚜

I peeked inside. Guests were scurrying to find seats in the two sections of white chairs that flanked the aisle, decorated by Candy Barr with ribbons and tasteful sprigs of baby's breath. The sounds reminded me of the lab at night. *How did I get here? How did I get here?* Mom had kept a wide berth since my meltdown. Candy told me not to worry, but Dad was running just a few minutes late. I had asked my parents to walk me down the aisle together. There was some grumbling from my mother, who said it was more traditional for the father of the bride to do the honors.

"It's not as if we're still married," she had said. "How's it going to look?"

"Just do it for me."

My mother met me in the hallway. Her pale blue eyes took me in, as cold as a Vermeer, her lips pursed tight, fighting the urge to cry with every muscle in her face.

"Mom, do I look okay?"

"Sweetheart, you look perfect."

A walkie-talkie crackled, and Candy Barr appeared, holding it to her ear as if she were Secret Service, then blurted, "He's here." Dad rounded a corner seconds later and stopped short. Oh, Bunny," he said. He pulled out his handkerchief and wiped away tears.

"You look so beautiful."

"Thanks, Daddy."

"I'm so sorry I'm late. Anita couldn't find her hat."

I took a deep breath in, gathering the strength not to break down. It had been a long time since my parents had been together in the same place, since we'd all been together.

"We done good, Lor," Dad said, and put his arm around Mom. They gazed at me together. "I would say so," she said. "I would certainly say so."

The question of Ollie's attendance hung in the air. She'd left Hunt at some point after the engagement party. I wasn't entirely sure she knew the date, but Dad said she definitely did. I could tell he hoped she would come. My mother wished she would stay away, though she wouldn't come out and admit it. Me? I wanted my sister; I just didn't know if I wanted Ollie.

Our arms linked, my parents walked me down the aisle. My mother lifted my veil, and they each kissed my cheek. I could smell my mother's makeup and the tomato juice on my father's breath. Marc was standing there with his phalanx of grooms-men, a cookie-cutter row of handsome and successful men.

I wanted to believe that I had been rewarded for being good. That my stupid solitary life had been a mistake, that my real life was starting now. As my parents took their seats, I listened for the caw of the crow. I cast an eye at the entrance one last time for any sign of Ollie before stepping forward to join Marc beneath the canopy.

As the justice of the peace cleared his voice and was about to speak, the great doors opened, light streamed in, and the congregation turned in unison. For a heartbeat, I expected Ollie to appear in Mom's wedding dress, disheveled and dirty, hair wild. Instead, I saw two figures in silhouette, stiff as bride-and-groom cake toppers. It was Josh and Ellen. Slight rumblings among the guests. Instead of finding seats, they stood at the rear. Josh slipped his suit jacket over Ellen's slim shoulders, a child swimming in her dad's jacket.

I joined Marc. He was trying not to cry, quickly thumb-ing tears away from his cheeks. Courtney fussed with my veil. Marc and I said our vows robotically so as not to stumble. I could feel the butterfly clasp of my grandmother's necklace dig into my neck.

The DJ blasted Madonna's "Holiday," and the dance floor filled. Along the perimeter, I saw Josh filling his mouth with stuffed mushroom caps until his cheeks were as full as a chip-munk's. Marc had made it clear that he didn't want Josh at the wedding, and I had refused to renege on my last-minute invitation. But after what had happened the night before, I couldn't believe he'd show up. Josh surveyed the room, thumbs tucked inside red suspenders, rocking back and forth on his feet, with Ellen sipping champagne beside him.

Courtney, Kira, and I had formed a little dance circle of our own; then I felt a shift on the dance floor as the sea of people parted. Josh had pushed his way in, clearing a path to the center. Everyone clapped and egged him on as he started to dance, incorporating moves from kung fu and John Tra-volta. The more they cheered, the wilder his moves. Then he approached me, pulled me close, and spun me around. The crowd went wild. When he dipped me, I was so dizzy that the twinkling lights on the ceiling looked like a great nebula. He kissed me hard on the lips, said congratulations, and left the dance floor, left the party, pulling Ellen along with him.

"What the fuck was that?" Courtney rushed to my side, straightened my veil.

"That was Josh."

Marc, glowering, sat out the next two dances, drinking with his groomsmen at one of the bars at the back of the banquet hall. Courtney, Kira, and I tried to pick up where we left off, enveloped again by the guests who had melded back into a single dancing organism.

Each day of our honeymoon I wanted to confess, but the more time passed without divulging my story, the easier it was to minimize what had happened with Josh. I tried to tell myself it was nothing, but a pervasive, discomfiting feeling prevailed: how easily I might have risked my life with Marc.

In the weeks after the honeymoon, during my sessions with Paul, I yammered on about small grievances from the wedding: Anita's fascinator hat with black feathers that crawled over her forehead like a tarantula, Anita pulling Dad onto the dance floor for a slow dance, her fingernails digging into his back. Courtney drinking too much as the night wore on, flirting with a bartender whose pecs bulged beneath his vest. My mother upbraiding a waiter for failing to supply cocktail napkins while serving hors d'oeuvres. I complained about my job, about my mother haranguing me to start on the thank you notes. Anything but Josh. When I finally told Paul what had happened, I downplayed the entire episode and my guilt. Paul suggested there was more to it.

"Like what?"

He suggested self-sabotage, but I literally couldn't hear it: my ears were buzzing. I had never cheated on anyone. On anything.

Paul suggested that what happened with Josh had to do with Ollie.

"I wish I knew what you're talking about."

"The chaos. Josh, in a way, is Ollie."

"It just happened. Things happen. They *happen!*" I cried, my voice pitched high, operatic.

Paul let that hang in the air.

"Aren't you going to say anything?" I challenged. "Or let me guess, you want to know what I'm feeling."

"Yes, I do," Paul said.

I thought of Ollie throwing the chair at Dr. Lucie and almost laughed. My big gesture: I gathered my bag and left before the session was up—without saying goodbye.

Sometimes it felt as if Marc and I were playing one of my make-believe games from childhood; I could have called it Grown-ups. Planning trips, charting interest rates as we eyed properties in the Hudson Valley, making the circuit of dinner parties, replete with hostess gifts, cigars, and bourbon. Marc had maintained friendships from grade school on. I asked him if he had ever dropped a friend, and he looked at me quizzically: why would he do that? He had sailing and hiking buddies, a racquetball partner, a regular poker game. Most weekends we'd meet his friends for dinner, brunch, or a baseball game. When we went away for weekends, the men would disappear for the whole day, fly-fishing, golfing, or mountain biking.

I had less in common with the wives, who had either stopped working or planned to when they had their babies. When they went into town to shop or cooked supper together, I'd usually beg off, claiming that I had to edit. At the end of the day, everyone would gather for cocktails, and Marc would fetch me.

More than once he admonished me for being standoffish or even rude to his friends. I found myself turning against what I came to view as self-important and self-congratulatory behavior. The Crate and Barrel of it all. After a particularly fraught weekend, I told Marc that his friends were shallow.

"Who are you to judge?" Marc said. "Maybe you're the one that's shallow. Did that ever occur to you?"

We both retreated into even longer work hours. He'd taken on more cases, I'd signed more authors. Marc was put out when I first mentioned that I'd like to skip the weekends away with his friends, claiming I had to finish editing a book, make a deadline.

"You can still go," I said. "You should."

"How is that going to look?" he asked.

"No one will care."

From then on, when I begged off, Marc would go without me. My mother was appalled that I didn't join him, and she scolded me.

"You shouldn't leave him alone. Men don't like that."

"It suits us," I said.

We congratulated ourselves for being independent and disdained couples who were inseparable. We must have known the marriage was foundering, but we had no way to talk about it. Instead, we grew polite, perfunctory. We still had sex from time to time, a brief reprieve from the distance we'd created.

"We're back!" Marc would say afterward, rolling off me like a log.

"Where did we go?" I meant it as an honest question.

"We shouldn't wait so long," he'd say.

"We shouldn't," I'd agree. But we did.

Ten months into the marriage, Paul suggested that we try couples counseling. Marc resisted, but once there, he was warm and forthcoming, while I found myself sounding stiff and judgmental. Marta Keller, in her seventies, wrapped herself in colorful pashmina scarves and wore patent-leather ballet flats. Marc admired her wall of Albers prints, with their brightly colored nested squares. I hated her chunky beads and the half-drained cups of tea on her desk. She had the warm energy of a kindergarten teacher, starting off each session by hitting her palms to her thighs and saying too brightly, "So, talk!"

At first Marc painted a picture of our marriage as happy. He pointed to our complementary work lives as young professionals, casting himself in the role of perfect husband. He was happy to gloss over the friction, the times we "agreed to disagree" (an expression he was fond of, which I hated for its forced bonhomie). I had seen with more clarity after we married that under his good guy veneer, Marc was cutthroat. With me, he had to have the last word. And at work, he had to win. "Am I vicious?" he rhetorically asked one time after a day of depositions. "If I have to be."

In subsequent therapy sessions, Marc revealed that he found it impossible to know what I was thinking or feeling, that he needed more feedback. He was baffled that I could stay silent for what he called an eternity. And over time his frustration came out in a series of escalating questions that grew sharp and nasty. No longer mysterious, my reticence appeared to him as ungenerous, withholding, and ultimately unbearable.

"Jesus, Amy, can you *say* something?"

"Could you nod your head?"

"Are you deaf?"

"Anyone home?"

He complained to Marta about how hard it was for me to say "I love you" and swore that I never said it first.

I denied this, and Marc spat out, "When? When did you ever say it first?"

I remained silent, and Marc pounced on that, too. "See! She can't answer."

Marc said he didn't consider himself needy; was it too much to want your wife to reciprocate? He appealed to Marta for an answer. She turned to me. "Amy, can you answer Marc?"

The first time Marc said "I love you" was after sex, and I had coyly replied, "You love sex."

"No," he said, "I love you, Shred."

I didn't say anything.

"What about me?" His voice in a little-boy register.

"I do love you, Marc Charles Goodyear," I said in an exaggerated Australian accent to lighten the mood, deflect the awkward imbalance.

I did love Marc, but I couldn't always return the serve when it landed in my court. I tried to explain to Marta that we never said "I love you" at home, but that didn't satisfy him.

"What about your sex life?" Marta asked. "Is it mutually satisfying?"

We had had sex all the time during the early months of our marriage. After, Marc would ask if I came, and I'd reply "Can't you tell?"—placing the burden of proof on him. Half the time I still didn't know, but his ardor moved me. I felt my body move in ways I'd never experienced. I wanted Marta to know about the good times, how we'd laugh in bed, eating bacon sandwiches and chips that Marc poured into the hideous Baccarat crystal bowl we'd received as a wedding gift. But Marc jumped in, saying he had to push for sex, coax me out of my moods. I always thought my resistance part of our thing, our mating ritual, our dance.

Marc said he never knew if he had satisfied me.

"I thought you could tell," I said. "Anyway, you don't have to always ask."

"I wanted to make sure you were satisfied, you asshole."

"Wow."

At the end of that session, I rode the elevator down, and Marc took the stairs. He ate in the kitchen, and I said I wasn't hungry. From then on, we managed to mostly avoid each other, even in our one-bedroom apartment, staggering the times we left in the morning and returned home at night, sleeping back to back, each clinging to the cliff of the mattress.

At the next session we retreated into more quotidian reasons to explain our failing marriage: our demanding jobs, my solitary nature versus Marc's need for friends and plans. In my sessions with Paul, he kept returning to Ollie, but I refused to believe that she permeated all my relationships or that I had retreated to the coldest part of myself the more Marc needed me. As to Marc's part in all this, he was a motherless child looking for unconditional love from his wife, from me.

Toward the end of what would be our last session, Marta twirled her watch around her thin wrist and glanced at its enormous face. I asked how much time we had left.

Marc stopped me: "That's rude."

"Why is that rude?"

We both fell silent.

"You guys want to tell me what's really going on?" Marta asked.

"You shouldn't have invited him in the first place," Marc spat out, as if the wedding had happened the day before.

"I can't believe you're bringing that up now."

"That's why we're here, isn't it?"

"I can't keep apologizing."

"Admit you're in love with him."

"It was a mistake inviting him," was all I managed to say. I wanted to blurt it out, come clean about the night before the wedding, but I knew Marc would explode and blame the failure of our marriage entirely on that one incident. He described Josh's swirling me around on the dance floor and kissing me in front of all our friends and family as a humiliating spectacle. I was prepared for Marta to side with Marc, but she suggested that he had agency, that he could have stopped it.

"Marc, why did you let Josh do that?" Marta folded her hands in her lap and tried to meet his gaze, but Marc's head collapsed in his hands, his body bent over. I couldn't tell if he was gathering anger or fighting tears.

"Amy, why do you imagine Marc let that happen?"

Marc lifted his head, his face contorted with pain. I told myself it wasn't my fault, but I knew I was responsible. I also knew that Marc had gravitated toward the law because it was black and white, and his keen sense of right and wrong left little room for forgiveness. There would be no second chances.

From a practical point of view, the divorce was cut-and-dried. The term "starter marriage" had recently come into the vernacular; it was no longer exceptional to end a union as quickly as it had come together. We had never merged our bank accounts. We didn't own property or have kids. I hadn't changed my name.

"Amy, why do you think Marc let that go on," Marta asked again. Marc sat up and shrugged, "See, she still can't say anything." Marc stood up, cracked his back. "Okay, I think we're done." I remembered urging Marc to invite his mother to our wedding and when he refused, I believed that he would always regret his decision. But it turned out that his only regret was marrying me.

PART III

Inchworm

14

A naked woman was drying herself off with paper tow-
els. Fiona rushed into my office to report what she
had seen: a homeless person washing herself in the
bathroom.

"Should I call Security?" Her voice verged on hysterical.

On some level, I had always feared this might happen. I
didn't know what it would look like or how I would handle it,
but now that it was here, I felt charged with what I had to do.

"I'll take care of it," I said, and pushed past Fiona. When
I opened the door to the restroom, Ollie was getting dressed.
"Ollie?"

"Oh, hi," she said, "give me a second."

She pulled on a pair of baggy jeans, a Janet Jackson T-shirt
two sizes too big, and a pink polyester vest with two lapel
pins on it. One said *I'm here to help*. The other, *Ask me anything*.
She angled her head beneath the hand drier, her hair blowing
in every direction.

"Done?" I asked.

"Done."

She seemed disoriented, jangly, but also docile. We took
a cab to my apartment, her head resting against the window,

staring at the rain. I made up the couch, put her in my pajamas, and she collapsed into sleep. Her pockets were empty
but for three dollars and change. Inside a plastic Rite-Aid
bag, I found a wallet containing a school photo of a young
girl with a bowl haircut; a hospital ID on a lanyard that
belonged to Mary McGrath, Aide, Albany Medical Center,
Psych 7; a copy of *The Cat Who Came for Christmas*; and some
used Q-tips.

Somewhere in the middle of the night, Ollie crawled into
my bed and spooned me. She woke at four the next afternoon, still subdued and somewhat confused as she surveyed
my apartment, admiring my books.

"You wrote these?"

"I edited them."

"Cool."

She ate three bowls of cereal and complimented the pattern on my plates, part of the wedding haul. Marc's two words
when we divided our belongings: Keep it.

I knew I should have called our parents. I felt guilty and a
little mean, but she had come to me this time. Though I wasn't
going to delude myself; Ollie needed a pit stop, a little time to
regroup, money. She stayed longer than I expected—almost a
month. At first she didn't leave the apartment, sleeping twelve
to fourteen hours at a time. She was foggy about where she
had been and how she had found me.

After a few days, I returned to work. Ollie promised she
wouldn't go anywhere. I didn't think she *could* go anywhere; still, I
tipped the doorman and asked him to keep an eye out. By the end
of the week, he was running across the street to buy magazines

and Starbursts for her at the corner kiosk. She ventured into the basement laundry and befriended our super, Luis. He taught Ollie how to fold sheets in tight squares, and they embarked on long, heated games of backgammon in the afternoons.

"It's your sister again," Fiona would say when Ollie called throughout the day, making a face that was part concern, part annoyance. Where was the remote? What should we order for dinner? When was I coming home? Could I pick up floss and conditioner? A week in, she started giving me long lists of grocery items for her vegetarian concoctions. Within days of eating the dark leafy greens and legumes that she seasoned with turmeric, cayenne, and ginger, my skin glowed and I slept better. Before we went to bed, she'd pierce a vitamin B capsule with a safety pin and rub a drop of its amber liquid into the creases between my eyes, dab it on my lips.

I called Albany Medical Center and asked to speak with Ollie's doctors: not allowed unless I was a parent, a spouse, or had power of attorney. I broke down and called Marc. It had been some months since we had signed the divorce papers. He grudgingly agreed to help me with the paperwork. We met at the diner we'd frequented on Lexington Avenue on Sunday mornings after nights of watching classic old movies, when we still had sex all the time.

"What are you looking at?" Marc asked as he squeezed into the booth.

"You look different."

"No, I don't."

His hair was shorter. He was wearing new glasses, with the clear plastic frames that were suddenly popular, and a green

Lacoste polo. Marc had despised status logos, free advertising for the corporations that were ripping us off.

"Are you seeing someone?"

"No."

"It's just the new look. The alligator?"

"Do you want my help or not?"

He unfolded his napkin and placed it in his lap. His hands were so familiar, the smooth pad on his middle finger blue from pressing his Bic pen too hard. He wrote briefs in long-hand because his mind worked better that way. I realized what was different: Marc was no longer mine. I knew the smell of him, the taste of him, the clockwise whorl on the back of his head that I had kissed and traced with my finger. Where does that go? You sleep side by side, breathe together, eat together, talk all night. After that, it's a half-remembered movie, a dream you wake from, the details vague and out of reach. Marc put the briefcase I gave him as a wedding gift on the table. I was proud to see he was still using it.

Marc read the menu and called out items that appealed to him. If he couldn't decide between two entrees, he'd ask the waiter's advice. *The veal chop or the Bolognese?* In the beginning of our relationship, I found it endearing. Later it seemed ridiculous, letting a waiter decide your meal. Now our life together was behind us. At our last session with Marta, she had said that one of the worst things people do in a divorce is internalize failure. "The marriage failed," she said; "you didn't." Marc warmed to this idea, but it struck me as idiotic. The fact is we had failed.

We finished eating, and Marc handed me a manila folder.

"It's all in here. Good luck with Ollie."

"Can I ask you something?"

"Sure."

"Are you still mad at me?"

"Let's not get into it." Marc looked down.

"You're seeing someone," I said again.

"We both made mistakes. Can we leave it at that?" Marc buckled his briefcase. I noticed that the gold initials embossed on the leather had all but worn off.

With power of attorney, I was able to request Olivia's medical record from Albany Medical and made an appointment to speak to the psychiatrist who had treated her. He explained that when she arrived she had been disassociated and unable to speak for a few days. Then she became aggressive, followed by a period of withdrawal and mild paranoia. He prescribed an antipsychotic, an antidepressant, and an antianxiety medication. He told me that after two weeks with no progress, she was a good candidate for electroconvulsive therapy, or ECT for short.

"Did you have her consent?" I asked.

"It's protocol for a nonresponsive patient."

"Protocol?"

"Remind me," the doctor said. "You're the patient's sister?"

"Sorry," I said, "I'm just trying to figure out what happened."

He said they had administered two of the usual twelve rounds of ECT. I imagined her body anesthetized, electrodes applied to her temples, her brain convulsed with current. He had hoped that the subsequent rounds would vastly improve her condition but then Ollie stole Mary McGrath's lanyard, vest, and wallet and fled.

Over the course of the month, Ollie filled in some of the missing pieces of her life. There was a sculptor named Thom whom she'd lived with for a few months on a houseboat in Seattle. A married Republican who arranged a stay at Silver Hill, a fancy psychiatric hospital in New Canaan, Connecticut— less than an hour from where we grew up—that looked like a small liberal arts college. She had crashed his vintage Jaguar into the house where his wife and kids were sleeping. She said he cared more about the car than his family.

She listed cities she'd spent time in: Pittsburgh, Iowa City, Eugene, Juneau. Hunt was the only person she returned to. Time and again he welcomed her back no matter the length of her stay: a few days, weeks or months. It was okay if she slept in his guest house or in his bed, if she holed up in the screening room watching movies or lounged by the pool reading screenplays. I couldn't tell if Ollie saw any difference between one scenario and another: sleeping on the floor of a bus station or in a suite at the Ritz-Carlton. Cleaning someone's house or leaving money for the maid.

She confessed that Albany was a new low. It had scared her. She told me she'd slept overnight in the train station and had been molested but didn't elaborate. A custodian found her unresponsive in a bathroom stall the next morning and called an ambulance. When I asked if she had reported it, she said she didn't want to make a big deal of it. I tried to hug her, but she pulled away, saying it wasn't the first time.

"The shock treatment was going to kill me," Ollie said. She had always maintained that she went off her psychiatric drugs because they felt like a wool cap on her brain. The ECT was another matter: "It literally fries your brain!" After the second round, she was determined to escape the locked ward. She waited for the shift change: "That's when they're paying less attention." With the cash from Mary McGrath's wallet, she bought a bus ticket to Westchester, and from there she hitched to NYC and found me at my office.

"What if I hadn't been there?" I asked.

"You were," she said.

We became a couple over those weeks. Ollie convalesced, recuperated, took refuge from her life. She was on the other side of her mania, a side I had never witnessed so clearly. She started using the gym in our building, walking on the treadmill at first, then running a mile, then a few, until she was back up to her usual six. One night she announced that it was getting too comfortable at 1298 Lexington Avenue and laughed. I knew what was coming, but I didn't know when. She was like a surfer waiting for the next big wave.

A few days later, Ollie slipped out of my apartment before dawn, while the city was still asleep, the streets slick with grime and morning dew. "Exploring," she said. "That's all."

Her early-morning wandering became a regular thing. She'd go to the Fulton Street market and watch the fresh catch cascade from the ships into the industrial containers below. She called it a silver waterfall. One morning she dragged me there; all the fishermen greeted her by name. Afterwards she'd go to

Chinatown, to a restaurant called Mon Sing Rice Shop, and watch the shopkeeper mop the floors and tables with oolong tea. Before long she was learning how to make dumplings. She proudly showed me her five-touch method, pressing her thumb into the hem of the dumplings. The man at the shop said she was an excellent worker.

One late afternoon, she dropped by my office with two shopping bags filled with dumplings. I was annoyed that she showed up without calling, but a colleague smelled the dumplings, and before long the conference room was filled with editors and assistants partaking of the feast. I introduced my sister, the dumpling queen, and the room applauded. Our publisher came up to us and said, his mouth filled with dumpling, "I didn't know you had a sister. We should do this more often." She chatted with two young, handsome guys from marketing; her tides were rising.

In early April, the tulips were in bloom along the Park Avenue median: from 54th Street to 86th Street, 60,000 bulbs in distinct blocks of color: pink, yellow, purple, red. Ollie took me there one predawn morning. She parted the carpet of flowers as she moved through them, dipping her hands into the sea of petals moving like waves. Hearing a police siren in the distance, I panicked. I wanted to take off, but Ollie wouldn't budge. She fell backward into the tulip bed and pulled me down with her. I felt the stems crush beneath me, petals falling on my face. Ollie threaded her fingers through mine. Twin Ophelias. Above us the sky turned indigo at the edges and the sun began its ascent. The police car, closer now, flashed its lights.

Ollie crouched, ready to run. I froze. She grabbed my hand and pulled me with her through the city's canyons.

Back at the apartment, Ollie couldn't sit down. She was fully charged, as if the walls of the apartment couldn't contain her. I knew she'd be leaving soon, and I couldn't do anything to stop her.

I floated the name of a highly regarded psychopharmacologist. "Been there, done that." When I tried to bring it up again, she was sharp: "I thought you were on my side." And later, "You really haven't changed." *Ollie straddling me, threatening to punch me in the face, pouring broth in my bed.*

"I want you to be safe," I said.

"There's no such thing."

Ollie pawed through a pile of clothes she'd amassed and took a few choice items, including a satin cadet's jacket she'd found in a dumpster near the Dakota. It had epaulets, fringe, and tassels, like the *Sgt. Pepper* album cover, and she was convinced it belonged to John Lennon. She left the rest behind, mostly things she had found on the street or possibly shoplifted. Like Josh, she was a great scavenger. *A snakeskin clutch, embroidered jeans, a paperweight with a thousand flowers bursting inside.* I checked the drawer beside my bed, where I kept a wad of cash tucked in an envelope; Marc had said it was good to always have a few hundred dollars on hand. She took the money and left Mary McGrath's two pins.

15

Courtney had something important to talk about. She said she waited until Ollie was "out of my hair." It was a Saturday morning, and she was hoping we could meet in person. I guessed that she had received a job offer at a competing publishing house. Courtney's reputation for picking celebrity bestsellers was well known in the industry, and it was inevitable that she'd be poached by another publisher. We met at Sarabeth's Kitchen. She loved the scones and pots of jam, lattes served in bowls big enough for a kitten to drink from. The walls were covered in chintz, and the tiny sconces had tiny pleated shades. The place was filled with women, multiple shopping bags pooled around their feet, some of them in tennis outfits. This, I'd learned, was a status symbol in Manhattan, showing off that you had married so well you didn't need to work. I despised it. Courtney, for all her success, aspired to it.

I squeezed myself into the banquette.

"Hey. What's up?"

Her shoulders trembled and she started to cry.

"Are you okay?" For a moment, I thought she might be sick. It also felt a little put-on. I knew Courtney well; she could work herself up over nothing in a matter of seconds.

· "Court, tell me."

She dropped her head.

"What is it?"

The words came out garbled. "Marc and I are in love."

She stopped crying, blotted her eyes with her finger, then fished in her bag for a tissue and gave her nose a good honk.

"What?"

"I waited to tell you."

"What? Since when?"

Courtney changed the date three times. "The New Year," she said.

"Around Thanksgiving."

And last, "I guess right before you guys ended it for good, last summer."

More words came out of her mouth: *I never meant for it to happen. It was so fast. I wouldn't have made the first move.* When I did not respond she issued more vapid, meaningless, insulting sentiments. *I would never do anything to hurt you. You are the best friend I've ever had. I would take a bullet for you, you know that?* Most galling, she said she had never been remotely attracted to Marc, even back in high school. It wasn't until after we separated that she saw him in a new light. *My light.*

I was suddenly sure that they'd been together even before we split, but when I challenged Courtney, she swore they hadn't been, and started crying all over again. Her tears hardened me. Then it hit me.

"You told him about Josh."

"No, I didn't."

"Courtney, what the fuck!"

"I mean I figured he knew."

I asked her to stop talking.

"Do you hate me?"

On some level, I had always been poised for this moment; Ollie was my first and best teacher in the art of betrayal. Only now was I in my mother's camp, having failed to see what was going on right in front of me. I couldn't tell if I was more ashamed or pained.

"I have to go," I said. Courtney begged me to stay, talk it through, but I didn't owe her anything.

"I didn't mean to," she pleaded.

My legs buckled as I tried to stand. Suddenly I was five years old again, when Ollie would take me to the skating rink. She'd skate backward holding my hands as I inched along on wobbly skates. She'd sing-song "Inchworm, inchworm," encouraging me to push forward, making sure I didn't fall. "Inchworm, inchworm," she sang over and over until we made it completely around the rink, where she'd hand me over to Dad. He and I would sit on the bleachers and watch her race around the rink, faster than the boys, skating backward and forward, weaving her legs in an elegant unbroken chainstitch.

I turned back as I pushed my way through the door. Courtney was signaling the waiter for the check.

TJ and I met at the Seattle Westin at the annual psychology conference. I went to a lot of academic conferences looking for potential authors. With Courtney out of my life as well as Marc, I was happy for any excuse to get out of the city. TJ's presentation was titled Empathy Project. It was the most well attended talk at the conference. He described empathy as a black hole in the field of social psychology. Most experiments designed to measure a person's empathy quotient relied entirely on self-reporting; his study challenged that approach. He was a fresh face, wearing blue-tinted aviator glasses, his thick, wavy hair pulled back into a ponytail. In academia he was a rock star.

A long line of students formed after his talk, eager to ask questions about his research. I waited at the end of the line, introduced myself, and gave him my card. Hoping my credentials as a New York editor would pique his interest, I asked if he'd like to go for coffee or a meal.

"How about now?" TJ said. "I'm ravenous."

We ate dry burgers in the Westin restaurant and talked until the place cleared out. TJ was eager for feedback, peppering me with questions about his performance, wanting to know what I really thought. "I can take it," he said. "Don't hold back. Be brutal!"

TJ knew his talk was the highlight of the conference, but I stroked his ego nonetheless. I had worked with authors long enough to understand their neediness and self-absorption. He basked in my compliments. When he seemed satisfied, he nodded in the direction of my half-eaten hamburger. "Are you going to finish that?"

"Go ahead," I said, pushing the plate toward him.

I watched him bite into my leftover burger, transgressive and intimate at the same time. I took in his blondish stubble, the fountain pen clipped to his breast pocket, his cuticles bitten to the quick. Of course, I also noticed his hammered gold wedding band. He wiped his mouth and asked if there was anything in his teeth, flashing them in a tight smile. TJ must have known from the start that I would be easy to seduce.

"Oh god, I haven't shut up," he said.

"No, it's fascinating."

"I feel like I can trust you."

"Of course," I said. *You can have me.*

TJ spoke more quietly, confessing that he might have compromised the research. The study utilized "decoys" dressed as homeless people panhandling at stoplights. Driver responses were ranked on a scale of 1 to 10, from disdain to compassion. TJ knew it was wrong to dress up as a decoy. "I just had to get out there myself and experience it."

Participating in your own study is frowned upon, especially among social scientists, because it potentially skews objectivity.

"You can't believe the footage!" TJ had caught people at their worst, showing disgust for their fellow humans, or their best, in a blend of sympathy and pity. "I know. It was crazy, but I had to," he said.

"I get it," I said, even though it went against all my beliefs about scientific methodology and integrity.

That night at the Westin, before our destiny would play out, TJ turned his bright light on me. "Tell me about yourself, Amy Shred, Editor, Rogers and Rogers," he said, reading from my business card.

I explained that I'd been recently promoted to full editor, that I worked closely with academics to turn their research into popular books. We were impressed with each other, both of us climbing the career ladder the way people do in their late twenties and early thirties, with so much to prove. The waiter left the bill and we both reached for it. I pulled the check from his hand and insisted on paying.

"I have an expense account," I said. "Besides, I'm wooing you."

"Is that what this is?"

The lights in the lobby dimmed. Going up in the elevator, we arrived at TJ's floor.

"You'll send me your thesis," I said and stuck out my hand. "It was great meeting you."

I wanted to follow him into his room and take off his glasses and his clothes and pull the rubber band from his ponytail, unfurl his beautiful hair, but I acted as if the dinner had been a purely professional transaction. TJ assured me he would send the manuscript after he put a few finishing touches on it and said good night. I rationalized that it was better this way, plus he kept twisting his wedding band.

The following week, TJ sent me his dissertation. I saw the potential, and we gave him a modest contract. He and I exchanged drafts until the book was ready for publication. It was a symbiotic relationship, a mutual admiration society. He loved my editing; I loved his revisions. Our notes in the margins of the manuscript became more flirtatious, more daring. Together, we had transformed his dry academic prose into a book for a popular audience. He compared me to Rumpelstiltskin, weaving his straw into gold.

"It's all you," I said. "The gold was there."

TJ called most days between three and four to go over my notes. I could hear Fiona chatting it up with him before sending the call over. It was annoying, but I knew he was an equal-opportunity flirt. I'd seen him charm the grumpy concierge at the Westin and make an elderly woman blush as he carried her suitcase to the curb. I'd close my door for our long editorial sessions, with TJ reading new pages aloud that he called "hot off the press."

I kept Fiona busy doing grunt work, reading the slush pile, clearing permissions for a five-volume book on physics. I never asked her to fetch coffee or make my appointments, the way Courtney and the other editors did. I considered myself one of the good bosses, but I discovered, too late, that Fiona was nursing a full-blown case of resentment, amassing a record of my offenses, and gossiping about me with the other assistants. I wondered if she could hear me laughing too loudly at TJ's jokes from inside my office, if she sniffed out my infatuation with him, but I was too caught up in TJ and our growing relationship to take heed.

TJ and I met for drinks at his hotel. He had come to New York to do publicity for his book, and he claimed to be nervous about doing interviews with NPR and other stations.

"You're a natural," I said and proposed a toast to his success, but TJ declined. "I'm not superstitious, but let's not jinx it," and we clinked to that. Our repartee was as quick and light as a birdie tapped back and forth over a badminton net.

"Can you stay for dinner? I don't feel like being alone." Not exactly the invitation I was hoping for, but good enough.

"Let me check my schedule."

We ordered hamburgers. TJ said it was our tradition, though it was only the second time we'd dined together. He added that his wife was a vegetarian. "It's a pleasure to dine with a carnivore," he said. I felt a flush of superiority over his wife, even though I knew it was ludicrous. He entertained me with stories of his grad students: the brownnosers, the grinds, the truly gifted. He talked about one young man who nearly lived in the lab. I confessed to TJ that I had been that person, the lead researcher at the Zuckerman Institute, as if I were the quarterback or the first violin.

"What were you working on?"

"I was trying to show how the freeze response works in the brain, like fight or flight."

He seemed sincerely interested and asked what drove me to choose that topic. I confessed that I had been so badly bullied in middle school and high school that sometimes I could barely move or speak. I told him about the time some boys found me in the band room eating my lunch. One of them, much taller than the others, with orange hair sprouting on his chin and legs, pushed over a few music stands and stood in front of me. He opened his fly. He had a poof of red pubic hair, and his penis was purple. It was my first encounter with a penis, and it terrified me. The other boys were barking encouragement. Cortisol flooded my nervous system, and I froze. The boy pushed his penis closer to my face, my mouth.

"Oh my god," TJ said. "What happened?"

"A teacher came in, and they took off."

"I'm so sorry."

"It wasn't great."

"I'm so, so sorry."

We ordered another glass of wine, and TJ confided in me about his daughter Daisy, who at three was already in treatment. She went into screaming fits and flapped her arms. TJ felt she would grow out of it, but his wife suspected she was on the spectrum and, having read everything she could find on autism, believed that early intervention was key.

"Sometimes I think Alice is making her autistic."

I knew you couldn't make anyone autistic. TJ said Alice had quit her lucrative job as a software consultant and was devoting all her time to Daisy. He was clearly building a "narrative" of marital discord, painting his wife as unavailable and obsessed with their daughter to the detriment of all else. But I couldn't be certain if I was reading the subtext correctly or manufacturing it, and the question hung in the air: would we sleep together? And if we did, what would happen, professionally and personally?

I wished he hadn't brought up his little girl. I was slightly crushed. Take that back: I was completely crushed.

The waiter came over and left the bill. I reached out to take it, and TJ grabbed my arm.

"No, no, this is on me."

"Don't be silly, it's a work expense," I said.

TJ was still holding my arm. "Do you want to come upstairs with me?"

His words loop-de-looped around my chest cavity. Deciding to sleep with a married man has to be a quick calculation, or you wouldn't do it. I didn't consider his wife or his daughter when we pulled off our clothes or, later, when we watched CNN and fed each other twenty-dollar jellybeans in bed.

TJ's publicist booked him on *Sixty Minutes*. It became one of their most watched segments that season. The videos of drivers (their faces blurred) confronted with the homeless decoys were riveting: locking their doors, rolling up their windows and turning away in disgust. Our national empathy, or lack thereof, was making headlines. The book went on to the bestseller list, and TJ was catapulted to fame. In a matter of weeks, he became known as the Empathy Guy. People stopped him in the street for autographs!

When he left for the airport to fly home, we didn't know what to say. I couldn't tell if it was the beginning or the end. They were heady days, with both of us caught up in the success of the book, which he sometimes referred to as "our baby." I tried not to imagine Alice and Daisy awaiting his return. I rode the Madison Avenue bus back to my apartment, my body raw and scraped out. I held my peacoat closed. I had torn my tights, and when I caught a woman staring at my bare skin, I glared back until she turned away. I was captivated by my reflection in the window. I was divorced, a successful book editor in New York City. I had a new lover, albeit one who was on his way back to his wife and child.

Alice called me at my office a few days later to let me know that I wasn't the only one. "Far from it."

She had had a feeling about me, she said, and TJ admitted it.

"He always comes back to me," she said. "And Daisy."

"I'm really sorry."

"Just so you know, he's using you."

I had planned to end it after Alice called, but it was harder to let go of TJ than I thought. I told myself that I was different, that I occupied an important place in his life. It was also hard to separate him from all the success, his and mine: I had been promoted to senior editor. All the important agents started calling for lunch dates, sending their A-list authors for my consideration. Of course, I knew that telling yourself you are special, the exception, should be a red flag.

Over the next few months, we'd meet up at academic conferences in cities where TJ was a keynote speaker. We'd play at being a couple, going to museums, strolling through gardens. In St. Louis, walking down a street of stately homes, we saw an "Open House" sign in front of one and decided to go in. The realtor, assuming we were married, started asking all kinds of questions. We supplied fictitious names from the annals of science for ourselves and our two children, later laughing at how clever we were.

We stopped by a bookstore, and the staff was happy to have TJ sign the stack of his books displayed on the front table. We ate barbecue back in our hotel room, still tasting the tangy sauce on our lips when we had sex.

On our last night in St. Louis, I woke up at four in the morning and TJ was gone. Something told me he was with the young woman from the bookstore. She had been so admiring of his work, so solicitous, holding open each book to make it easier for him to autograph. As she leaned over, there was just enough cleavage showing under a pretty camisole. Was there anything else she could do for him while he was in the city? She wrote her number on a promotional bookmark. I didn't have proof, but I changed my flight and left early that morning before TJ returned. I wasn't prepared to confront him, or myself.

When I discovered that he was also sleeping with his publicist, I berated myself for being so stupid. Did everyone at work know? Doubtless they did. Surely Fiona helped spread the word. Maybe he'd slept with her, too. I saw that TJ was a coward, and I knew I was too. Our passion was ginned up, the repartee hollow, the sex good for being raw and desperate but not much else. I believed that was enough for me, all I deserved.

I'd been skipping my sessions with Paul, using work and travel as an excuse. I didn't want to face him or what I imagined would be his disapproval, even though he was never judgmental. He didn't need to be; I knew my behavior was wrong, and I was punishing myself. Nonetheless, when I did show up for an appointment, I'd act surly and put-upon.

"Why don't you say what you're thinking," I'd challenge him.

Paul would circle his foot.

"Just say it. It's not as if I don't know."

"I'd like to hear from you."

"I'm a fool," I'd say, pivoting, trying for sympathy.

Paul remained quiet. I closed my eyes. *A sequence of cells replicating. Minerals crystallizing. Anita's hand wiping my father's mouth. TJ pushing my head into his lap in the back of a cab.*

"I can't do this," I said, trying not to cry.

"You are doing it. This is the work."

I never really understood how therapy was work. The refrain of Lorraine Shred in my head: *if people spent less time working on themselves and more time doing their jobs, the world would be a better place.* Paul asked if I ever thought about harming myself.

"No, no," I said, too ashamed to admit to flashes of stepping in front of a bus or jumping off the roof of my building.

"It's my responsibility to ask," he said, sounding apologetic. Now I couldn't stop crying.

"Amy, would it be helpful to come more often?"

"I don't know, maybe."

"We can also think about medication."

Prozac was the new miracle drug; it was even on the cover of *Time* magazine. People who had been depressed for decades suddenly woke up to smell the flowers. I'd grown dubious about medications, having seen everything thrown at Ollie to no avail. So I agreed to see Paul twice a week during those "crisis" months.

At the end of my session, I gathered my things and thanked Paul.

"We'll continue next time," he'd say, providing both comfort and cliffhanger.

"Can't wait," I'd replied.

Slowly, I came to view my actions with more leniency and less judgment. It wasn't a wide lane, but there was more room to maneuver. During that time, I joined the Y and started swimming regularly. I admonished myself: *sink or swim, Shred.* I became part of a group of dedicated morning swimmers, women who would greet one another in the dressing room, complain about the men who hogged the lanes, the high levels of chlorine, the weather, as we dressed and went on to our jobs. After a while I learned the others' names and they knew mine.

Courtney was desperate for my forgiveness, my blessing. I avoided her at work, didn't return her calls for a full six months after our showdown. I knew she hated being shut out and felt guilty about Marc, but she had taken a calculated risk with me, knowing that our friendship might not survive. One day in the company cafeteria, I spotted her at our old table by the window and joined her. I didn't think about it; I just did it.

"I've missed you, Shreddy," she said.

It was remarkable how easily we slipped back into our old roles, gossiping about coworkers and complaining about authors. As we were about to bus our trays, Courtney lowered her voice. "I don't know if you want to hear this," she said, "but we're going to get married. At City Hall. No big wedding or anything."

"Congrats."

"Maybe this isn't okay? To talk about?"

"No, it's fine."

In fact, it was torture. Paul suggested that I was punishing myself, but I believed that forcing myself to hear about their life together would make me stronger, more impervious to pain. I also knew that Courtney gave Marc what I couldn't: her whole self. She marched in and made your life better. She had done that with me, mentoring and encouraging me. She taught me everything about publishing and cheered loudest when the books I worked on hit the bestseller list or won a prize. Courtney had even managed to broker a détente between Marc and his mother. She got them talking on the phone, and now his mother and her partner were coming for Thanksgiving. Courtney, convinced that the three of us could be friends again, instigated a meeting between Marc and me. We met at the Bethesda Fountain in Central Park. I went with the best of intentions, but after a few pleasantries, I couldn't hold back.

"You slept with Court when we were still married, right?"

The question instantly pissed him off, and he scowled at me. He remained adamant that nothing had happened until after we split up. He reminded me that he had spent hours on getting me the power of attorney for Ollie, and I hadn't yet thanked him for the favor. And that he had done it for free. I took this as deflection and asked Marc again: "Did you?"

He refused to answer. How many times had I heard Marc prepare a witness: keep it simple, use plain language, say you don't know if you don't know, and only answer the question asked. People got into more trouble by answering questions no one asked, blathering on out of nervousness, guilt, or stupidity.

"Why can't you answer?"

"We fooled around, okay?"

"I knew it! I knew I was right," I said, with too much conviction, giddy over Marc's admission. "'Fooled around' meaning you fucked." I started laughing. "I knew it. I *knew* it."

"Okay, are we done?"

"It's kind of perfect. I mean, your high school crush!"

"Is this a joke to you?"

"That my husband and best friend were sleeping together when we were married. No, it's not. I'm just asking you to be truthful."

"The way you were about Josh?"

"At least we didn't fuck."

"You win, Amy. Are you happy now?"

TJ's questionable participation in the Empathy Project was leaked by a graduate student and reported in an academic journal. As a result, the study was scrutinized, and a symposium assembled in what was essentially a takedown of all his research. Not since B. F. Skinner raised his daughter in his experimental Skinner Box had the scientific community been so up in arms. The last time I spoke with TJ, he was licking his wounds, saying he stood by his work. Plus the book remained on the bestseller list, and a TV series was in the works. His academic reputation was tarnished, his ego bruised, but not much else.

"You're still proud of our baby, right?" he said.

I didn't answer.

He said he missed my blue pencil, he missed my tits (those small, perfect orbs).

"There's a conference in the Keys," he said. "We can go to Hemingway's house, see the great man's desk, his fishing rods, his inbred cats."

I was tempted. I was lonely. I declined.

16

I was at work when Mom's "man-friend" called me in a panic. That's what she called Sid Gottfried, the widower she'd met in the condo complex. They'd officially become a couple sometime after I got married and were still going strong. Though when I asked Mom if she loved him, she replied, "He's better than nothing." She said he was someone to go to the movies with; he was a decent bridge partner. One thing was clear: Sid loved her. He doted on her, opened doors for her, brought flowers on Friday night. She played it down, but I knew she cared for him.

Mom had a fall while giving her weekly docent tour at the Center for British Art. It happened in front of her favorite George Stubbs painting of a black-and-white zebra standing in a lush English forest. I'd watched my mother give this tour a few times, impressed with her style and how well she hit her scripted marks. The zebra, she'd explain, was the first one brought to England from South Africa, a gift to the young Princess Charlotte in 1762. "Imagine," my mother would say, "a horse with stripes!"

That day her legs suddenly gave out, and she fell, hitting her head on a corner of the painting and crumpling to the concrete floor. She was carried out of the museum on a stretcher.

In the days after the fall, my mother lost most of her motor coordination. She was dizzy and extremely nauseated. She slept twelve or more hours a day in the hospital, in and out of lucidity. Then her vision started to fail. Sid cried every time he visited, and she instructed him to stay away if he couldn't control himself. An MRI revealed a mass in her brain that had probably caused the fall. My mother chose to go into a nearby hospice facility. She was not prepared to spend the rest of her life unable to walk, talk, or toilet herself. I called Dad. He said it was quite a blow, but he didn't offer to come.

I moved into Mom's condo to be close to her. Every morning when I arrived at the hospice facility, she had a list of errands, from checking the oil in her car to donating her clothes to Goodwill. ("And don't forget to take the receipt! It's tax deductible!") Her once beautiful script had devolved into illegible scratches. I executed her orders perfectly, as if that would keep her alive. In the evenings before I left, she'd ask for Ollie. I checked with Dad, but he hadn't heard from her in quite a while. It was Hunt who came through for me. He tracked Ollie down in South Dakota, riding horses.

She arrived two days later, wearing denim and a cowboy hat and boots, smelling vaguely of hay. Ollie kissed my mother's cheek and said, "Hi, Mama." *Mama?* We never called her that. She drained the entire pitcher of water on Mom's bedside table and asked where she could wash up.

Our mother spent the days in a semi-twilight state. Ollie and I sat beside her bed, laughing and crying, playing gin rummy, and eating Tootsie Rolls from the hospice gift shop. To the nurses, we must have appeared as devoted, loving daughters, and I was glad for that. The illusion, if nothing else, was comforting.

Ollie stayed with Mom during the nights. In the morning, I would arrive with coffee for the two of us and find her asleep in bed with Mom. My mother had adamantly maintained that what Ollie had done to our family was unforgivable, but in those last days I saw how she needed Ollie and how natural it was for Ollie to soothe her as death drew near. I had been afraid to touch Mom, but Ollie polished her nails, combed her hair, swabbed her mouth with a sponge on the end of a stick. Was all forgiven, her golden-haired child returned on a crescent moon?

The day before she died, my mother patted the bed and asked both of us to sit with her. When we were little, she'd read to us separately at bedtime, calling us Bedbug 1 and Bedbug 2. Ollie would only listen to adventure stories: *Gulliver's Travels* and *Robinson Crusoe*, while I loved *Charlotte's Web* and *Black Beauty*. The one story we both could agree on was *Great Expectations*. Mom would impersonate the convict Magwitch, her impression so convincing that we'd scream and beg her to stop.

When Mom patted the bed, Ollie didn't hesitate and plopped down.

"Please, Bunny," my mother whispered to me.

I acquiesced, half sitting, half leaning against the bed. She reached up to touch our faces and said, "I wish you girls were married."

Ollie promised that we would take care of each other.

"That would make me very happy," Mom said, "to see you girls get along."

It wasn't a matter of getting along. We had long since jetti-soned family traditions like sharing holidays, sending Christ-mas gifts, making birthday calls. Mom had claimed that we would be best friends when we grew up, which struck me as a bit ambitious. In dark moments, I wondered who would be responsible for Ollie when our parents were gone, who would claim her body if she was found dead somewhere. How was it that we never spoke about that? My mother was a planner. It made no sense. Long ago, Dad had alluded to a trust if I needed financial help with Ollie. What did that even mean? Wasn't Ollie supposed to take care of me? The baby, the bun?

The nurse said Mom was getting close, maybe a day, two at most. Ollie took a cool compress and gently dabbed her forehead. Kissed her. As our mother drifted off, Ollie said over and over that she loved her. Then she abruptly announced that she needed some air and would be right back. She had been slipping out a few times each day and getting high on the Letting Go Trail, a winding asphalt path behind the facility, where patients could be walked around in their wheelchairs. She'd return reeking and assured me that the pot was medici-nal. Did I care? Along the path were stones painted with the words *Love, Angel, Stars, Dream*. The one time I took my mother on the trail, she said, "What a load of crap." The nurse and I stood by Mom's bed. She asked if Mother would want a rabbi or priest present. I tried not to laugh.

"I think she was waiting for that big sister of yours," the nurse said. "It's remarkable how people can hang on, waiting for that special person." I thought of pushing her and her pink breast-cancer pin down the stairs. Still adrift on a wave of morphine, my mother expelled a few short breaths in rapid succession, stopped, and started again.

"Should I get her?" I asked the nurse, attempting to quell my panic. I knew Mom would want Ollie, and I was terrified to witness her death. Suddenly, Mom took a few enormous gulps of air as if she were about to go underwater and hold her breath. Her head and neck tilted back, and her skin turned paper-white and taut, as if reversing years of aging. The nurse put her hand on my shoulder. "She's gone." No human sound came out of me.

I expected Ollie to be upset, missing what my mother sometimes called the Grand Finale. But when she came back to the room, she said, "Oh, wow."

Hunt flew from California for the funeral. Marc and Courtney drove up from Westchester, where they had moved after the twins were born. Courtney had traded in her career for the girls, a red Volvo, and a Labradoodle. I knew it was nice of them to come, but it made me a little sick, seeing my ex–best friend and my ex-husband together at my mother's funeral. They both had gained weight, so there was that to be happy about.

Kira came but was on her phone half the time. Sid's three adult sons were there or, as my mother referred to them, Huey, Dewey, and Louie. Colleagues from the museum, my mother's manicurist, her hairdresser, and a few of the drivers from the lumberyard were all there to pay their respects. The ladies from my mother's bridge club came even though they had stopped playing years ago. Another of my mother's aphorisms: "Everyone loves you when you're dead." Anita had a kidney stone, so she and my father stayed in Florida. I was outraged, then relieved.

There were around thirty people in the chapel at the funeral home; the funeral director quickly removed the empty chairs so the room would appear full. Ollie had put together a slide-show; watching the washed-out ghostly slides flash by, you could mistake us for an intact family. Even a happy one. My favorite, the four of us at the 1964 World's Fair, my mother's scarf caught in a bit of wind. My mother's ashes were in a handsome urn with a Jewish star carved on one side. How many times had she said we were bad Jews: never going to temple, not having bat mitzvahs, celebrating Christmas. Sometimes she said we would burn in hell—she made it sound deliciously appealing.

My mother had left instructions: she didn't want any pomp, just a simple service followed by a small but elegant shiva back at the house. The rent-a-rabbi asked us about our mother; we said she loved art, she loved bridge, she was a great cook. She asked if she was a good mother, and we agreed. Sure, why not? From this she scraped together a passable eulogy. I thanked everyone for coming and made a few remarks on behalf of Ollie and myself. I talked about how brave my mother was and praised her for always pushing me, for having high expectations. I said she had lived and died on her own terms, though that was a lie. Life had offered her a set of terms she could not abide. I had more written down, but I didn't finish—it was as if I heard the music that comes on when an actor's acceptance speech goes on too long. Olivia rested her head on Hunt's shoulder. He took her hand in his.

Back at the condo, Sid had ordered a platter of lox and bagels and whitefish salad and babka. A neighbor at the condo, a widow my mother was convinced had her eye on Sid, lent an enormous coffee urn that served endless cups of hot coffee, though the cream ran out early on. My mother would never have let such details slide. In the months and years after she died, I often saw the world through her eyes, as if I had inherited her mantle of judgment, her scoreboard in the sky. Those were the times I missed her most.

Before long, the solemn gathering morphed into a party. Sid broke out the whiskey, and people were joking, talking about *Seinfeld*, the popular new show about "nothing." One of Sid's sons did a Kramer imitation over and over, entering the room as if he had a gerbil in his pants. Marc and Courtney peeled off early: the babysitter! I thanked them profusely, as if they had cured world hunger, and I waved with both hands as they climbed into their Volvo.

My mother's manicurist trapped me on the deck. "She was a great lady, your mother."

I nodded.

"A great lady."

I hadn't cried during the service, but now the pressure behind my eyes started to build.

"She worried about you girls."

I wondered what exactly my mother had confided in this tiny Russian woman with too much blue eye shadow, week after week during her standing appointment. Now, imagining the intimacy they shared, there was no holding back my tears. The manicurist took my hand in hers; my nails were chipped like shale.

I visited Sid one time after my mother died. He was in his robe at eleven in the morning, and I asked if I should come back later. He insisted I come in. I recognized the woman who had brought the coffee urn eating a Danish at the breakfast table and paging through the circulars. Mom had called it. With Anita, she hadn't seen it coming; she was certain not to make the same mistake again.

She had told me that Sid would get snapped up, and she hoped he would. "Some people don't have the knack for being alone" is how she put it. "They're not strong the way we are." I never viewed my ability to be alone as a strength. It was more of a default. My mother would never admit that she had had a breakdown in slow motion after the divorce. The few times I suggested she talk to a therapist, she said she'd had enough of therapists and psychiatrists for a lifetime. Mom had chosen the unexamined life and stuck with it to her dying day.

Sid handed me a worn Saks Fifth Avenue bag. Inside was the accordion file I had found so long ago with our report cards. In another shopping bag, growing a fine fur of dust, was the pink neon sign for Ollie's bakery, Dough. I took that too. On my way out, Sid asked if I wanted her Nissan Versa, which I did not. Then he asked if I knew anyone who would take it off his hands.

17

It was captured on a security camera, but the image was too fuzzy to identify: a man harassing our doorman, shoving him, and storming off. I suspected it was Josh. Some months after my mother died, he and I had started talking again. I was lonely, and he would turn up with a box of miniature cupcakes; we'd stuff our faces watching old episodes of *The Honeymooners*. We went to the Cloisters in upper Manhattan, and he introduced me to the floor-to-ceiling tapestries known as the Hunt of the Unicorn. The final tapestry depicts the unicorn in captivity, encircled by a wooden fence. It struck me that the fence was too low to imprison the horned creature, but there he remained, bound by his mythical affliction. Outside in the medieval-style garden, we sat silently for a long time staring at the Hudson and the Palisades beyond. You could have mistaken us for an old married couple who'd run out of things to say.

Other times Josh seemed distracted or furtive. One night he came over for Chinese takeout and left before the food arrived. Another time he asked to borrow a hundred dollars, and when I said I had no cash, he asked if we could go to an

ATM. He grabbed the stack of twenties and ran off, saying he'd call. He showed up at my office completely obsessed with a potential book project. He'd found a secondhand copy of Hesse's *Siddhartha* that had belonged to the beat poet Allen Ginsberg. The pages were covered with Ginsberg's drawings, doodles, and lines of poetry. Josh wanted to publish them in a book: could I help? I wasn't immediately enthusiastic, and he said forget it, he'd find someone else.

Josh's dad was turning sixty, and his mother had planned a surprise birthday party at the Jersey shore. Josh asked me to rent a car for him. I offered to drive and go to the party with him, but he insisted on going alone.

"Unfinished business," he said.

I didn't want him driving a rental car under my name with an expired driver's license, but I gave in to his pleading. Josh returned the car on time, so I assumed my worries were unfounded, only a week later I got a letter from the New Jersey Transit Authority, reporting that the car had been tagged for going through a tollbooth near Atlantic City without paying. I called Josh for an explanation. He'd gone to the casinos; he didn't even try to deny it.

"You didn't go to your dad's party?"

"I'm a shit."

"Josh?"

"I couldn't face him."

"Are you kidding me?

"I mean, you met him," he said, as if that would make it all right.

I decided I wouldn't lend him any more money or let him crash on my couch. The next time he asked, I said, "Sorry, I can't."

"How's my sunshine?" Every morning, the man in the coffee truck outside my office building greeted me with a big smile, no matter how glum I looked. "Milk, one sugar, am I right?"

It struck me that in the middle of New York City, there was exactly one person who knew how I liked my coffee, and I couldn't decide if that was wonderful or pathetic. I had read in a women's magazine that having someone ask how you are every day boosts the immune system. Did the coffee man count?

I was heading in to work when Josh stepped out from behind the coffee truck wearing a filthy trench coat, his face partially obscured by a baseball cap.

"Josh, what the hell!"

"I need money."

"What the fuck, was that you at my apartment?"

"I'm sorry, I'm sorry."

"You can't come to my building like that. I live there."

"I'm really sorry."

"What are you on?"

He didn't answer. I bought him a cup of coffee and a giant glazed bear claw, and we went to a nearby park—not really a park, a half block of scummy café tables and a few trees that looked like upside-down brooms. He wolfed down the pastry, then threw up in a garbage can.

"Jesus, I'm sorry."

I searched for a napkin or tissue. His eyes and nose started leaking, and he used his sleeve to staunch the flow.

"Josh, I can't help you if you don't tell me what's going on."

As the herd of commuters stampeded by, the subway rumbling below, Josh admitted that he'd taken meth. "Love at first sight," he said. He was fired from his job; friends dropped away. Then Ellen had kicked him out. He lost or sold off his belongings and squatted in an East Village tenement until the building was razed. Then he joined up with a bunch of other addicts in Tompkins Square Park. He punctuated his monologue with the frequent refrain, "I know this is my fault. This is my fault." And he kept apologizing for all the times he'd hit me up for money.

"You asked me for money five minutes ago."

His lips were cracked, and his shoes were taped together with duct tape, like clown shoes. There was a faint pinprick in his earlobe where an earring used to be, probably pawned. He told me he had spotted his sister on the street. He was sure she recognized him, but she kept going. He saw disgust on her face, disgust on the faces of people passing by. He wanted to call out to her but feared she would reject him, tell their parents. He said it was like a movie of his childhood in some bizarre rewind: going back up a slide, falling up a flight of stairs. He had woken up that morning crumpled in the vestibule of a Fifth Avenue office building as a security guard approached, kicking his shins, telling him to move on.

He started heaving, but I didn't cave. He was looking for his next fix, not help. Perhaps he had already fished in my purse and nabbed my wallet. He stopped crying, having worn himself out like a newborn, and was wiping his face with a napkin. Josh used to carry a pressed handkerchief, sometimes wore suspenders and a fedora, affectations from previous decades. He called it panache. Sometimes he pulled it off, other times he appeared to be playing dress-up. He couldn't face me. He started sobbing and said he wanted to kill himself.

A few days later, after I'd made all the arrangements, Josh and I headed out to a Pennsylvania rehab. On the way, we got married in a church the size of a porta-potty and about as fragrant. It cost a hundred dollars, fifty for the marriage certificate and fifty for the ceremony, performed by a teenager wearing a Mötley Crüe T-shirt and a white satin vest. Josh, already in the early throes of withdrawal, could barely stand. Back in the car, he crawled into the back seat, threw up in a Wendy's bag from our last pit stop, and dozed on and off until the next craving kicked in.

I knew this plan was dicey, bordering on perilous, but he didn't have insurance; getting married was the only way to get him covered. The night before we left, Josh insisted we get grilled cheese sandwiches and milk shakes from the diner near my apartment. I wanted to pick up the food, but he insisted. Then he remembered that he needed money to pay for it, so I fished out a few bills from my wallet. I could feel his eyes on the money. He asked me to trust him. For the entire time that he was gone, I was convinced that he would buy drugs and reenter the addict's demimonde. I was prepared to never see him again.

Josh had already finished one of the milk shakes by the time he returned and was drinking mine. He couldn't eat any solid food. He told me he needed the bathroom; the next thing I knew, I heard the shower running. I ate my grilled cheese sandwich and stared at the shelf of books I had edited. I took TJ's down and read the dedication: For Alice and Daisy. Josh emerged from the shower with a towel around his waist and complimented the water pressure. He was so skinny. He had pulled out most of his chest hair, leaving only random tufts along the sunken floor of his chest.

A newly published biography of Brando described his psychoanalysis. Josh lay down on the couch and started to free-associate as Brando: riffs on food, booze, sex, drugs, acting. I suggested he stage a one-man show called "Brando on the Couch." We talked about renting a black-box theater. We'd hang posters in the middle of the night all over Soho and Tribeca with buckets of glue and fat brushes. We both knew none of it would happen. But that was our way of spinning dreams.

Having exhausted himself, Josh stretched out on the couch and fell asleep, his body covered in bruises, his arms scratched as if by thorns. He turned to the side, and I noticed what looked like a row of white satin buttons on a wedding dress down his back: they were the knobs on his spine.

On the drive to rehab, Josh needed to use a restroom every forty or so minutes. I was unaware that he had been snorting meth in the dank roadside bathrooms all along the interstate, and only realized later that he had been doing it in my bathroom the night before, covering the sound with the shower. After each stop, he would get back into the car, pop on his sunglasses, and fiddle with the radio or talk nonstop in his barely passable Brando accent, then crash. Going through Wilkes-Barre, he found a rock station. He rolled down the window, craned his head into the wind, and screamed the chorus: *And I still haven't found what I'm looking for.*

"Sing with me!"

I kept my eyes forward.

"You're no fun."

"You're kidding, right?"

"This could be your last chance." Josh closed his eyes and started dancing in his seat, until I reluctantly joined in. He gave me the hugest smile. That's one picture of him. Shortly after, he crashed again, sleeping with his head mashed up against the window, his hair flattened like a bug.

At the rehab, Josh nodded out during the intake interview; the social worker, who had seen this a million times, poked him in the arm with her pen, then let him sleep. She directed her questions to me, his wife. Treatment history, medical history, education, mental health history. Alcohol, substance abuse, suicide attempts. I made it up as I went along. There was only one question that tripped me up: how long had we been married? Um, three and a half hours. The social worker wrote it down. I figured we were hardly the first duo to have cooked up a similar scheme. She searched through Josh's bag and confiscated a few packets of meth, dropping them into a bag labeled *Substances.*

"Funny, they usually finish everything before they get here." She said Josh would be assessed. It would be a week or two before I could visit.

"He's got to detox first," she said and winked. I had no idea why; were we sharing a secret? She explained that there were groups during the week if I cared to participate. "I have to get back to my job," I said, "in the city." "It's not mandatory, but it usually helps both you and the addict," she added. She mentioned Al-Anon meetings and placed a brochure in front of me: "Codependent No More." The social worker was sorry she couldn't give us any time alone. They were ready to take Josh for a body-cavity search. "I don't make the rules," she said.

Why was it that the same people who didn't make the rules took such perverse pleasure in enforcing them. I felt as if they were taking Josh to the gas chamber and could barely watch as the orderly escorted him out. Josh turned back in abject terror, his face completely disorganized. I felt like his executioner.

"One more form," the social worker said, pushing a neon-yellow paper toward me. They wanted to know who to call in the event of an emergency.

I filled the tub with warm water and Epsom salts. My back was aching from the eight hours of driving there and back. Staring at the crumbling grout around the tub, I vowed to look for a new apartment. I avoided our doorman, hated the tinted mirror in the elevator, the lingering smell of someone else's cooking in the hallway. Memories of Marc, happy and unhappy.

Too keyed up to sleep, I picked up the phone to call my mother, then remembered she was dead. That happened often. I was so used to calling her, either in the morning before the office sprang to life or at the end of my workday, when I knew she'd be sitting down to the evening news. Sometimes I'd just stare at the phone. I would have given anything to hear her distracted voice, "Hi, Bun," as she filled in her beloved crossword. Sometimes, standing in a line at the bank or supermarket, I would fall into a mini-trance and fail to move up as the line advanced. The person behind me would gently tap my shoulder, as if awakening a sleepwalker.

I picked up the Saks bag Sid had given me and riffled through the tabs on the accordion file. Tucked behind Ollie's report cards was a file from The Place, fastened between brown covers with her name and case number on a label curling at the edges. The pages were wavy and stiff, as if they had survived a shipwreck. At the bottom of the first page was the date of her release, an embossed seal, and Dr. Simon's signature, his florid script taking up half the page. I sifted through a bunch of forms and disclaimers before I found a page titled Psychiatric Assessment:

Patient disregards authority.
Patient oppositional/defiant.
Patient believes she is exceptional; rules do not apply to her.
Patient lacks the capacity for introspection.
Patient exhibits impulsive, risk-taking behavior.
Patient exhibits hostility and outbursts of intense anger.
Patient needs to dominate all situations and people.
Patient lacks remorse.

Also listed were the medications Dr. Simon had prescribed over the course of her stay: mood stabilizers, antidepressants, antianxiety and antipsychosis medications. They sounded like elements on the periodic table: Thorazine, Lithium, Prolixin, Amoxapine, Clomipramine, Haldol. As soon as the long fingers of an active ingredient reached Ollie's brain circuitry, she rejected it. When none worked, Dr. Simon labeled her "treatment resistant." His diagnosis: Borderline personality disorder.

Dr. Lucie's meticulous notes followed. He had seen Olivia three times a week for fifty-minute sessions. He must have known that she was falling in love with him, but his notes were couched in cold medical parlance: *transference, projection.* If she wasn't overtly flirting with Dr. Lucie, she was full of bravado, talking about the other patients, how easy it was to dominate them, how they feared her and did her bidding, as if she were a Mafia don. She loathed Dr. S. and referred to him as a fascist, a pedophile, a limp dick, and power-hungry. The social workers were sorry excuses for human beings, with their clogs, corduroy skirts, and Swatch watches. She loved the orderlies, especially Jimmy, always ready with a light. These were her people.

Dr. Lucie had attempted to get her to talk about her childhood, our parents, but she stuck with generalizations: she loved our father and couldn't stand our mother. She said I was annoying but loyal. Dr. Lucie's notes described Ollie's body language, her grooming, and behaviors.

Patient wears provocative clothing.
Patient exhibits romantic feelings toward practitioner.
Patient flirts with practitioner.
Patient boasts of sexual conquests.

Patient seeks information about practitioner's private life.
Patient's transference is expressed in romantic/sexual terms.
Patient propositions practitioner.
Patient simulates masturbation.

Olivia!

He observed that she was often elevated and animated, but also occasionally subdued, tamped down. Contrary to Dr. Simon's assessment, his diagnosis was Bipolar Type I. He also described her as a "rapid cycler." Unlike people who sustained long periods of mania and depression, Ollie could fluctuate between highs and lows over months, weeks, or within a single day, or hour. This, he noted, was why she was difficult to diagnose and even more difficult to treat.

In summation, Dr. Lucie described my sister as funny, observant, quick, and intelligent. He believed that with ongoing therapy and the mood stabilizer lithium, she could lead a productive life.

I wondered what Ollie's life trajectory might have been had she followed Dr. Lucie's recommendation, stayed on the medication long enough for it to be effective, level out in her bloodstream, stabilize her moods. Or would it have been another ghost we were chasing? And who's to say Ollie didn't find her life satisfying? You could say she lived on her own terms, or you could dismiss her as mentally ill, the woman who continues to dance after the floor clears and the lights go down, listening to music only she can hear.

Washing up in my apartment that evening, I saw a mouse dart behind the toilet, and I jumped. How many mice had I killed in the lab? I imagined the bathroom filling up with flesh-eating mice, an army come to kill me. I climbed onto the toilet and wished that Marc were there to save me. The mouse didn't move. On closer inspection, it turned out to be a little brown baggie of meth. I flushed it down the toilet. I couldn't believe Josh, my first true friend, had gone so far out on a ledge.

I was awakened the next morning by a call from my boss. I had slept through the editorial meeting, and she was checking to see if I was okay.

"You never miss," she said. "I was worried." She suggested I take the day off.

My bed was covered in documents from the file, including a row of Ollie's school pictures, like Tarot cards with nothing to divine. I had forgotten that I'd had plugged in the *Dough* sign. In the daylight, the lurid pink neon cast a faint glow.

I decided to go to Sarabeth's Kitchen for breakfast. The hostess chirped, "Is someone joining you? I can't seat you until your party is complete."

"Just one," I said quietly.

I ate a waffle the size of a tennis racket and tried the four syrups in each of the waffle's quadrants. Just as I finished, the waitress asked if I wouldn't mind giving up my table. The line was "crazy," she said, slipping the bill between the sugar bowl and the miniature creamer.

I took a manuscript out of my tote, started reading, and asked for another coffee. The waitress and I locked eyes. Having lived as a couple, I understood that it conferred privileges, while being single invited speculation, pity. Some people in the line glared at me, while others vigilantly protected their place. New York was a Darwinian struggle for everything from parking spaces and corner offices to reservations and real estate. I thought about staying at my table until closing, watching the busboys mop up. As the waitress poured my coffee, she regarded me the way a parent silently scolds a child. I imagined she took as many dance and acting classes as her tips would pay for and that she would never make it to Broadway, not even as one of the kids in the chorus. The city would flush her as it did all of those chasing fame. I had come to New York for its abundant anonymity. No matter what your desires, this was a city of chutes and ladders.

On the D train to Coney Island, I gave up my seat to a pregnant woman with a toddler, watched a woman in a shearling coat put on an entire face of makeup, as if she were in front of her bathroom mirror. Josh loved the amusement park and beach, the much reduced but dedicated band of freaks who performed at the famous sideshow, the elderly Russian women, arms linked as they slowly strolled the boardwalk. He would take my arm and talk in a Russian accent about Pasternak and Pushkin. We'd go to Brighton Beach for pierogi and borscht. Today the boardwalk was empty, gulls circling and crying in the cold November air. I stared at the bleached slats of the boardwalk, the closed concessions, the carcass of the Cyclone in the distance.

Fiona's cubicle was cleaned out when I returned the next day, and there was a message for me to go to Human Resources. I felt like I was waiting outside the principal's office except for the brochures on retirement and 401K plans. When Dennis Bowman, the HR director, opened the door, an enormous fake smile crossed his face. His bald head was glossy, and he wore a deep blue shirt. "Amy, come in." I took a seat, and he struck a casual pose, leaning against his desk.

"As you've probably gathered, Fiona has left her position."

"What happened—is she okay?"

Dennis closed the door, instantly raising the stakes. I couldn't imagine what happened to Fiona. Then he sat down and knocked his knuckles together.

"She filed a complaint."

"What?"

"She said she couldn't work with you."

"What? Why?" I prayed this wasn't about TJ.

"She said you were rude and dismissive."

I cough-laughed.

"Actually, she has a long list of grievances."

"Really?" I couldn't tell if I was burning with shame or anger.

"She said you didn't include her in projects, that you barely said hello or made eye contact."

Where was this going? "I'm sorry, what?"

"Please don't get defensive," Dennis said, instantly ratcheting up my defenses.

"You can't be serious."

"I know it's hard to listen to." I was convinced Dennis was enjoying this.

"Sorry," I said.

"Fiona claims she handled all the work when your mother passed and that you never acknowledged her efforts."

"She's using my mother's death. That's rich."

It was true that I was behind on all my projects after taking a month off to be with my mother before she died. Fiona had kept the office on track, attending my meetings and sending me fastidious minutes. She had edited a few chapters of a manuscript and sent it to the author without my permission. I didn't know if I should praise her for taking the initiative or admonish her for usurping my job. Instead I punished her with my stoniness.

"Amy, let me finish." Dennis let out a sigh. "She said you were mean." Of all the accusations, that stung me the most. I knew I couldn't defend my actions. I had been mean and withholding. I'd been cold.

"We're reviewing resumes for a new assistant, but this does go in your file. You're fortunate she didn't want to take it to the next level."

Next level? File? I'd never had a single mark against my name.

"I'm recommending a few sessions with a counselor here in HR."

"I'll pass."

"It's not optional," Dennis said, blinking slowly.

"I don't need counseling."

"It's corporate protocol after a complaint has been officially filed."

I stood up to leave, the back of my shirt soaked with sweat.

"You're an important member of our team," Dennis said, a sentiment lifted from an HR handbook, followed by a more personal but equally unctuous note: "And Amy, I'm sorry for your loss."

It was a Saturday morning, and I was on my couch working on the crossword when the phone rang. I had gotten the hang of doing the puzzle and felt a kinship with Mom as I penciled my answers in the squares. The person on the line introduced himself as the patient relations officer. He sounded official, scripted, and he delivered the news in the deep, steady voice of a TV anchorman: my husband had died early that morning. My husband? Marc? He kept talking, but his voice was a stream of white noise—inaudible frequencies across the spectrum of sound.

"Ma'am, are you there?"

I'm not here.

"Is this Amy Shred?"

No.

"Ma'am. Is anyone with you?"

Please stop calling me ma'am.

The man said he wasn't at liberty to disclose the cause of death until there was an investigation and autopsy. He was obliged to mention body removal and options and liability for the rest of the first thirty days, as per the contract. I realized then that he was talking about Josh. A flock of pigeons exploded off the window ledge, scattered in the sky, then disappeared.

I called Josh's parents. It wasn't for me to arrange his removal, bury him, or have his body cremated. He was no longer mine. He belonged with them. His mom invited me to the funeral.

I said I'd be there but I didn't go. I couldn't face Josh's father, who had taken every opportunity to humiliate and diminish his son. Was he happy now? His mother sent me a note, thanking me for being a friend, extending an open invitation to visit the grave and have lunch at their home. When the autopsy report arrived, it showed both heroin and methamphetamine in Josh's body. Apparently, nowhere on earth were drugs more plentiful and easily procured than in our nation's rehabs.

The one weekend I had visited Josh at the rehab, I thought he was getting better. I realized now that he was putting on a show for me, making me laugh. He called me "wife" and "woman," and kept asking if I would be there when he came home, as if he were a soldier away at war. I participated in a group family session that reminded me of Ollie and The Place. The same concepts and stock phrases: self-acceptance, one day at a time, self-care, brutal honesty. I could barely sit still, listening to each tale of woe while Josh nodded off. One of the social workers was arranging pastries on a tray off to the side. I watched her lick some icing off her finger.

Visiting hours almost over, Josh and I had parked ourselves at a picnic table on the perimeter of the grounds. I noticed a grove of birch trees, whose peeling white bark reminded me of ancient scrolls. Seeing some bird poop on the table, I mentioned our family's aborted trip to DC and the pandas I never got to see. Josh promised to take me to the zoo. As with all our fantasies, I knew it wouldn't come to pass, but that wasn't the point. He hugged me hard. I could feel my chest heaving against his.

A loud bell rang. "Five minutes, people!" someone called out.

I saw Josh take the stage. He was in makeup and costume, top hat and tails. Everything that was about to happen had already happened. The spotlight found him. He tapped his cane: Five, six, seven, eight.

"You're gonna be great," I said, no longer able to contain my tears.

"Good as new," he said, and pressed his forehead into mine, conjoined twins for the last time.

Couples and families were moving toward the parking lot, as slowly and heavily as a herd of elephants. We hugged one last time.

"I love you, Shred."

"I love you, too," I said.

The final bell rang, and I pushed my body up the grassy hill toward the parking lot.

18

Ollie didn't know she was pregnant. She was as reckless with birth control as with everything in her life.
Plus, she often missed her period for months, so she
didn't suspect it and didn't start showing until her fifth month.
When it became clear that she would have to keep the baby,
she showed up at Dad's condo unannounced, wearing designer
jeans and pink Uggs as if she were home for the holidays. Dad
asked if Hunter was the father.

"Don't know," Ollie said.

"Where is Hunt?" Dad asked.

"Where he always is."

As ever, Dad took Ollie in, stopped asking questions, no
further accountability required.

"You're enabling her," Anita told my father, using the new
addiction vocabulary that had seeped into the mainstream.

"What am I supposed to do, disable her?"

For all of Anita's tough-love talk, she too fell under Ollie's
sway. She couldn't go to the store for milk without picking
up a little rattle or toy for the baby. She started calling Dad
"Gramps" and referring to herself in the third person as
"Nonie." Through an acquaintance of Anita's, Ollie got a job

working at Juice World. Anita found a small but pretty two-bedroom apartment for her on the beach, furnished the nursery with a crib and changing table, and had a mural of elves and fairies painted on one wall. Dad was happy to write the checks. Ollie grew close to Anita during the final months of her pregnancy. Dad said she appreciated Anita's help decorating the apartment, finding an obstetrician, picking up prenatal vitamins at the drugstore.

We all hoped that Hunt was the father. He'd never stopped loving her. He'd produced a movie based on a comic book Ollie discovered at a flea market. The movie turned out to be a hit on the indie festival circuit, picking up a few prizes, establishing the career of a young quirky director, and launching an unknown actress who had a shaved head and a raspy voice. Hunt had asked Ollie to marry him many times, but after the success of the film, he bent down on one knee and presented a ring. Didn't their success prove what an amazing team they made? Ollie told Hunt to marry a normal girl and have a normal family. He shouldn't wait for her. She could never be that person, and she was gone the next day. It had been over six months since he'd heard from her.

I flew to California under the pretense of meeting an author, but I was there to see Hunt. I called him against Ollie's wishes; she didn't want me to tell him about the baby that was due in two months. He picked me up at my hotel and drove out to the beach. It was late afternoon, overcast. The only people on the beach were a few fishermen, their poles planted in the sand, and a man throwing a ball into the water as his dog wildly crashed through the waves to retrieve it.

Walking along the frilly hem of the waves, Hunt confided that after Ollie rejected his proposal, he'd made a series of impulsive decisions that turned out to be disastrous. First he started dating a film and television agent, Ivy Cross, a rising star in the industry. Six weeks after they started going out, they drove to the Strip on a whim. After two days and nights of heady and intoxicating connection, sexual and otherwise, they waltzed into the Clark County Marriage License Bureau, like so many doomed couples before them, and on to the Chapel of Love.

Ivy fell in love with a three-bedroom house built in the forties on two acres of premium Malibu real estate. "The realtor said Spencer Tracy lived there when he was shooting *Father of the Bride*. They'll tell you anything out here."

We walked back to the car and watched the sunset, blurry through the fog. Hunt told me he had kept his home in West Hollywood, having convinced Ivy it was a bad time to sell; he would keep it for investment purposes. Of course, the real reason was Ollie; the idea that she would turn up at the house and find other people living there was unthinkable to him.

Ivy wanted to start a family, Hunt said he needed time.

"I bolted. I went to Prague. I used the excuse that one of my indie directors needed me on set. Total bullshit. I'd watch the dailies alone at night, all the lights off, guzzling vodka." He added, "I'm not proud of any of this."

Seven weeks later, when he returned home after the shoot wrapped, Ivy revealed that she had fallen in love with one of her actor clients. Hunt laughed uproariously at this. "An actor loving anyone other than himself, ha!" He admitted that their affair should have ended in Vegas. It had been a desperate, misguided attempt at marriage between two people who were clearly better on paper than in real life.

"Tell me about it," I said.

"And I was just so pissed at Ollie."

That's when I told him about the baby. I saw him count the months backward in his head. "Is it mine?"

"I don't know," I said. "You tell me."

Everyone at Juice World loved Ollie. Dad and Anita would stop by the store, happy to wait in line (no special treatment!) and watch Ollie press juices, wipe down the counter, banter with the customers. Many asked when the baby was due and what she was having. Ollie didn't want to know the sex of her baby. Had she come up with any names? Yes, she said and rattled off the names of juices: Mango, Papaya, Carrot, Beet. The customers found this hilarious. One month after getting the job, Ollie was promoted to assistant manager. She had two sets of keys, one to lock up the place, the other for the register.

Dad was so proud. I asked him if he was worried about her having keys and access to the cash register; he asked me to keep my negativity to myself. He said her life was on track. Plus he was going to be a grandfather. In the end, Dad said, what do we really leave behind but these little people with our DNA?

"What about the seventy thousand she stole from you?"

"Don't worry, you'll get your share."

"That's not what I'm saying."

⚜

Ollie and Anita went to Lamaze classes, which Ollie claimed were a waste of time. "Humor me!" Anita said. Ollie wasn't interested in natural childbirth; for all her fearlessness, she was terrified of pain. She said she'd get a C-section. Madonna had one, she reported. "Lots of actresses have them to stay intact."

Anita wanted to shop for maternity clothes; instead, Ollie bought some men's pants at an Army and Navy store and they served her throughout the pregnancy. Anita loved taking her for checkups. "She's way more excited than I am," Ollie said. She hated the changes pregnancy wrought on her body. Her dark, enlarged nipples. The line that ran from her belly button to her pubis. She said she was grossed out by her belly button, now a fat twisted knot.

The Lamaze teacher assumed Ollie and Anita were mother and daughter, and they didn't correct her. There was a gay couple in the group, two men who were preparing to be in the delivery room with the surrogate giving birth to their twins. They took turns stuffing a pillow under their shirts during the breathing exercises.

Ollie became friends with Al and Gerry, who lived on a canal and had a rooftop terrace where the three of them spent long relaxing evenings. They served her pregnancy-power foods: berries, raw almonds, yams, and Al's special three-bean salad. Sometimes Ollie would show up with a bag of Burger King, and they would flip out while she languidly dragged a French fry through the ketchup.

When Gerry and Al's surrogate went into labor, they asked Ollie to stay in their home and take care of the dog, also named Olly, "with a Y!"—a coincidence that further sealed their friendship. She felt calm on their rooftop watching the sun go down. I remembered when Ollie didn't have the patience to watch sunsets. She went back to keeping a journal, and I imagined her flicking a pen between her fingers like a mini-baton, the way she did in high school.

Ollie and Anita decorated the house with pink and blue balloons when Gerry and Al returned home with the twins. Ollie admitted to me that she felt guilty; here were these two men who had depleted their bank accounts and retirement funds in their quest to have a family. Ollie had become pregnant without trying. She wasn't even sure she wanted it.

I went to Florida a week before the baby's due date; Ollie had asked me to be her birth partner. She was grateful to Anita for all she had done but said she needed me in the delivery room. No matter how desperately I always wanted Ollie to choose me, I resented it when she summoned me. She had skipped my high school and college graduations, missed my wedding—and my divorce, for that matter. I didn't appreciate how our dad had deemed her god's gift to heredity. What had she done but screw some guy? Probably a stranger, on a train or plane. I had contemplated not going. I was so conflicted that I called Paul between our regular sessions, something I had never done.

He asked what was keeping me from going.

"Self-preservation!"

On top of that, I said, I didn't know anything about child-birth. Paul, who rarely offered advice, directed me to get on a plane as soon as possible.

"Why should I?"

"You'll regret not going."

"We're home!" Anita and Ollie came through the door with shopping bags labeled "BUYBUY BABY." My plane was early, and they weren't expecting me yet. I stared at Ollie, thirty-eight weeks pregnant, standing in the doorway in a crop-top T-shirt that said JUICE WORLD, her belly enormous.

"Don't say anything," Ollie said.

"What."

"I'm ginormous."

When Anita wasn't around, Ollie and I gossiped about her. She infantilized Dad, she dyed her hair too dark, and what was with the name Nonie?

"Did you know she lost a baby?" Ollie asked me.

On one of their car rides home from Lamaze, Anita revealed that she had been married before, a secret she had kept from our father. She confided that she had become pregnant when she was in college, and her parents forced the young man to marry her. The baby was stillborn, and her husband of six months stopped coming home at night. Anita imagined he had taken off with another woman, but learned that he had moved back in with his mother. Anita fell into a depression, or, as she put it, "postpartum depression minus the baby." The marriage was annulled. She went back to school, received a degree in design from the University of Cincinnati, and worked for a local architect. It was by chance that she met our dad at a design show in Boston.

❖

Ollie was frantic. Either her water had broken or she peed herself, she couldn't tell which. We had been watching a movie at her apartment, and she started pacing in circles.

"I can't do this. I can't do this. I can't do this."

When we arrived at the hospital, she was already nine centimeters dilated, too late for an epidural. Ollie asked to have a C-section.

"You're ready to give birth, my love," the doctor said, then turned to me. "Are you the partner?"

Ollie screamed as another contraction zippered through her body.

"I can't do this. I can't."

Ollie had also asked if I would be the child's guardian if anything happened to her. She knew Anita would want the baby, but she said it had to be me, and she hoped the kid would get some of my brains. She apologized for taking my money and leaving New York without saying goodbye.

"I don't care about the money" was all I could think of saying. "Lame Aim," she used to call me. Ollie believed she would be a terrible mother, that she didn't have any maternal instinct. She was convinced that when the baby cried in the middle of the night, she wouldn't hear it, or she'd forget the baby in a department store or lock it in the car on a broiling August day. She didn't trust herself.

She shouldn't trust herself! I had no idea what to tell her. She had left a trail of hurt, all in service of her restless, fevered, formidable mind. Live free, or what?—Live like the rest of us, live like me? For Ollie there seemed to be an unlimited cup of possibility, a bank of brilliant clouds against a perfect blue sky, a taut ribbon flickering in the distance. As Dad always said when Ollie crossed the finish line, "Your sister is a winner."

The baby's crown appeared, and the doctor urged, "Now, push!" Ollie pressed her eyes shut, and her body became a muscle, the tendons in her neck taut. My sister the athlete. *Soft gravel beneath her feet, crowds cheering from the bleachers.* She grabbed my hand and pushed again. I knew I was supposed to encourage her, tell her "You're doing great," and "Just a little more," but I froze. The doctor told Ollie to push again. Dazed from the pain and exertion, she fell back against the pillows and started to cry. "I can't do this. I can't do this."

I leaned in and whispered in her ear, "Inchworm, inchworm."

"This is it," the doctor said. "*Push*, Olivia!"

She squeezed my hand so hard that the bruises didn't appear until a day later. The baby entered the world.

"You did it," I said, and Ollie opened her eyes.

19

The groundskeeper gave me a map marked with X's, something a child would draw with crayons for a treasure hunt. He'd offered to drive me in his cart amid the shovels and hoes, and for a second I imagined he might murder me *and* dig my grave. I thanked him, saying I'd prefer to find Josh's grave on my own. He said it's a free country.

It had been a month or more since Ollie had given birth and returned to LA, to Hunt. I couldn't identify a reason for wanting to visit the grave; it was just something I felt compelled to do. It started to drizzle as I walked up and down the rows of headstones, longing for the earth to give up her secrets. I hoped that Josh would materialize and we would take shelter in one of the granite mausoleums as the wind picked up. I found his headstone and my breath caught; fat tears fell. The anger I felt when Josh overdosed swelled again, and I wanted to kick over the tombstone. I remembered the boy in my class who died of leukemia. He didn't have a say in the matter. He would never go to college, fall in love, kiss a baby's round head. I wished I hadn't taken Josh to rehab. I believed I had hastened his death, signed his death warrant. I would never forgive myself.

The rock I brought to leave on his grave was dark gray with a white line around the middle. As children, Ollie and I called them wishing stones and believed they had magical powers. I gave the best one in my collection to Mom for Mother's Day. Not the biggest, but it had an unbroken ring. These were said to be the most powerful, and if you made a wish for someone else, all your own wishes would come true. I begged Mom to tell me what she wished for, but she zipped her mouth and threw away an imaginary key. As she tucked me in that night, she leaned over and whispered in my ear, "I wished that all your dreams come true." I later learned in geology class that the stripe around the stone was formed by an imbalance of minerals; liquid quartz and calcite inside the rock filled the fissures and cracks. I warmed the stone in my hand before leaving it on the grave.

Josh's mother picked me up at the cemetery. She couldn't thank me enough for coming and I didn't know what to say. She had cooked up a feast and I could barely eat. Josh's dad was working, but he'd be home soon, she said. His sister and her fiancé were visiting, but they were not interested in me or the fact that I had visited Josh's grave. They were planning their destination wedding. I wanted to ask his sister if she had seen Josh on the street that day in Midtown when he believed he saw her, but I was too polite. At one point during lunch his mother told me, apropos of nothing, that I was a beautiful girl and she wished Josh had married me. Before leaving, I asked if I could see Josh's room. It was much smaller than I remembered. The tea stain on the ceiling was still there. *Please walk through the door. Please come back.*

Josh's father returned just as I was getting ready to leave. I wanted to call a cab, but he insisted on taking me to the train. His mother gave me a huge hug and told me to come back any time. Then she handed me a shopping bag filled with food wrapped in foil and a manila envelope on top. I tried to decline, but she insisted.

On the way to the train, it seemed as if Josh's father had something he wanted to say, but we rode in silence. As we pulled into the station, he urged me to open the manila envelope. Inside was Josh's Boy Scout sash with six badges sewn on, memorializing all things noble and worthy: Archery, Astronomy, First Aid, Pioneer, Life Saving, Citizen of the World.

"We bought the uniform, all the camping gear. He had his mind set on getting all twenty-one badges to make Eagle Scout."

I ran my finger around the stitching.

"He never finished anything."

I couldn't make eye contact. I didn't thank him. I knew he'd lost a son, but even now he couldn't pass up an opportunity to register his disappointment in Josh.

I got out and started walking toward the platform. Josh's dad got out of the car and called me back.

I kept going.

He caught up as the train pulled into the station and handed me the shopping bag. "You forgot this," he said. When the conductor came around and took my ticket, he asked if I could smile for him. *No, I can't.*

Back in my apartment, I was putting the food away when I noticed something underneath the foil. It was Josh's battered leather jacket. It held the shape of his body, the shoulders and elbows. I put it on half-expecting to burst into flame. At the bottom of the bag, I found a book of Walt Whitman poems that Josh must have swiped from a library, the call number pasted to the spine. Many pages were dog-eared, and I flipped through them until I landed on a poem titled "As I Lay with My Head in Your Lap Camerado." As I read the poem, I began to understand what Josh and I were to each other: not lovers, not husband and wife, not even best friends. We were *camerados* on the high seas. Josh couldn't accept a higher power. He didn't believe he was powerless over anything. He didn't want to live one day at a time. He didn't want to live one day.

"Get on the next plane," Anita commanded. "Your dad had another stroke."

He'd had the first one shortly after Ollie gave birth. He was on the fifteenth hole after sinking a putt from five feet; the sound of the ball dropping into a cup was what my father lived for, a little thumbs-up from the universe, a perfect plunk. He had slid back into the golf cart, preparing to record his score when, he said, his brain locked up. Later, he would admit that he'd been having little warnings. Numbness in his face, blurry vision while driving, balance problems. His buddies lowered Dad onto the putting green, and the ambulance drove right up to the hole.

After the hospital, he was sent to rehab, where we learned that he would spend the rest of his life in a wheelchair, his sharp mind a step or two behind. On top of that, he had to pay for resurfacing the fairway where the ambulance had churned up grass. Even more insulting, the hole came to be known as Shred's Stroke.

Anita told me to pack a dress and call Ollie, who was in LA, living with Hunt and the baby, now a year old. When I reached Ollie, she said she would take the next plane, but when I suggested she pack something black, she refused. "Dad will be okay," she said. I wasn't sure what there was to hope for. After his first stroke, Dad was already confined to a wheelchair and had little interest in life. He'd stopped watching television, lost interest in most foods apart from Pizza Bites. Anita tried to get him to play poker with the guys, but he couldn't hold the cards and refused to use a card holder.

"It was emasculating," Anita said.

Ollie and I believed he was depressed, but Anita said it was cognitive impairment. He had become dependent on her for everything.

"Where is he now?" I asked Anita, trying to picture what was going on.

"He's in an ambulance. I'm on my way to the hospital."

"How bad was it this time?" I asked.

"Not good."

It was night when I arrived. I found Anita sitting outside Dad's room. Her eyes were closed, and I thought she might be asleep or praying. When I touched her on the shoulder, she jumped.

"Amy! You scared me."

"Sorry."

She looked at her watch. "You made good time."

"How is he? How are you?"

"How do I look?"

"Can I go in?"

"He's not responsive," she said. "You can talk to him, though. The nurses say he can hear us."

Two thin tubes kept oxygen flowing into his nostrils; drugs dripped from a plastic bag into a port in his arm. On the monitor a green line zigged up and down. Dad's thick head of hair hadn't diminished, though it was whiter. Mom had always been taken with his hair and his height. Getting closer, I saw that his skin was gray, the stubble on his face a fine dusting of first snow.

I tried to speak, but I felt self-conscious. I remembered being so proud when I trailed behind him selling brooms door-to-door for the Lion's Club, with a cigar box to collect the cash. The song "Windy" popped into my head, singing it in the car with Ollie cranking up the volume. I half believed the song was about her, the girl with stormy eyes. Now, when I attempted to hum it, nothing came out. I tried again and a thin sound choked in my throat. I touched his hair. I cupped his hand. I wasn't sure if I believed the nurses that he could hear us but I rested my cheek against his and whispered, "Hi Daddy. It's me. Your Bunny."

Anita and I settled into a booth at a Red Lobster and ordered lobster rolls. "I never eat French fries," she said, "but what the hell."

"Go for it," I said weakly.

"You know, your father is a good man," she said, unfurling her napkin, the cutlery spilling out on the table. My hand was resting there, and I flashed on her stabbing it with a fork. I told her I was grateful to her for taking care of Dad. "Thank you, Amy, that means a lot."

⚜

Dad died alone in the middle of the night. The nurse told us he went peacefully, and Anita thanked her.

"Do you think they say that so you don't feel guilty for not being there?" I asked Anita.

"I don't feel guilty," she said.

I picked Ollie up at the airport later that morning. She looked beautiful even after an all-night flight, her hair in a messy bun. She took one look at my face and knew.

"Fuck," she said. "Fuck, fuck, fuck." Then, "How's Nonie taking it?" and we both cracked up. True to her word, she had packed nothing for the eventuality of Dad dying. On the way back to the condo, we stopped at Neiman Marcus and Ollie purchased a sleeveless black linen dress. I mentioned that Mom would not approve of a sleeveless dress at a funeral.

"Then it's perfect," she said, and handed the salesclerk a credit card.

"How did that feel?" I asked as we left the store.

"What?"

"Paying for something."

"Ha ha. I'm on the straight and narrow now, Sis."

"Good to know."

"You don't believe me."

"If you say so."

She threaded her arm through mine. "Benefit of the doubt?"

"Sure," I said, and we picked up the pace.

⚜

We buried my father on a humid day. Hunt flew in with Raine. (Ollie named her Raine, shortened from Lorraine, after our mother.) Four men holding thick straps lowered my father's casket into the ground in incremental drops, the way an elevator jolts before it lands, causing the same sick feeling in my gut. Then they retrieved the straps and wound them around their hands in tight coils. Anita leaned over and asked if we had to tip them.

As I waited in the driveway for a taxi before flying back to New York, Anita said that Dad was very proud of me and my career. She said he loved receiving the books I had edited and would read out loud the passages in the acknowledgments pages where authors often thanked me.

"Thanks for telling me that," I said.

"By the way, in case you're wondering, after I die, your dad's estate gets divided two-thirds to Ollie and one-third to you."

I didn't know what to say. Ollie and Hunt had plenty of money, while I was living on an editor's salary. It wasn't even the money, though it also *was* the money, all the cash Dad had fronted Ollie over the years. It was just so wrong.

"You don't have any children," she said by way of explanation.

"Right," I said, though later, in the cab and on the plane, and then for weeks and months to come, I replayed all the things I wish I had said in the moment, starting with "Fuck you, Anita" and ending with "You don't have any children either."

"We decided it was fair."

"We?"

"Your dad and me."

I was certain it was Anita's idea and not my cognitively impaired father's. I knew that she resented me the moment Ollie designated me as her birth partner and Raine's guardian. And long before that, when I intuited that she was sleeping with Dad and stopped coming to the lumberyard, stopped being her little friend. It was also more convenient for me to park the blame with her than deal with my feelings of having been abandoned. (Paul's insight. Thank you, Paul.)

On the day of my wedding, Dad had said, "Be happy, Bunny." And when I divorced, he said, "Welcome to the club." We both laughed, though he for a little too long. Then he asked if I needed money for a lawyer. I said I was trying to get rid of a lawyer, *ha ha*. My father wrapped me in his arms and said, "That guy just lost the best thing he ever had."

I wished I had been kinder to Dad after he left my mother. I had been too hard, and now it was too late.

The cab company called and said they were running late. Anita asked if I had sunscreen on.

Hunt never took a paternity test; he didn't care if he was the biological father or not. This child had brought Ollie back to him. And he was smitten.

In the weeks and months following Raine's birth, Ollie struggled with debilitating postpartum depression. Hunt hired a woman named Lillian to take care of the baby. But Lillian's true gift to their family was healing Ollie, who at first refused to see or nurse Raine, icing her breasts with bags of frozen peas to keep the milk from coming in, keeping the blinds drawn and the TV on without the sound, her room bathed in the artificial blue light of a squalid aquarium. Lillian could only get her to drink smoothies that she laced with protein powder and Omega-3 fatty acids.

I called Hunt almost every day for updates. Ollie refused to get on the phone. Lillian prepared teas and salves and foot massages, which she swore by, believing they activated the nervous system and released endorphins. Gradually she let a little more light into Ollie's room each day and urged her to try some gentle yoga stretches.

After a while, Lillian started to bring the baby to Ollie's bed for her afternoon nap. Ollie would stare at Raine as if she were a tiny alien from another galaxy. One day she kissed her forehead, then her tiny feet. Lillian eased Ollie into taking a few steps outside, eventually pushing the baby in her Silver Cross pram, a gift from one of the studios. Hunt said Lillian was a miracle. And he managed to persuade Ollie to meet with a psychiatrist, who prescribed lithium, the mood stabilizer Dr. Lucie had recommended all those years ago. Ollie agreed to try it.

"What changed?" I asked Hunt.

"Raine. That little girl saved her life."

Ollie had never used the word "depression" when she crashed. She'd say that she needed a break, she had to regroup, her brain wasn't working, she couldn't get into gear. Sometimes she'd go back to Rocks and wait it out. She said riding horses out west was the best therapy.

One time, in LA, when she had stopped functioning, Hunt took her to Cedars-Sinai, even though he had promised never to hospitalize her. She had warned him that it was the worst thing he could ever do. She refused to see him when he visited, and after she was released, she took off and didn't call him for months. She described these low periods by their physical manifestations: stale breath, funky armpits and groin, crusty scalp, flayed cuticles. She said it felt as if someone had pulled back on the brake. *The carousel screeches, children scatter, a horse's eye beats down like a vicious marble.*

The psychiatrist explained that Ollie's stability (and happiness) during pregnancy was likely due to the high level of hormones her body was producing; the severe postpartum was a result of those hormones plummeting. That information came as a huge relief to Ollie. She had believed the postpartum depression was a message from the universe telling her that she wasn't fit to be a mother. Much later, she confessed that she hadn't wanted to see the baby because she believed she might harm her. Hunt said she completely broke down in tears after they returned from the doctor's office. It was the first time he had seen her cry.

"We both bawled our eyes out," he admitted to me. Those months after Raine's birth were more terrifying than Hunt had admitted during our calls.

"I wasn't sure your sister was going to make it," he said.

Ollie promised Hunt and the doctor, but most of all this tiny creature, that she would stay on the medication and wouldn't leave them. I wanted to believe her. *Olly Olly Oxen free.*

Ollie bonded with Raine on their longer and longer walks pushing the pram around the neighborhood. She found herself talking and singing to her baby, eliciting smiles that on their own might have changed Ollie's brain chemistry. At four months, Raine started to reach for her ankles and grab hold, rocking her body back and forth, a happy Buddha. In a book on baby development, Ollie learned that this stage was known as "finding your feet." She crowed to me as if her little girl had won an Olympic gold medal.

When Raine turned two, I flew out to LA for her gala birthday party. Ollie invited Anita, Gerry and Al and the twins, Lillian, some neighbors and a few of Hunt's colleagues including a sprinkling of celebrities. It was pure Hollywood. Two ponies, a clown, a jumping castle, an aspiring actress dressed as Snow White with chirping birds sewn into the sleeves of her dress. The food was catered by a posh new restaurant, and the many-tiered cake was iced in rainbow colors. Gerry and Al soaked up the LA vibe, drinking watermelon margaritas, as the twins turned somersaults in the jumping castle. I noticed Lillian and the caterer hitting it off. Hunt was filming, while Ollie kept an eye on Raine, a kind of force field connecting them. Our mother would have deemed this party the height of pretension and completely unnecessary, given that the child wouldn't remember any of it. Her rule of thumb: age one, one guest. Age two, two guests, and so forth. What my mother wouldn't see was that Hunt and Ollie were also celebrating themselves; they had become a family.

I'd been dating Ian, an architect I'd met at the pool where I did my morning laps, he in the fast lane, me in the medium. His body would whoosh by mine, sleek as a seal. We started walking together from the pool to work, our offices a block apart. Then we decided to get breakfast, and eventually that led to dinner, then movies, then sleeping together.

Ian was my fifth official lover. It had been a long time since I'd undressed with anyone, and I forgot how vulnerable it felt. How naked it was! Ollie told me to bring him to the birthday party, but I told her it was too soon. "I'll bring him next time," though I suspected our relationship was more of a bridge, two people biding their time, waiting for something better or, in my case, a way back to the land of the living.

The night before the party, Ollie and I were filling glittery goody bags in the pool house: glitter headbands and wands, miniature crystal unicorns (yes, from Swarovski). She tied the bags with pipe cleaners that she twisted into hearts.

"Since when did you become Martha Stewart?"

"I know, right? I wish Mom was here to see this."

"Me, too."

"I miss her," she said. "God, I gave her a hard time."

"You were pretty shitty." I said it half-jokingly to take the sting out.

"Fair enough," she said. No attitude.

"Sorry," I said. "Can I take that back?"

Mom's long ago prediction that we would become friends had finally come to pass. Now we spoke nearly every day, Ollie starting each call with a report of Raine's accomplishments. If Mom were alive, she would have reveled in every step: new words, potty training, singing loud in Mommy and Me classes. I tried to stand in for her, wildly applauding each new development. I loved being an aunt. I sent Raine books, Beanie Babies, and stickers. In a trendy kids' clothing store, I found a T-shirt with the famous Pink Floyd album cover on it. Ollie sent me a picture of them in matching sunglasses, smiling in the sunshine, Raine sticking out her chest, wearing the shirt.

The pool pump clicked off, amplifying the silence between us.

"I love you, little sister. I hope you know that."

When I failed to respond in kind, Ollie returned to her assembly line, filling the last of the goody bags.

"It's okay," she said. "I know you love me, too."

After dinner, cleaning up the kitchen, I watched my sister twist the cap off an orange vial, pop three salmon-colored pills into her mouth, and swallow them without water. Was it possible that my sister's stability and happiness was predicated on taking a single drug?

"No fuss, no muss," she winked.

Demon seed, changeling, imposter, thief.

On some level, I never stopped wishing for an idyll that had ceased to exist long ago: the four of us together. Four fortune cookies. Four fortunes. *Don't hold on to things that require a tight grip.*

Hunt came into the kitchen and relayed that Raine had asked me to read to her and put her to bed. An honor like no other. I attempted to blink back a tear, but it was too fast.

"Really?"

"She requested you specifically," Hunt said.

"Go," Ollie said. "I'll finish cleaning up."

My sister swims beyond the ocean crest, part-dolphin, part-girl. Gulls circle and fill the air. A cloud asks, what do you know? No one will love you more or hurt you more than a sister.

20

Kira Banerjee asked me to be in her bridal party. I couldn't say no, though accepting the invitation meant multiple celebrations at which I was supposed to smile and giggle with the eleven other women in her bridal party. She asked if I wanted to bring a date. I declined. Ian had ended our relationship via answering machine after a college love had rekindled.

Over the course of those three days at her parents' home on Long Island, I grew fond of her women friends and cousins, including a CEO of an apparel company, a litigator, a few stay-at-home moms, a PhD candidate in astrophysics, a physical therapist, a documentarian, and an insurance auditor. Kira introduced me as her Caucasian friend, and the women fussed over me and helped me tie my sari, applied makeup and curled my hair as if I were a doll. Confession: I loved it.

Each room we entered in her family's mini-mansion was spritzed with rosewater. A buffet of Indian appetizers and creamy stews, constantly replenished, was always on offer. There was a mehndi ceremony, in which henna was applied to Kira's hands and feet. After it dried, the intricate design appeared in a rich tobacco color. Kira added her own twist, a henna "tramp stamp" on her lower back with a stencil of

Tony the Tiger, an in-joke between bride and groom. Some of the other women participated in the ceremony, but I was afraid the henna would never come off.

The second night before the wedding, the families gathered and sang folk songs, many of which I learned were meant to tease and embarrass the bride. Kira embraced it all. The past was the past; she loved being at the center of the festivities, her cynicism shelved, making her family happy and proud. Most important: Ari had given her a second chance.

Kira dragged me out of bed just as I had finally fallen asleep. She took me to the remnants of a childhood fort in the woods behind her house and took out a joint.

"I used to play castle here when I was little," she said, lighting up. "I gave my first hand job here, too."

"You're gross."

Kira handed me the joint.

"You know I don't smoke."

"It's my last night as a single girl, come on."

I took the smallest puff imaginable and started coughing.

"I wouldn't be getting married if I hadn't listened to you."

Kira called it her re-arranged marriage.

"I didn't do anything."

"No, you did."

"How?" I asked.

"You got me into therapy."

Kira tamped out the joint and put it back in a small brass box.

"I learned two things from my therapist," she said. "First, I'm not that bad. And second," only she couldn't remember the second thing. "Shit, I'm stoned."

On the third and final day of the ceremonies, over four hundred people filled a massive catering hall. In our lavender saris, the twelve of us looked like a sea of phlox. Kira wore a traditional red sari with gold embroidery, her hair fashioned into a crown of braids tied with gold ribbon. She gave each of us a bracelet with a gold lotus charm symbolizing beauty, prosperity, and fertility. We hugged and cried and put them on. I had become a part of this chorus of women I hadn't wanted to join, and now I was afraid that it was all going to be over too soon.

The crowd suddenly became quiet. One of the women grabbed my hand. "Do you hear that?"

In the distance a steady drumbeat and a flute piping a melody could be heard. As it came closer, I saw Ari surrounded by brothers and uncles and little boys dancing beneath a brightly striped canopy: the groom's procession to meet his bride. Under an altar festooned with flower chains, Ari and Kira faced each other, trembling, as if meeting for the first time, resplendent in their wedding garb. Parents and families gathered close behind: two small armies about to join forces. The emotional current was overpowering, and for a moment all the joy and sadness in life pooled inside me and I longed for everyone I'd ever loved. Ari placed a garland around his bride's neck, and she in turn placed one around his. Her father's eyes were brimming with tears as he placed Kira's hands in Ari's. After prayers were offered and vows exchanged, the couple fulfilled their final ritual by tying their garments together and circling the ceremonial fire seven times. The solemnity of their task gave way to uproarious cheering, rice spraying the air.

The guests were ushered into a hall decorated with thousands of blossoms. Kira had dropped many hints about wanting a flash mob at her wedding, and we obliged. One by one, each girl strutted across the stage to "Dancing Queen," Kira's favorite song. She screamed and whooped as the guys arranged themselves in a half-moon behind us and dipped us backward. I was paired with Dev, an analyst at Morgan Stanley, and I wondered if we might have some chemistry, but by the end of the night he was making out with another bridesmaid behind the chocolate fountain.

I stood alone, suddenly feeling ridiculous in my sari, nursing a melting mojito. A man I hadn't noticed before approached and asked if he could refresh my drink. I declined, saying I had to cut myself off.

He asked if I wanted a piece of cake, and before I could decline a second time, he put up his hand. "Don't move."

He came back with one piece of cake and two forks. Out of habit and curiosity, I glanced to see if he was wearing a wedding ring.

"I'm not married," he said and held up his left hand, flipping it front and back.

"Was I that obvious?"

"You're Amy."

"Do I know you?"

"I'm Ravi. Kira has been trying to fix me up with you for a long time."

"Really? How long?"

"I was married, to be truthful. An arranged marriage. Total disaster. It took a while to, you know, recover."

Ravi and I fell easily into conversation. Our failed marriages became badges of honor: we were soldiers on the battlefield of love, burned, battered, but still here, or so we said. There was one last bite of cake on the plate.

"You," I said.

"No, you."

I held his gaze and ate the cake. Then he asked me to dance, and I didn't make my usual fuss. As we arrived at the dance floor, the fast song ended, and "Lady in Red" came on.

"Are we doing this?" I asked, trying to strike the right blend of irony and interest.

He took my hand, put his other hand on my back and pulled me toward him. His neck smelled of sandalwood, his pocket square impeccable. I felt that jolt my mother spoke of when she first met my dad at a dance: "That's when you know." I counseled myself: Only a very foolish girl would mistake an evening of flirtation at a friend's wedding for anything more than a moment of magical thinking. The DJ announced the last song, and we watched as Ari and Kira, exhausted, sweaty, and in love, danced to "Love Is All Around." The guests made a circle around the bride and groom and started moving together like the great skirt of the whirling dervish.

I believed that Kira and Ari would grow old together. Their mettle had been tested, their garments knitted together. Before I left, Ravi asked if he could call me, and Kira thanked me for being her friend and bridesmaid. Then, hugging me tight, she whispered in my ear, "I remember the second thing my therapist said: you have to forgive yourself."

✠

I ended therapy with Paul some months after Kira's wedding. I announced that I was ready, and he agreed. I immediately wanted to take it back.

"So that's it. That's how it ends. Just like that." I hadn't expected it to be so easy.

"You've been coming for five years. You've worked hard."

"So, you want me to leave," I said, trying to keep it light, trying not to cry.

Paul had been the most consistent person in my life. Sometimes it seemed as if he had more recall about my life than I did, reminding me about previous situations or emotions I had conveniently blocked. Paul had been attentive and caring no matter how dense or ill-tempered I was. He never wavered, never asked more of me than I could handle. I recalled our early sessions, when I'd ask if he preferred the door closed or open for his next client, and how vexed I was that he left it up to me. Eventually, it became a useful metaphor in our work together. We named it the Riddle of the Door; it stood for every fork in the road.

At the end of our final session, Paul broke the fourth wall and hugged me. His sweater smelled like the cedar in our family's front-hall closet. I don't know how long we stood there, a minute, a mile. *The spider plants and their shoots multiplied inside the room. The planet was a blue marble as seen from the moon.* Patient and kind to the end, Paul waited for me to let go before he took a step back. I walked out the door for the last time and knew that whatever I did next was up to me. I left the door open.

Acknowledgments

Heartfelt thanks to Ilan Zechory, Anne Dailey, Leah Hager Cohen, Erin Hosier, Rosemary Mahoney, Jenefer Shute, Colin Campbell, and most of all Jill Eisenstadt for reading early drafts and offering comments and support.

My editor Elisabeth Schmitz is my Maxwell Perkins, the publishing gold standard. She helped me make this book better in every conceivable way. Laura Schmitt has provided constant good cheer, feedback, and assistance. Thanks to the Grove team: Morgan Entrekin, Peter Blackstock, Deb Seager, Justina Batchelor, Natalie Church, Judy Hottensen, Rachael Richardson, Mike Richards, Jenny Choi, Miranda Hency, Sal Destro, and Norman Tuttle. Thanks also to Peg Anderson and Michael Mah for copyediting and proofreading, respectively. Georgia Petersen and Chloe Knapp provided invaluable assistance. Many thanks to my film agents Howie Sanders and Ryan Wilson for their enthusiasm. Ongoing gratitude to my agent David Black for his unflagging support and expertise and his team at the Black Agency: Susan Raihofer, Anagha Petrevu, and Anna Zinchuk. Special mention to Leigh Stein, in a league of her own.

I have had the good fortune of a long career in publishing and can never fully express my debt of gratitude to my partners at DCL, Henry Dunow and Jennifer Carlson, my authors, clients, and colleagues who have generously shared their knowledge and passion with me over the last four decades and from whom I've learned so much.

My beloved sisters Nina Palmer and Gail Lerner gave me an early thumbs up to publish this book. My daughter Raffaella Donatich provided a close read along with her generosity and warmth. Deepest gratitude to my husband John Donatich, my first and best reader.

In memory of George Arnett Hodgman (1959–2019)